THE CONDUIT CHRONICLES SPECIAL EDITION:

TWO LEGENDARY PREQUEL TALES

ASHLEY HOHENSTEIN

I am dedicating this special edition to my outstanding team! They have made this publication possible and together they make me a stronger woman and writer every day! You are my tribe, Beks, Rebekah and Darah, I love each of you.

A NOTE TO READERS

THE LEGENDARY PREQUEL TALES SPECIAL EDITION is the compilation of two stories that take you into the more fantastical aspects of the Conduit world long before the events of *FOUND* transpire.

I believe you can read this story as a standalone and enjoy every twist and turn but it is written to be read between Book IV, *FATED* and Book V, *FOREVER* of The Conduit Chronicles.

The two prequel tales happen simultaneously, at times the characters cross paths. I would highly suggest you read *THE ORIGINALS*, first. But if you desire to be a rebel, go ahead. I have always liked rebels. That being said, the epilogue at the end of *THE QUEEN*, does have some spoilers.

Consider yourself warned.

A CONDUIT CHRONICLES STORY

Chapter One

"My Queen, your daughter goes into labor. The trolling will be here soon," Goutel announced when she entered my room.

"Very good. How is the father?" My anxiety had been mounting as the hours passed leading up to my daughter giving birth to her first-born. Frozen by fear in some ways, I remembered my own labor and how her inception led to the demise of her father, my partner Itzalo.

"Spitzle is weak, but still holding on." Goutel watched me knowingly as she reported his status. She had been my most trusted confidant for more years than either of us could count anymore. A troll's life was vast. My parents lived well into their eleventh millennium, passing of old age and willing their bodies to expire together. They were found holding hands in my mother's shuttle, as though they had only fallen into a deep slumber. But in fact their flesh had turned to stone, the gentle passing of two strokes that were no longer to be painted within the circles of this life. It was a different death than that of my Itzalo. His strokes were abruptly ended during the birth of our child, Tazzle.

It's the risk a troll pair has to take when they decide to breed. As a queen you have no choice but to procreate; it is written in your fate—no matter the perilousness. The crown must be passed on to a daughter of the line. The power it possesses can only be activated by the true queen.

Itzalo knew when we fell in love that it was a risk we would have to take. But had I known what I would lose to gain my daughter, I may have navigated things differently. I never wanted Tazzle to endure what I had.

"My Queen," Goutel interrupted my reverie. "Certainly you wish to go to your daughter, to meet the next of the line."

"Yes, of course. Bring me my crown." It would be unbecoming to be seen by the trolliage without the sign of my status upon my head. Goutel quickly brought me the beautiful gold ornament—that was how I thought of it most days, a shiny trinket that represented a mountain of responsibility. I adjusted it on my scalp. It fit perfectly since the day it was handed down to me. The crown formed to its commander, adjusting to my individuality in its structure to reflect my strengths. Malarin had created it in this way, a gift to the leader of his first-born children. "Take me to them, Goutel," I said once I was adorned.

We walked out of my chamber and down a long corridor—no need for light in my palace within the walls of Listy, the great troll city. Trolls thrived in the depths, in the dark. We were built this way.

I heard the parturition before we entered the room. Deep guttural groans, the familiar sound of the male troll willing his strokes into his prodigy, the painful process of animation. My mind shot back to the moment Itzalo died. My heart throbbed with loss.

I held our daughter Tazzle in my arms. I had created her form. My strokes duplicated and molded into a beautiful infant she-troll.

But it was Itzalo who must bring the strokes to life. He had to perform the inception. The inception was a dance between life and death, where the father gave his life force to his child. If he gave too much, he would turn to stone. If he gave too little, the being would never breathe life.

We turned the corner and my knees nearly buckled at the sight. It was too familiar, too painful. Tazzle lay on the bed, holding the small troll form. Spitzle stood hovering over both of them, his hands embracing the infant, his strokes moving from his center, through his arms, and visibly into the child. I gasped when I saw that Spitzle's legs were stone. He was losing his life force—my daughter would suffer my fate.

I grabbed Goutel's arm before we approached the bed. "This must stop," I whispered. "Look, he will pass into the Tins. He isn't strong enough."

My daughter heard me. Her head turned. "Mother, my Queen, trust in the painter. Spitzle will prevail." She looked lovingly at her partner. He was battling an internal struggle, walking the tight rope of giving without sacrificing himself.

Tears streamed down my cheeks as I watched on in horror. The inception was complete when the infant's eyes opened. There was no sign of completion by way of the tiny face.

Spitzle moaned in pain and the stone moved farther up his large thighs. I began to pray. Cry and pray.

Chapter Two

Spitzle's groans were choked off as the stone snaked up his spine and began to encapsulate his lungs. Next would be his heart and he would be gone.

"We must do something," I whispered as I looked on in terror. My daughter could not suffer the same fate as I did—she could not lose her husband for the sake of their child. I looked at Goutel and repeated myself. "We must do something."

Just then the door behind us flew open. "My Queen, OAD, King of the Powries, has arrived to celebrate the legacy of the trolls."

Goutel turned on the man servant. "Can you not see that this is no time for disruption!" she scolded. The male-troll's expression transformed into mortification as he began to close the door.

"Wait!" I shouted over the loud gurgling noises coming from Spitzle. "Bring me the king! Immediately!"

The door slammed shut and I tuned to the tragedy in front of me. He had moments to live. Tears streamed down Tazzle's face as she watched her husband sacrifice his life for the animation of their daughter. Resolve emanating between them, they had clearly discussed the likelihood of this outcome and agreed the price was worth the gift—an heir, a daughter, a legacy. But they did not truly understand the cost. No one did. My right arm grew warm. It was King OAD. He had arrived in the chamber via the teleportation power of flame.

I turned to him as he manifested. "Save him… I will do anything. Save him."

"Anything?" He cocked his head at me inquisitively. "To save a male troll… Is his death not a righteous one, a common occurrence for the bloodline of your kind to stay intact?"

"Can you do it?"

"I will not use my life-force. Whose shall I syphon?" he hissed as he looked around.

"Mine."

A maniacal grin spread across the powrie's face. "Very well, dear queen." He quickly stepped between us. Spitzle's body was stiff. The gurgling had stopped, replaced only by the sobs of Tazzle.

OAD held his pikestaff in one hand and outstretched his lanky arms encased in brown leathery skin. His long, stringy hair limply hung to his shoulders. I could not bring myself to look at Spitzle so instead I admired the king. His build was burly and stout, his nose long and crooked. Beedy red eyes darted between my son-in-law and myself until my vision went dark, the room went eerily silent and my body seized. In the back of my mind I knew what was happening. He was draining my life-force, transferring it to Spitzle. *Was this what it felt like for Itzalo before he was no more?* The thought no sooner crossed my mind than consciousness slipped away, and I knew not what would become of any of us.

Chapter Three

My legs were stiff when I moved to my left, rolling over in my bed to see the familiar eyes of my daughter Tazzle and the innocent eyes of her newborn.

"You saved him," she said. "I can never repay you."

My voice was hoarse when I spoke. "Was there a cost to be paid?" I looked down at my feet. They appeared in working order.

"Not one we can see, but nothing comes for free. OAD must have required a toll."

I nodded. There was nothing else to be said on the matter. I would square away with the king and be eternally grateful for his assistance. For it was in the strokes that one of the only creatures created by Malarin that could save my son was present when he was needed. There are no coincidences, only divinely orchestrated moments of fate. "What is her name? This fierce one who nearly depleted her father and surely took some strength from her grandmother."

Tazzle looked down at the bundle she held in her arms. "Fetzle."

"Fetzle?" I looked at Tazzle, surprised. "The procurer of unity? Interesting meaning. Do you believe we are in a time of dissension?"

Tazzle shook her head thoughtfully. "No, but I had a dream that Fetzle would someday carry the burden of unification."

"Dreams are always to be considered, and you, dear daughter, have always had profoundly important dreams. Fetzle suits her," I agreed as I kissed the trolling's soft head. "Where is Spitzle?"

"He sleeps. The Pythoness says he will slumber for many more hours. He was nearly taken by the stone." A tear rolled down Tazzle's cheek. I wiped it away. "We thought we were prepared for the sacrifice."

"I know, I know, we all think we are until it is upon us," I assured her before pulling her and my granddaughter in close for an embrace.

Chapter Four

Goutel buttoned my robe. I hated it. It was cumbersome. I preferred my bare skin. It was bad enough that I had to dip in the thirteen baths—an outdated ritual I had always intended to abolish when I became queen but forgot about it until I was faced with the ceremony of having company. Trolls did not entertain others very often. The city of Listy had drifters, of course. It was, after all, the hub of every troll shuttle in the world. But company was an entirely different production. Because trolls did not have many offspring and even more rare was the birth of a queen, there was much cause for celebration.

Long ago, painted in the strokes, formality and rituals originated. My mother loved the observance of it all. My father was much like me—chagrinned. The robe I wore was weighted down with heavy gems, mostly obsidian. The couturier of the dwarfs had made it for the first queen—thoughtful, but burdensome.

"You look majestic." Goutel beamed. "You should wear it more often."

"When might that be? For shuttle rides?" I laughed and she chuckled. "Can you imagine?"

"I see you are, of course, wise and jocular."

"You know I hate it."

Goutel simply nodded, always patient with me. She was my closest friend, my bodyguard, my truest advisor, and clearly had terrible taste in fashion.

"Who has arrived for the feast?" I took a seat on my ottoman at the end of my bed. It was a useless piece of furniture most days but today it suited me as well as any throne.

"As you know, OAD, King of Powries, arrived first. Following him we have greeted Hewit, Goddess of the Minotaurs; Ka, King of the Dwarfs; and Bracin, King of the Pixies. We await the company of the fae trio, the centaur king and the griffin queen. It is early yet."

"Then why am I dressed in this monstrosity?" I moaned.

"Because you are a queen of the highest order."

A rap on the door interrupted my next barrage of complaints. "Enter," Goutel asserted.

The same male-troll who'd interrupted the labor entered my chamber. "My Queen, King OAD requests an audience."

Of course he did, and he deserved it. I had mixed feelings about the powries in general but there was no denying the value that OAD had provided by saving Spitzle. I would be fortunate to repay him.

"Tell the king that I will meet him in the crystal cavern in a half a length's time." With that the male-troll shut the door.

"I suppose I have to wear this thing to meet the king now?" I grimaced at the thought of it. Goutel's expression pulled me out of my disgruntled mood. "What? What is it that has you concerned?"

She waited to speak—unusual for my dear friend—making me all the more concerned.

"Out with it, Goutel," I demanded.

"What do you think the powrie king will request for payment?"

"I haven't the faintest. Why is this upsetting to you?" I stepped toward her and took her hand. "It is my burden to bear. King OAD made right by me and my family in a moment of desperate need. Whatever the price, it will be worth it."

"You, my Queen, have had little dealings with powries." There was a tone I was not accustomed to.

I pulled my hand away, feeling shamed although uncertain why. Goutel would never purposefully wish to hurt my heart. "I have had enough dealings, I assure you."

In truth, I had had very few happenings with the powries. They kept to themselves, only every so often chartering a shuttle to get from here to there. OAD had been king since my grandparents' rule, so I knew they had very long lifespans. I surmised that, because of their long lifespans, they felt no need to meddle in other creatures' affairs. As I understood it, they kept to themselves in their villages of dirt. Powrie populations stayed close to the surface of the earth. I had never considered why that was. Their communities were relatively small in number, pods of them dispersed all over the world. Listy was massive in size and population comparatively. We trolls preferred to congregate with one another, join in fellowship and merriment. I loved my people.

"I love you, my Queen, but you do not have adequate knowledge of the desires of the powries," Goutel insisted. "They feed off carnage. That is why they settle so close to the surface. Their power is tied to the sorrow and devastation of others."

This was new information for me. "But how would this affect me and the repayment I make to OAD? He cannot expect me to perform such deeds."

Goutel lifted her brow in a 'can you be so sure' way.

I threw my hands up. "What would you have me do?"

"There is nothing to be done except pray to Malarin that the strokes be in our favor."

CHAPTER FIVE

Goutel's warning knotted in the pit of my stomach as I walked to the crystal cavern. It was one of my favorite rooms in the palace but today it gave me no joy to convene in its grandeur. The cavern had been built by my great-great-grandfather, King Kazzle. My own daughter's namesake came from his memory. King Kazzle was known for his ability to create beauty. The crystals were given to the king by the Goldhorn Buck of the great mountains, each one hand-selected from his treasury, each one unique and priceless. Many were in the shape of stalactites, others dripped from the ceiling like glow worms. The ambience challenged any I had yet to see in the world.

The door loomed closer. I calmed my nerves by reminding myself I had no reason to believe the king had any ill intent for me or my people. OAD had never demonstrated anything that should lead me to believe he held any rancor towards the trolls. After all, he was here to celebrate the birth of our next heir.

I rolled my shoulders back, bracing for whatever may come,

knowing I could handle it, when out of nowhere the Pythoness stepped out of the shadows and into the dim candlelight.

"My Queen," the old crone hissed, "be leery of what seems like a fool's errand. Much will be discovered. It will alter all of our fates forever. He asks the favor that will lead to the rinsing of the strokes in the River Tins—Dalinkas will not spare us the new beginning." Then she slinked back into the darkness from where she came.

What must I do? Surely she was referring to OAD's request. *Can I just ignore his bidding?* I was in a state of shock, so it took me a moment to hear the powrie king.

"Queen Peozleo? What keeps you?"

I looked up to see his beady red eyes glowing in the dark. My hands shook, so I clasped them together in front of me. This was the duty of the queen—to make commitments and keep them. I could deter any ill-fated actions. We are all only one decision away from a totally different outcome. If I made a deal with the devil, surely I could make it right. I reasoned this all in my head in only a moment, plastered a toothy smile on my face and stepped toward the king.

"Sorry to have kept you waiting. Someone caught me in transit. Shall we?" I gestured toward the cavern, hoping he did not notice my tremors.

"Of course. I know well how difficult it is to find time for simple audiences. The job of a monarch is never finished."

"You would understand," I agreed as we both took a seat among the brilliant crystals.

"Entirely." He crossed his legs, still holding his pikestaff firmly in his left hand. "That is why I will make this quick."

I nodded.

"Do you know what I carry in my hand?"

"It is a weapon, a status of your reign over your people."

"You are partly correct. It is the Staff of Banishment."

My eyes got wide.

"Aye, you know what that is." He nodded with satisfaction. "It is my status symbol, just as yours is your crown atop your very head. But it is more, much more. By the look on your face you know the origins of the Staff. It was the Rittle created by Fih, the very one that would impale his brother Tindle. Henceforth Fih was banished to his forest where he was meant to stay. His brothers took the Staff, along with the other Rittles, deep into the caves of Cataphet the original, where she agreed to keep them safe—or this is how the story goes."

"How do you possess this cursed object?"

"Because stories are not always as they seem. Remember, after Tindle fell, his blood spilled about him, and his brother Priloc lay by his side, willing him to live. Powries were of some of the first strokes; not like you or the originals, but our creation followed shortly after. We lived in the dirt, small, discreet creatures, not even visible to most eyes. When Tindle's blood soaked the soil, we grew, and I developed into what I am today. The painter saw this and believed it was good. From malice sprouted expansion, from grief and betrayal begot growth. Chitchakor blessed the powries, making me king and bequeathing me the Staff which held the raw intention of Fih and his duplicity. As long as I hold this Staff we maintain our powers. We are further fed by the daily atrocities that feed the earth. It is our absorption of this pain that balances the strokes."

Goutel was right; they did feed off the terrible parts of the world. I tried to maintain a neutral expression as he continued—to hide my disease.

"You see, it is imperative that I carry the weight of the Staff of Banishment. When the brothers woke, they carried all but the Staff down into Cataphet's lair and I have held it ever since. Can you understand why the painter honored me with its safekeeping?"

"It would seem it was made for you, or you made by it—either way, you seem inseparable. How is it that I am to help you with what you already have?"

He flipped the Staff upside down, showing me the blunted end. "Fifteen hundred years ago, someone stole one of the blades."

I replayed the fable in my head and did recall the Staff was described as double-bladed. "How could someone have stolen it from you? I have never seen you without it."

"There was a time when I was more frivolous with its locality. That has changed, I assure you," he hissed, then regained his composure. "Without the entire Staff the strokes are off balance. I have failed Malarin in my folly. No matter where I have looked, I have not uncovered the culprit or the blade. It is rightfully mine, and the world is better for me having it. I need you to find it and bring it to me."

"If you have not discovered its whereabouts over the last fifteen hundred years, how will I fare any differently?"

"Trolls see many creatures, they hear of many things… I trust you will find a way. After all, I saved your son and your daughter anguish—did I not? You are merely returning what is mine back to me."

He slowly flipped the Staff back around, blade once again upright. His grip was noticeably tighter and his eyes shimmered with a glint of impatience. *Do I have a choice? Is this the seeming 'fool's errand'?* It actually felt like a nearly impossible task. The Pythoness must have been referring to something else.

"Queen, there is no negotiation here," OAD growled.

"I am aware of our agreement, King OAD, I assure you. I was only calculating a strategy." It took all I had to keep my voice calm. It would do no good to meet his agitation with my own.

His shoulders relaxed visibly. "That is a blessing to hear."

"I hope this task can wait until after the festivities?" It was said as a question but that was more as a courtesy to him.

"Certainly," he said as he got to his feet. I followed his lead, towering over him when I was erect. I considered the difference in our stature, in our nature really—we were painted from very different strokes.

We bowed slightly and I moved toward the door.

"Dear queen, do make haste. I have never been a patient man." There it was, just the hint of a threat. I opened up my mouth, prepared to take a whiff of his aura to be sure I heard the real intention behind that statement.

"No need to try and smell my aura. We haven't one."

My face grew hot with embarrassment. "You haven't an aura? I have never noticed." The truth was I had not ever tried to detect his energy and its intention.

"All you will find is maleficence; after all, that's what I feed on. It is also what we exude."

My eyes narrowed and I breathed in with my senses despite his warning. He was right; I tasted nothing but sour, bitter malignity.

"Told you." He pushed past me, into the hall. "I look forward to the festivities."

I wondered as he walked away, did he not have an aura or was he just that defiled?

CHAPTER SIX

I walked back slowly to my chamber. Goutel would be there expectantly and I was not certain how I felt about the arrangement with OAD. *Do I tell Goutel about the Pythoness' warning? Would it just fuel her worry?*

"Mother!" Tazzle shouted from down the hall. She was adorned with similar atrocities to my own but she favored it. Beside her stood Spitzle, holding Fetzle in a plush velvet blanket. By the strokes, even the trollings had to be put on display.

"Queen Mother." Spitzle bowed as they approached. The men only wore a sash. It was light and looked bearable. I examined his body; he appeared unscathed. I exhaled. Who knew how long I had been holding that breath in? He was healthy—that was all that mattered. Everything else would work itself out. I pulled my grandchild and Spitzle in for a hug. Tazzle wrapped her arms around all three of us.

"It is good to see you well," I whispered in his ear. "This child needs her father."

"I have you to thank for that. You are the most generous being I will ever know." I felt his tears touch my shoulder and I too began to weep. It would all work out. It had to.

"Stop that, you two!" Tazzle playfully scolded. "You'll ruin the robes."

I gave him one more squeeze, kissed the little one's head and wiped away the tears. "She has the bluest eyes," I observed and caressed her cheek with my finger. "They remind me of your father's."

"Really?" Tazzle had to hold back her own tears this time.

She wanted to celebrate, lighten the mood. I knew my daughter well. "Hey, hey, do not ruin the robes."

She smiled and the tears that had crept so close to the surface gave her reprieve.

"We went to your chamber and Goutel said you were away speaking to OAD. Is everything all right?" Spitzle asked.

That was a tough question to answer but right now, looking at my family intact, I could confidently say that everything felt perfect. "The king and I worked out the rest of our arrangement. We are both very satisfied." That was true—as long as I would be able to find the missing blade.

"Wonderful!" Tazzle cheered. "Then tonight truly is a celebration."

"Of course it is," I assured her, but Spitzle looked skeptical. "I must collect Goutel. She will be furious with me if I left her in my chamber and attended the events without her. She thinks I look queenly," I joked.

"But you all do, all of my ladies." Spitzle kissed his daughter's head and her eyes blinked affectionately. Priceless. This moment was priceless.

"I thought I heard you out here," Goutel's voice echoed down the hall. "You were going to attend without me. So that I could not see everyone's expressions of reverence upon your appearance."

"She always thinks the worst of me," I whispered to Fetzle.

"The child can't save you. Now come here and let me make certain your crown is on straight."

Everyone laughed as I sheepishly walked toward my dearest friend. She was great at lightening all manners of moods. When I got good and close, only then did I see the worry on her face.

I met her stare and knew I needed to reassure her because no matter what happened, this was my burden to bear and she needn't worry on a night like tonight. I mouthed the words so that only she could see.

'All is good.' Her shoulders relaxed some. It wouldn't be enough to assuage all of her fears but it would do for now.

Chapter Seven

The pageantry was tedious. We paraded in one by one and took our seats in the communion hall. All of my trolliage were in attendance and that was what mattered most to me. My people, my family, my community desired to celebrate their new queen.

The kings and queens of the other attending creatures, along with their constituents, were shown to their seats one by one on an elevated stage surrounding our table. The rest of the trolls took to the tables a level below, talking among themselves and carrying on. Rightly or wrongly, I appreciated that most of them did not appear dazzled by the spectacle. I never ruled from a golden throne or with an iron fist, nor had any of my predecessors—we were one with our people. Many of the other leaders here had very different ways of presiding over their people. I felt it wasn't my place to judge.

Dinner was a myriad of delicacies, a different dish to match each palate present. From the raw newt brains, a treat prepared for the pixie King Bracin, to the firefly wings prepared for the fae trio, Raven, Abbot and Simone.

It was a funny thing to partake in, because no creature in the hall required food to sustain their life-force. I always wondered why Chitchakor had created humans with such fallibility. *Was it out of trickery or disdain?* Perhaps the painter wanted humans to cherish every moment in a way that only those who were mortal could do. Everything tasted much sweeter when it could be your last bite. Whatever the case, food was no requirement for those of us with unusually long years. We chose to eat when ritual demanded it or, in my case, on the rare occasion I had a craving.

I raised my glass to Ka, the king of the dwarfs. He was by far one of my favorite guests to entertain. The dwarf king could drink with the best of them. He always made for a jovial time. Swade, the leader of the centaurs, sat beside him. They were an unlikely pair; Swade was a much more reserved creature. He towered over the dwarf king. His horse body was double his size. But they were endeared to each other; that was very obvious by way of their shared laughter.

Goutel leaned in. "Did you see that the Kraus couple arrived just before the ceremony?"

"Where are Cane and Sorcey?" Goutel pointed to the table of fae. Cane sat between Abbot, a muscular winged angel fae with chocolate skin and translucent eyes, and Raven, a thin tall female faerie who had long white hair and pale blue skin. Their third sat beside Sorcey. Simone was amphibious in nature. She could live just as comfortably in water as she could on land. Her skin was sleek and slippery in appearance, and she had gills along her arms and chest. I waved when I was able to catch Sorcey's eye. When the feast was over I would say hello.

"You did not know if they would make it," Goutel reminded me.

"Right. They have their own happenings, with the Katuan Trials approaching. Please do not let them leave without me saying thank you."

"I won't." Goutel clinked our glasses together in a small toast.

"Those two guests actually deserve a moment of your time. They came as supporters, not out of obligation."

I turned to my friend. "You are so strange. You love dolling me up in this ridiculous formality but don't value the venerated traditions of our guests of honor?"

She just rolled her eyes.

I laughed and thought about my special relationship with the Kraus family. About a hundred years ago I was transporting them, along with several other Conduits, to a gathering they were having outside the North lands covered in snow. We came along an accident in the line. One of my young trolls had hit an obstruction, causing her to hurtle to a stop. Because she had only just received from a traveling fae a toll that happened to be a vial of Squonk saliva—an acidic substance that could burn through anything, including our nearly impervious skin—the poor shuttle driver lay there crying and writhing in pain. Sweet Sorcey was able to mend her raw chemical burns. From then on, I made it a point to shuttle them if they were in need of assistance.

Goutel interrupted my reverie. "Have you smelled the aura of the goddess of the minotaurs, Hewit? She has been up to some very sensually arousing things. It is all about her."

"By the strokes, Goutel! Let the goddess enjoy her pleasures without judgement."

"I am not judging. I am only going to ask her what her pleasure practice is."

I laughed so hard I thought my belly would burst. "You do that… for both of us."

CHAPTER EIGHT

I woke up with a headache. Too much dwarf brandy wine. "You outdid yourself last night, my Queen." Goutel stood over my bed with a glass of moss root in her hand. "I pureed it and added cinnamon."

"It still smells awful." I sat up and took the glass in my hand. "Thank you." I was grateful, even if the cure tasted terrible. Moments after I consumed the moss root I would feel completely back to normal. It was a miracle, a medicine that treated nearly all ailments. I opened my mouth and swallowed the contents in one gulp, gagging slightly as it went down.

"Do not purge this cup. It will only make the next dose all that more unbearable." I could hear the smile in Goutel's voice. She was enjoying this a little too much. But no matter, the headache was gone and the taste in my mouth would wash away soon enough.

"Thank you," I repeated.

She took the cup and handed it to a male servant who quickly excused himself, and with him went the moss root smell.

I scooted over. "Sit… Tell me, what did you think of the night? Where are our guests? Are they in worse shape than me?"

"Only one fairs worse than you. Swade. He and his entourage are still asleep. Sorcey and Cane left last night." Goutel sat and gave me a sideways glance. "Everyone has left except OAD."

I instinctively turned away, knowing the next thing to come would be questions. Questions I did not entirely know the answers to. I cut her off at the pass. "Before you start, there are more questions than answers. The errand OAD would have me do in repayment is obscure. He wishes I find a blade that has gone missing from his spike Staff." *Do I tell her the whole truth? Do I share the Pythoness' warning?* On one hand I trusted no one more than Goutel, on the other hand she could make herself fraught with worry. I wanted her in my corner, as I knew she would be, but I did not need her to fill my head with doubts and fears.

"That is all? He wishes you find something that is already his?" There was much suspicion in her tone. "That seems simple."

"It would seem, but he hasn't a clue who stole it. He expects that as trolls we will have better luck, since we are in the company of many travelers."

"You do not think we are more likely to discover its whereabouts?"

There was something the king had not told me. Even in his muddled aura energy, I sensed it. I did not know yet what that was but something was amiss. At the very least, he should have an idea of who had been present when the blade went missing. This led me to believe that either he knew who took it and simply could not reason with them, or worse, that he knew who took it and they were dangerous.

"I believe that if this was a simple errand, the king of the powries would not utilize it to collect on a debt of this caliber."

"That stands to reason," she agreed and then wandered off in thought. We sat there in silence for a few moments, a thousand questions swimming in my head. "Why does he linger?"

I shook my head. "I do not know. Has he asked for an audience?"

"No. He has not left his chamber."

"I should go to him." He clearly was waiting for something. I pulled my blankets off. Goutel stood and moved toward the door, picking up my robes from the night before from the floor.

"I will have these cleaned."

"Why bother? It will be another five thousand years before anyone touches them." Or at least one could hope.

She scoffed and was almost out of my sight as I entered the washroom.

"My Queen, be careful." Then she shut the door and I ignored the uneasy feeling in my gut.

At the end of the hall and to the right was the guest chamber of King OAD. I took long, deliberate strides, with each step assuring myself there was nothing to fear; he and I had already made the arrangement. I knew my part. I would do everything in my power to see it through. The door was in view when it cracked open.

"Come in, Queen Peozleo," his familiar voice filled the space between. That was the second time he'd felt my presence. *Or am I just imagining that?*

"I hope I don't find you indisposed, King OAD," I said as I entered his chamber.

"Oh, no, I am in perfect spirits. In fact, I am brighter than I have been in hundreds of years, knowing that you are on the hunt for my missing blade. Take a seat," he said as he moved to the other side of the room, his glowing red eyes watching me intently.

"Do we have more to discuss?"

"Only a lead I just came across."

That is convenient. Far too convenient.

"Is that so? Please share."

"I would begin your search with the Niffler."

"The Niffler? Why would I bother him?"

"It has just come to my attention that he has been seen out and about in recent years. After centuries of being dormant in his tunnels, Hewit spoke of seeing him on multiple occasions."

"But your blade has been gone for many decades."

"Of course, but the Niffler is the huntsman of all the world's shiny objects. If the blade has been accounted for, he would know of its keeper."

I could follow that logic. "I will see to the Niffler. He was old friends with my father."

"Perfect! The strokes are in our favor." OAD moved swiftly to my right, taking my hand in his free one, never once putting down his Staff. "Queen, I am looking forward to what you discover. Please keep me abreast of your progress."

"How would you have me do that?"

"Please take this." He handed me a marble. "My messenger hawk will know to look for you. She can carry any correspondence needed between us. Speak to the stone, throw it in the air and the message will find me."

"Will that be all?" I was growing more and more uncomfortable with his presence.

"It will."

He let go of my hand and I casually walked to the door, not wanting him to sense my discomfort.

I bowed slightly. "We will be in touch."

"In fact, we will." His eyes lit up wickedly red and I shut the door.

I wanted that creature out of my palace as soon as possible.

Chapter Nine

Goutel packed my bag. "What will I tell your daughter? How do I explain your absence to the trolliage only days after the next heir is born?"

"Let my daughter deal with the politics. This will be good practice for her reign." I sighed, hating this errand more and more with each second that passed, knowing that when I returned Fetzle would be more grown than the day I left and begrudging every moment away from her. "The most important thing is that no one find out my debt to OAD. It would stir doubt among the trolliage. We have never been beholden to another creature before. I do not wish to burden our community with unwarranted fears. Besides, there may come a time when I must ask for every troll who shuttles to be vigilant for clues; that will be troublesome enough."

"You should tell Spitzle and Tazzle."

I took Goutel by the shoulders. "Do not tell them. They will blame themselves for my debt. It was my choice and it is my responsibility." I used my voice of authority, not one I took often with Goutel, but she knew it well and her expression confirmed what I had hoped. She would not overstep and tell my family what I was doing.

"I understand, my Queen. But then tell me, how can I assist you—if in no other way, with an alibi for an extended absence?"

"Today we will only concern ourselves with my reason for leaving. I am going to take Swade and his party back on my shuttle. The king needs some special care after his illness following the celebration." Returning Swade to his kingdom was an easy excuse for departing the city of Listy, and not unheard of for one royal to help another. Indeed, some royals insisted on only being shuttled by me. Of course, Swade was not one of them. He was far more informal, and I liked him for it.

A knock on the door interrupted our conversation. A male-troll entered. "My Queen, King Swade is ready to depart."

"Thank you."

Goutel excused him. "Tell him we will be right there. He can meet us at the queen's shuttle. You can escort them."

"Of course." Then he was gone.

"You are all packed," she said as she handed me the small bag. "I need you to be careful. We do not know the disposition of this Niffler."

"I will be careful." I smiled to ease her fears. "I have to find him first."

"I have no doubt you will." Goutel pulled me in for a hug. She always saved the most intimate affections between us for private quarters. She felt it wasn't appropriate for servants to display that type of intimacy in public. But everyone knew she was no servant of mine. She was my dearest friend. I held her close.

"I will be fine."

"You will be safe," she asserted.

"I will be safe."

"Now be off with you, before your daughter finds out you're leaving. She will make this much harder than I ever could."

Goutel was right about that. It was time for me to make my escape.

Chapter Ten

I dropped off King Swade and his entourage in the forest of Lost Leaf. It was a grand forest with huge trees, the largest in the world. I could see why Swade spent much of his time among them. Hundreds of centaurs inhabited the lands throughout the gigantic trees. Swade's nine wives were happy to see him upon our arrival. I barely got to say farewell before they swept him away for a merry reunion.

Back in my shuttle, I was not sure where to begin. The Niffler was a curious creature. The only one of his kind, he was secretive, leading a life of seclusion. My father and he had a pleasant relationship after they ran into each other—literally—many, many years ago. The Niffler was burrowing one of his tunnels and my father's shuttle happened upon the freshly dug passage. What could have been a battle turned out to be the start of an unlikely friendship.

My father did not speak of him often, but every now and again he mentioned that the Niffler called upon him for counsel or maybe just company.

I did not even know what the creature looked like, only that he collected shiny things. He was a treasure seeker. *Where would a treasure seeker scavenge for items he deemed worthy? What is treasure to a Niffler?*

My shoulders slumped in defeat. A lead was no good to me if I had no idea what to do with it. Goutel had packed the most recent map of the shuttle passages. Perhaps there would be something on it that would inspire a starting point.

I rummaged through the bag and felt something unexpected. I pulled out the map, and with it my crown. On the back of the map was a note handwritten by Goutel.

You insist that I cannot help you, but I insist that I must.

How else will you coax out a seeker of fine things but with a fine thing?

I packed your crown for you to trap the untrappable.

You're welcome.

I laughed out loud. She was the smarter of the two of us, without a doubt. *Now where does one set the bait for a Niffler?* That was the important question. I unfolded the map and, once again, was blown away by Goutel's foresight. She circled a length of shuttle line between the Solomon Islands, the islands of the giants and Antarctica, and next to that was a small notation.

This is where your father first ran into the beast. You're welcome.

Maybe I should have brought her with me. I laughed again. She would have already made contact with the thing. I folded the map back up, stuck my crown in the sack, and prepared my shuttle for the coordinates she indicated. I could be there in a matter of minutes.

Luckily for me, it was a remote shuttle line. The giants shied away from our services or from leaving their islands at all. This meant there would be very little traffic on the lines. I was being blessed by the strokes in more than one capacity today.

“Thank you, Malarin,” I said to the ethers. Then I sent my shuttle in the right direction.

Chapter Eleven

Moments later I arrived at the intersection indicated on the map. The best I could do for now was to sit and wait.

I looked around my shuttle. I loved it. It was the only thing as a queen that I'd made myself. All trolls created their own shuttles because they were an extension of our beings. It was our essence that fueled the transport. That was why we negotiated our tolls with magical tokens or morsels of energy—they filled our reserves so we could continue our service. Plus, it gave us the advantage of having a variety of other elements at our disposal. Things like communication, healing, and much, much more.

I often wondered why the painter had made us in this way, with the ability to express other creatures' gifts. As far as I had ever known, there were none other that possessed this ability. My shuttle alone carried thousands of tolls. I never knew when one would come in handy.

I walked over to my collection. My mother always said she knew I would be an organized ruler by the way I kept my shuttle. Every toll was accounted for, categorized and stored for safekeeping. I also kept my shuttle pristinely clean, unlike my daughter Tazzle. I laughed and shook my head at the thought of it, imagining who my granddaughter Fetzle would take after. There was a pride in the building of one's shuttle that only a troll could understand. I wanted my guests to feel at ease when they entered, and it was conveyed to me by many that in fact they did.

Shuttles were built from elements of the earth. My chosen element was granite. I had a rainbow of different speckled stones throughout my space, shelves with gold and black specs of color. These shelves held my tolls. Benches of black and grey granite circled a large white-stone firepit.

Perhaps it was time to start a fire. I ambled over to the large basket I kept my firewood in. It was no ordinary basket. This basket had been woven by the sisters, the CiGuaPa. Beautiful in their form, they looked much like humans or Conduits, but they were not. The CiGuaPa sisters had pale blue skin and feet that pointed in the opposite direction than those of a human. I rather liked the look of it. Ci, the eldest sister, had red hair. Gua, the middle sister, had yellow wavy hair, and Pa had deep royal-blue hair. Together they wove their hair into an assortment of items with many different gifts. My basket, for instance, would never be empty of whatever I chose to put in it.

I took several logs and threw them in the pit, quickly lit a match and tossed it on top. The wood went up in flames. I did not need the fire for warmth. Rather, I enjoyed the company of it. My favorite chair rocked slightly as I took my seat and kicked my feet up on the ledge of the firepit.

I closed my eyes, only listening to the crackling of the fire. The image of sweet Fetzle filled my mind. She took after both her parents. A she-troll, royal and strong, but those pale blue eyes, those were what captivated me—just like my Itzalo's. The trolling had the clear white thick skin that would someday be covered in dirt, just like most trolls were. Three rows of needle-sharp teeth for chewing through flesh. We didn't need the meat, but if given the choice, most trolls would choose biting into still-living flesh. There was something about the energy exchange that occurred. It had been years since I, myself, had eaten anything that was still alive. It wasn't fitting for a queen to act with that type of barbarism.

But I did remember and cherished the last time I'd fed in that manner. My father and I had hunted an elk.

"Make it a swift death, Peozleo. We are merciful killers. Honor thy prey..." His words trailed off in my head. Maybe I could take a nap. Sleep was not something I needed either, but I certainly loved to dream. With that, I trailed off in a state between consciousnesses.

Chapter Twelve

Sometime while drifting through consciousnesses I was startled awake. I felt a jolt, then again, this time harder. My entire shuttle shook violently and I was grateful I had properly secured all of my magics, because not one fell from its place. I heard a loud brushing sound sweeping above me quickly.

This has to be the Niffler, right? If it were not, I would need to abandon my plan of action and discover a new way to make contact with the elusive beast.

"Niffler!" I asserted. The brushing stopped but the silence made me feel no better about the situation at hand. "Niffler?"

Still there was nothing. My shuttle shook again, rocking back and forth, making me nauseous from the motion. *Dare I step outside to truly assess the scene?* It was either that or run—and running wasn't an option. It only prolonged the inevitable task at hand.

I moved toward the door, took a deep breath and quickly unlatched the lock. The hatch lifted and I was met with two huge black eyes. I took the sight in as quickly as possible. An enormous rodent stood in front of me. Grey-brown hair was matted with dirt, the nose was black as night, and long, ropey whiskers jetted in every direction.

"You are not Feyol! You are a she-troll!"

The creature turned to scurry down a dark hole in the distance. "Wait! Are you the Niffler? Feyol was my father. I am his daughter, the queen of the trolls, and I need your help!" I let the desperation leech in; anything to get this animal to stop, to hear me out.

It did not stop but it did slow down.

"Why would your father send you when I have not seen him in centuries?"

"My father has long been stone."

"That is nonsense!"

"It is not, I am afraid. He and my mother entered the River Tins many years ago."

The beast's pace had all but stopped but it didn't turn around to face me as it spoke. "That explains why I have not seen him in many centuries." I saw in the shadows that the rodent's head hung low. *Is he mourning my father?*

"He expired in the arms of my mother. They chose to pass on together. It is the highest honor among our people to go in this way."

"There is no honorable way to die, she-troll!"

"Is there not an honorable way to die as a Niffler?" I was hoping it would confirm what I suspected—that he was the beast I was looking for.

He turned his gaze to me once more. "There is no honorable way to die when you are the only one of your kind. When I go, there will be a Niffler no more. Who, then, will collect the world's treasures? Well? Who will do it?"

"You cannot be the only creature that accumulates treasures, or if you are, then perhaps you have located one I am pressed to discover and we may negotiate a price."

A shrill laugh echoed off the walls of the cave around us. "You came here to see my treasure trove? You are a woman." The Niffler laughed again.

"Pardon me?"

"Your father knew better than to be so bold, so brazen. You will never set foot in my treasury, foolish she-troll."

"I am a queen!" I had had enough of this beast's disrespect. Niffler or not, manners were always necessary.

"What does that mean to me? You are just another silly female."

"My father would be appalled by your behavior. I am his only child. I require help from his long-time friend, and all you can do is insult me. I assure you, you are not the company my father usually kept if this is the best hospitality you have." Something in me knew this Niffler would have no respect for me unless I demanded it. I had to meet him at his level to earn his trust. It was a level I didn't enjoy but desperate times called for desperate measures.

"You do speak plainly for a feminine nature." The rodent slowly walked toward me, sniffing the ground as he approached, and I realized the sweeping sound was his enormous whiskers brushing the stone. He stopped a few feet away, towering over me, and it dawned on me for the first time… I did not know what a Niffler ate. I could be swallowed whole by this beast. *Show no fear,* I thought. "You have your father's golden eyes. His eyes always looked like treasure to me, another shiny thing to add to my collection."

I heard the sadness in the Niffler's voice. It made me miss my father as well.

"I miss him too."

We stood there in a long silence. What was going through the Niffler's head, I would never know. I could only hope it wasn't a consideration of how I may taste.

"What do you seek?" the Niffler hissed.

"A blade."

That shrill laugh filled the space again and goose bumps danced up my neck.

"A blade," it mocked. "A she-troll wishes to find a blade. What would a female do with a blade?"

"By Malarin's strokes, Niffler, what is this offense you have of the feminine gender?"

The black eyes looked back at me with a strange blank stare. "Well, I am not one of them."

The astonishment on my face must have said it all because he recoiled ever so slightly.

"What? There is only one of me and the painter made me male—clearly the masculine is superior."

"Where I come from, the male-trolls are smaller and less powerful than the she-trolls, so it would stand to reason that the painter favored the females."

He just shook his head in disgust. "That makes no sense. No sense at all."

"You may believe what you wish, but I ask that you keep the snide comments to yourself—assume I am doing my best as a troll. I do not need your insulting remarks."

He just glared at me.

"This is a special blade."

"Are they not all special? If they have caught my eye, they are of an extraordinary caliber, I assure you."

I was uneasy telling the Niffler all that I knew. But is there another way? How can I convince him to help me?

Just then I felt another earth-shaking jolt. This time it was all around me, coming from the earth itself.

"May my strokes be damned! I must get out of here!" the Niffler shouted and ran towards its dark abyss of a hole. My chance to get information from him was slipping away.

"Wait!"

"I cannot! I should not be this close to the islands."

The islands?

A thunderous noise came from overhead. I darted back into my shuttle. The earth above me collapsed. I was going to be crushed or entombed here for some time, at the very least until I could repair the shuttle line.

Then I heard what could only be described as an animal brawl before it when deathly silent.

Chapter Thirteen

I waited for what felt like an eternity. Silence. Nothing but silence. It was time to see the damage. Would I be digging myself out, repairing my shuttle, or worse, reaching out to Tazzle to come assist me? Her involvement was the last thing I wanted.

The lever on the door moved with ease. That was a good sign. I pushed, and dirt and rock fell about the hatch but it moved—another good sign. Then I saw it, whatever it was… Another gigantic rodent. This one had a bushy tail. It was tying the Niffler's four paws together. He appeared to be unconscious. *What in the strokes happened to him?*

I took a deep inhale, smelling both of their auras simultaneously. Fluffy tail was courageous, righteous, while the Niffler was selfish, indignant. The fluffy-tailed rodent spotted me. There was nowhere to go, nowhere to hide. And the truth of the matter was, I needed to be wherever the Niffler was, whether I liked the look of this situation or not.

"Who gogogoes there?" the creature stuttered.

"My name is Peozleo. I am the queen of the trolls," I asserted with confidence.

"P-P-Peozleo? Are you acquaintances with this p-p-pest?"

The stutter wasn't from fear, it was an impediment. "Hardly. I am in need of his assistance, however, in locating something of great importance."

"D-d-did he steal from you as well?"

Oh, now I understood what this was about. My mind jumped ahead quickly. Perhaps if I could help the Niffler out of this situation, he would be more likely to assist me. Or even better, maybe this creature intended to raid his treasury. "Possibly. I need to see his treasure trove to be certain."

"Y-y-you will be hard p-p-pressed to find it. This f-f-fiend is very clever." The beast yanked on the Niffler's binds, tightening them so that, should he wake, there would be no getting away.

"And you, my friend? Who are you?"

"I-I-I am Ratat-t-toskr, hired by the giants to deliver the th-th-thief."

"Like a bounty?"

The creature nodded and I saw a glimpse of its face. Suddenly I remembered who Ratatoskr was. He was the enormous squirrel who was responsible for weaving all of the roots of the world's trees into the core of the earth herself.

"You are the great Ratatoskr. I have heard of your repute. How have you come to do the bidding of the giants?"

"I-I-I am very illustrious indeed," he agreed with pride. "My b-b-brother here has been creating problems. It is up to m-m-me to bring him to j-j-justice, since our s-s-sister Adanc c-c-cannot travel on land."

Adanc was the great sea monster. She traveled in every body of salt water, keeping peace beneath the waves. "You three are siblings?" I was astonished.

"C-c-created from the s-s-same stroke." Ratatoskr shook his head and looked down at his brother. "S-s-something went wrong with Niffler—h-h-his strokes are pervaded."

I found myself pitying the rat monster; he was not even cared for by his siblings. His relationship with my father must have been very special to him. I knew now that I had to go with them and do my best to get him out of this debacle, whatever that may be. I did not much care for the giants. They did not much care for trolls. None of that mattered at the moment.

"May I go with you?"

Ratatoskr looked at me skeptically. "H-h-he will not help you. H-h-he helps no one."

"I must try."

"W-w-well, if you must. I am n-n-not one to stop you."

I turned back and looked at my shuttle. It was in working order, but because the giants did not care for us, we avoided creating lines near the Solomon Islands. It would be best to leave it here and come back for it after I sorted things out with the Niffler. I grabbed my bag and, just before I was going to step out, I remembered I had a translation serum. Once again, I was grateful for my system. I knew exactly where it was. I quickly swiped the small bottle that I had gotten from a faerie many years ago and shut the hatch. I kicked some of the rocks out of the way, gingerly making my way to Ratatoskr's side.

"I will follow you."

Chapter Fourteen

These tunnels were different than shuttle lines. They were taller, wider, and far closer to the earth's surface. They served a different purpose. They were passageways for the giants to get from island to island without entering the sea. Giants did not much like water. The rumor was that was because they could not swim. They only sank. I could not say if there was truth to this rumor. In my lifetime I had only met one giant. We trolls were large but giants could grow three times our size. That was not our grievance with one another, though. It went back much further than that. When the first giants were created, a she-troll named Xieleo fell in love with the Emperor's son, Kaness. Since this star-crossed affair, the giants preferred to keep their distance from our trolliage.

I'd never felt any animosity toward the giants. It also never bothered me that they kept to themselves. So it was anyone's guess how this encounter was going to go.

"How do you know the giants, Ratatoskr?"

"Empress D-d-dafnee knows my s-s-sister well. Adanc called on me when this d-d-deviant stole a f-f-family heirloom."

"What did he steal?"

"I d-d-don't know; only that it w-w-was important."

"You and Adanc are close?"

"V-v-very close."

"How does she know the empress?"

"Th-th-the sea, of c-c-course."

Apparently Ratatoskr was not one for elaboration. My nerves were getting the better of me and I wanted to make myself busy with chitchat, but he was not obliging me.

"Are we close?"

"Y-y-yes."

A thought occurred to me. "Do you speak trollish?"

The question stopped the squirrel in his tracks. "Wh-wh-why is it that every creature th-th-thinks that it is I wh-wh-who speaks their language?" He shook his head and then began to walk again. "N-n-no, Ch-ch-chitchakor created our strokes with n-n-no language of our own. S-s-so we speak all languages. W-w-we are exceptional."

"That is exceptional," I agreed, because it was. I had learned many languages over my centuries inhabiting this world, mostly because it was expected of a queen to do as much. With the help of many different magics, it became even easier, but by no means was I created with the ability to understand and speak to all beings. Not even the dragons could speak to all beings, yet they were blessed with the ability to understand all languages. Dragonian was a lost language to all but the lineage of trolls. We were the last creatures to understand the originals without assistance. I often wondered how I sounded to those I spoke to. Cane once said that when I spoke Asagi all my words ran together. *What do I sound like speaking trollish?*

"W-w-we are here."

He interrupted my thoughts and I looked up to see a very steep staircase in front of us.

"Are they expecting you?"

"Th-th-they will recognize my entrance. Y-y-you will be seen as an intruder."

I held my head up and squared my shoulders. There was no turning back now. I looked at the Niffler's limp body and wondered what his brother had done to knock him out so hard. The squirrel put the ropes in his mouth, exposing his two large front teeth. They had to be over half my height. It made my skin crawl. Ratatoskr took off at a quick speed and I had to climb the steps two at a time and at a sprint to keep up. I was starting to regret bringing my bag.

The ascension took some time. When we reached the top of the staircase I was winded.

A loud feminine voice greeted us almost instantly. "Ratatoskr," was all I understood. The rest of the words were lost on me. I quickly rummaged through my bag, found the serum, uncorked it and swallowed the contents. *I sure hope it doesn't make me sick,* I considered as an afterthought.

My head got swimmy and my mouth dry, then my ears popped and I could understand the voice perfectly.

"Why? Explain," the female voice demanded. "We do not condone the company of trolls here."

Ratatoskr started to speak but I interrupted.

"I am sorry. I only came to get to the bottom of a theft myself."

"You speak giant? How is this?"

"It's fae magic, a toll I collected for a shuttle service."

She scoffed. "It is almost its own form of thievery, your tolls."

"Excuse me." I meant to bite back the words, but they just came out.

A moment later the silhouette of a large female appeared in a corridor ahead. "Since you can understand me, I suppose introductions are in order." When she moved into the light there was no doubt that she was royalty. Three times my size, she had long white hair that was braided to one side and over her shoulder. She almost looked human except for her size and huge-browed forehead. I was not judging, however. I preferred to be created with unique characteristics. We trolls were one of a kind. The giants had been created before humans or Conduits, so it was safe to say the painter mimicked their strokes, *but then would it be true to say that he felt he did better with the renditions to follow?* I smirked to myself. The woman wore the hides of large mammals to cover her groin, her breasts were bare, but her neck was weighted down by many necklaces, an assortment of boulder-sized stones strung together and almost completely covering her nipples.

"I am Empress Dafnee." Her purple eyes assessed me. I looked for a crown on her head. She didn't have one but she did have several gold ropes woven through her braid, definitely a sign of affluence and power.

"I am Queen Peozleo."

That caught her off guard but she quickly recovered.

"We are hosting the queen of the trolls? To what do we owe this pleasure? Or am I to understand you keep the company of thieves?" Another backhanded insult.

"On the contrary, I was hoping to admire said thief's collection and assess if he is in possession of an item I know to have been stolen." I paused before adding the last part. "For a friend."

I was still uncertain how forthcoming to be with this mission.

Ratatoskr just stood between the two of us, still holding the ropes in his mouth.

"Well, it seems we both have a stake in this creature's 'collection', as you kindly refer to it. I prefer to call his methods what they are, pilfering of what is not his to collect."

"I am not arguing that with you, Empress. I meant no ill intent." She was ready to condemn anything I said that didn't entirely align with her assessment and I didn't care to rumble with her. The Niffler was a thief; it was that simple. He must have stolen something exceptionally valuable from the giants for them to commission his capture and for her to be so sensitive—or maybe it was the sight of a troll that agitated her.

"What spell do you have him under, Ratatoskr?"

"I g-g-gave him root of the sleeping vine. It w-w-will take him a day to rouse, Empress."

I wondered if he was speaking in giant now. It also occurred to me that I did not know how long this serum would last. May the strokes be in my favor, since it would seem I would be here for, at the very least, a day.

"A day? Could you not have been more sparing with the root?" The empress propped her hands up on her hips. "It matters not now. We are in this predicament without an easy solution."

Aww, I was the predicament.

"I can return, Empress," I suggested. I did not necessarily wish to stay here either.

"That would be foolish. Besides, we giants have a hospitality code. Once you enter this hall you will have all your needs attended to for the duration of your stay. It is why we do not invite trolls down here."

Respect was clearly not part of the giants' code. I thought about arguing with her but it seemed like an impossible battle. She didn't want me here, yet she would be aggravated if I left and broke her code.

"Then I would be honored to be hosted by you and yours, Empress." I nodded politely.

She turned to Ratatoskr. "And you will stay as well. We owe you much gratitude, and your sister will be excited to see you."

Adanc is here? They must have been good friends.

"Of c-c-course, Empress. I l-l-look forward to seeing Chaness t-t-too."

The Empress smirked at me. "I think our new friend here will appreciate meeting the princess as well."

Not if she is anything like her mother, I thought.

CHAPTER FIFTEEN

I threw my bag down on the floor. It was a nice room, very comfortable because it was meant for much larger guests. I had all the room in the world to spread out. Tall ceilings and clay walls kept it cool. There were huge murals on each wall, painted with a sundry of bright colors. Ocean scenes, mountains and lands of ice and snow. I could appreciate the art for hours and probably still miss many of the details—it was impressive.

A knock on my door. *Already?* I thought. I had only just entered. I opened it and saw a huge bear-looking creature on the other side.

"Dinner is at dusk. The empress wishes you wash yourself and wear this robe," the bear said flatly, handed me a black furry garment and turned the other direction.

I shut the door and wondered how I would know when it was dusk. There were no windows in this room. It was preferable to me, of course, to have as little light as possible. I spent most of my time underground. Too much sunlight and I found my eyes hurt.

When I turned back around to face my bed and put the robe on it, I saw a large tub manifest before my eyes. *Giants have their own tricks.* Immediately the tub began to fill with water. I did not have an aversion to baths but this was a lot of pampering for me in only a few days. I internally huffed and desperately wished Goutel was here to help me navigate this situation.

The water stopped a few inches from the top of the tub. I tested the temperature with my hand. It was perfect. There was an oil in it, rose oil—by the strokes, I would smell like this for weeks. I stepped into the bath, surprised to find it wasn't too deep. They had a troll-sized tub after all. It proved to be more relaxing than I would have thought. I soaked for a long time but was pulled from my tranquility when the water began to drain on its own. It must have been on a timer, so this was my cue to get ready for dinner.

A towel that I hadn't noticed before lay on a bench just outside the tub. I dried off and looked at the black furry robe. It was a pelt of some kind. I detested wearing clothes. *Did the empress know this somehow?* I would not put it past her.

I pulled it over my shoulders and it proved to only be a little too large. That was another surprise. Once the robe was on I looked for a mirror. There were none, so I would just have to pray the empress approved of my appearance, since I could not make an assessment of my own. My chamber door opened. I peered into the hall. No one was there but it seemed like I was being led by some invisible force so I stepped into the vast concourse. I was about to shut my door when I realized this might be the appropriate time to wear my crown. I darted back in my room, dug out the crown, silently thanked Goutel for her wisdom and foresight, and reentered the concourse. This time someone stood at the other end of the long passage. By their silhouette I could assume it was a giant. That was until they called out my name.

"Queen Peozleo? Is that you?" a familiar voice echoed.

"Cane?"

He quickly ran toward me in his gigantic form. Cane looked just like a giant except he was not one. He was a Conduit who expressed the gift of growth.

"What in Malarin's strokes are you doing here? The giants are not particularly fond of trolls," he stated the obvious and laughed. I appreciated Cane on a good day, but on a day like today I was ecstatic to see a friendly face.

"This was an accident, I assure you. What are you doing here, my friend? Do you converse with giants often?" I asked, realizing for the first time that he might. "You and Sorcey were making arrangements for the upcoming Trials when I saw you only yesterday, were you not?"

"I have spent a fair share of time down here. I get to really immerse myself in my gifts. The High Priestess requested an audience with me. The timing could not be worse; the Katuan Trials are set to begin in just short of a fortnight. But when a High Priestess calls upon you, I dare say you answer." He leaned down and gave me a hug. "It is wonderful to see you again so soon. How is your granddaughter?"

"It is good to see you. The trolling is well. I wish I was home with her right now but that is a story for another time." I was not going to go into all that had happened with him right now. Not here, where I was not among friends.

"Let me fix your crown." He adjusted it gently. "There, now you look like the queen you are."

"Thank you. There are no mirrors in my room."

"It may be for the better. The giants have strange traditions with their robes."

I looked Cane over and realized he was wearing nothing but a small loincloth over his genitalia, not his usual garment choice. There was no point in making him feel any more insecure than he already did. He was by all accounts a handsome man—sandy blonde hair, soft fair skin, striking hazel eyes. I didn't much care for his characteristics but I could appreciate the beauty of the creature. Besides, he had great broad shoulders, the type you would find on a she-troll—definitely his best feature.

"You wear leathers very nicely. And I should know, since I am at groin height." We both laughed. Suddenly torches began to light along the corridor. "Can we assume that is our escort?"

"Indeed, we can." Cane smiled his warm smile and I was grateful for his friendship.

I took three steps to his one but kept his pace. We turned a corner and the hall opened into an enormous banquet room. Everyone else was already seated. We were late to the party, hence the torch chauffeur. The empress stood and everyone else stood with her.

"Welcome, honored guests." I looked up to see Cane smiling. He truly felt honored. I wished I could say the same. "Please take your seats."

The giant beside the empress gestured with a sweeping arm. "Cane, you must sit by me. I insist." By the look of him, he was the emperor. With everyone standing, I could not see another vacant seat, until I could. The color drained from my face where there had been so little already.

"Queen Peozleo, you will find your seat here, beside Princess Chaness."

My feet wouldn't move. They couldn't move. Princess Chaness was a giant-sized troll.

Chapter Sixteen

What kind of sorcery is this? I watched the enormous troll in disbelief. In all my days, with everything I have seen over the vast lifetimes I have lived, never could I imagine such a thing. When I sat, everyone else around me took their seats. I was dwarfed, surrounded by giants and Princess Chaness. Her eyes were glued on me. I could feel them burning with her own curiosities.

The empress was on my other side, and my ally, Cane, was yards away.

"Princess, let me formerly introduce you to Queen Peozleo."

I swallowed the knot in my throat and turned to greet the Princess. "Princess Chaness, it is lovely to meet you."

She smiled and I realized she did not have the layers of needle-point teeth we trolls had. Her teeth were those of a giant—square, blunt, and she only had one row. "The pleasure is mine, dear queen." This close, I also noticed that her eyes were more proportionate to her head and slightly more almond-shaped. But there was no mistaking her nearly translucent white skin that was distinctively troll. Her head was as bald as mine, as well, a stark contrast to the giants around us. In my quick assessment of her body, and while she wore more clothes than I would ever be comfortable in, I detected her form was more slender than mine but absolutely more muscular than the empress'. I suspected that while I made my own appraisal, she was in fact taking inventory of my characteristics and similarities as well.

Empress Dafnee interrupted our silence. "I intend to leave no mystery about it. Princess Chaness is the daughter of Kaness, the first emperor's son, and Xieleo, the she-troll."

The thought had crossed my mind, because there seemed no other explanation. But that would make the princess extremely old—four generations my senior, to be exact. *How can that be?* Giants did not live very long, especially in comparison to a troll's life span.

"How old are you?"

"A hundred span."

I did not know this measurement.

The empress elucidated without me asking. "We giants live a life span of about three hundred years before our bones get brittle and we turn to dust. Chaness has lived through a hundred of our span, making her over thirty thousand years old."

"Astounding." There were no other words. She was incredible. Half-giant, half-troll, and a complete anomaly.

Chaness smiled again. "The Priestess says I may live forever."

"We should be so lucky," Dafnee said at my back. I could not take my eyes off the princess. "If you wish, you two may take some time away later this evening, but for now let us eat. The High Priestess has invited a special guest, Queen Peozleo—Cane Kraus."

I finally tore my eyes away and looked beyond the two royals at Cane, who was enjoying the company of the emperor very much.

"Cane and his wife are very good friends of the trolls."

"They are good friends to all," the empress contended, and there was no arguing that. "Our Priestess requires we engage in ceremony, and the first of that is breaking bread and drinking wine. Communion creates an energy that is used to fuel the conjuring." Dafnee lifted her glass in the direction of three women dressed very different than the rest, across from our table.

All three women had long black hair woven in an assortment of thin and thick braids. They could have been sisters, and for all I knew they were. Their skin was bronzed, sun-kissed. Their high cheek bones and slightly varied nose structure made them look distinctly similar. The middle one wore a black cloak with gold inlays threaded throughout. It gave her an appearance of mystic power, and I knew she must be the High Priestess.

The empress handed me a chalice. It was almost the appropriate size for my grip. "Drink up. The time for merriment is now."

We clinked glasses and I raised my cup to the High Priestess, who in turn gave me a wicked grin.

CHAPTER SEVENTEEN

I had to admit that the giants knew how to have a great time. It helped that I really enjoyed Chaness' company. The empress became a brilliant hostess once the food was served, and she flitted about, filling the hall with laughter and conversation, so that gave Chaness and I time to talk. We kept the conversation lighthearted, an unspoken agreement between us. Or perhaps it was the empress' statement that we would have time alone in the future that abated my desire to dive into more in-depth matters. Either way, our conviviality was pleasant.

"You are wearing my childhood robe," Chaness pointed out after several glasses of wine.

I laughed so hard I thought I would spray the table with red wine. "I am not!" I asserted when I could use my words again.

"It is true. You are wearing my robe from when I was a youth. It was all they could find to fit you." She patted me on the head playfully. "You wee little troll."

My belly hurt, I laughed so deeply.

"I cannot wait to tell my daughter that I was called a wee troll by a giant princess. She will be tickled."

"Are you two close?" There was a tenderness in Chaness' question that caught me off guard.

"Very. I would do anything to see her be happy and thrive." It was true; after all, that was what had brought me here.

"She is lucky to have a mother like you."

"Were you and your mother close?" I had to assume Xieleo had died some years back. She would have lived longer than a giant, but unless she had been enchanted, she would not have lived as long as her daughter appears to have done.

"I never met my mother. She died bringing me into this world."

That was the emotion I'd felt. She was doleful about her mother's passing. The thought had not occurred to me until then that perhaps a troll-giant offspring would be difficult to animate. Come to think of it, I wondered how she did come to be born.

"How was your mother's labor?"

Chaness opened her mouth to speak when the empress interrupted. "I said you would have time to speak in private later. Tonight we make merriment." Her voice was stern.

"Of course, Empress," Chaness agreed. I gave her a sideways glance, hoping to convey that we would return to this conversation.

I looked about and noticed that all of the conversations around us were full of choruses of laughter. This must have been some sort of requirement for what the empress referred to as communion energy. It was a beautiful way to fuel magic, but I sensed a level of facade to it now. I realized that for now I could not follow the natural flow of my conversation with Chaness into matters that were not necessarily pleasant but could deepen our understanding of one another.

Ratatoskr came over to converse with the princess.

"P-p-princess, how have y-y-you been?"

I gave them their privacy and turned to see that Cane was free for a moment.

"Come, tell me. I am curious, do you speak giant?"

He nodded and I could tell by the exaggerated gesture that he was feeling a little sloshed. "I do. I am fluent in giant, trollish, Asagi, and mediocre in several other tongues. You seem to be quite fluent. How, pray, tell did you manage that?"

"I have a few tricks up my sleeve."

"A toll or two if memory serves." He leaned over the two vacant chairs to clink glasses. "May the strokes be in our favor!"

"May they be!"

Just then the High Priestess stood and the room got quiet. Cane was instantly enthralled by the spectacle as well. We both adjusted ourselves to face her. Ratatoskr quickly excused himself back to his seat.

The Priestess moved seductively to the center of the room, where no tables had been set. It was a circular space, and now that my attention was drawn to it, I noticed the carvings in the floor—several overlapping circles, some small and some large. The design was beautiful. I saw a few of the giants look up, and only then did I realize that the ceiling was made of reflective glass so you could watch the Priestess' movements from above. Her sweeping gestures were even more captivating from this vantage. There appeared to be gold sparks that flew behind her cloak as she traced some of the circles with her steps.

"She's magnificent, isn't she?" Chaness whispered.

"Shhh!" the empress scolded as she sat. Their dynamic was peculiar. I would ask Chaness about it when we had privacy.

The gold sparks turned into flames as the Priestess skipped faster along the lines. Her movements were fluid, graceful, sensual, like a dance without music. Smoke began to fill the room. It wasn't normal smoke, though. It was sweet and tasted like strawberries on the tongue. The Priestess moved faster still, and the flames no longer chased behind her but instead the golden fire remained in the etched markings and the woman danced through them. This was the most beautiful magic I had ever witnessed. Her aura grew as she performed the rites. I had never tasted anything like her energy.

The other two Priestesses began to chant, quiet at first but gaining in volume as their leader moved faster. "Aho, hum ta ho, heh tum ho." Even with the serum in my blood, I could not translate the words. Louder and louder their voices rose, and when the chanting was nearing yelling pitch, they stopped, as did the dancing, and the High Priestess fell to the floor. Flames crawled onto her cloak, animal-like in nature, consuming her fallen form, and I thought for a moment we were going to watch her be burned alive. But suddenly she rose from the ashes, naked, with her eyes closed. I took my stare form the ceiling to the woman who stood in front of me. Her back was too me and I admired her shape. It was voluptuous, very feminine.

Without warning, the Priestess turned and darted forward, landing on the table in front of Cane like a lioness crouched and ready to strike.

"Your son will unite the circles!" The words came out in a flurry. Then she was in front of me. Her pupils, her whole eyes, were black.

"You cannot give him what he seeks. The strokes were painted long ago. You will dismantle his Staff. You must, or all you love will perish."

Then her body went limp. She fell from the table onto the floor. One of the other Priestesses came to her aid while the other scooped up the ashes of the cloak she'd been wearing. Only, when she brought the ashes to the High Priestess, they had somehow transformed back into the black cloak with golden thread.

They covered her body and began to lift her to her feet. She mumbled something. "Empress, the queen will go with you to the Niffler's trove."

"High Priestess?" the empress whispered.

"She will go," she repeated. "As will the Conduit Cane." Then she was swept away.

CHAPTER EIGHTEEN

I was still reeling from the ceremony as I walked back to my room. Chaness had stayed in the hall to see to the empress, or so I assumed. Cane was in a daze when I approached him. He just stared off in the distance and waved me on. So I left. The High Priestess' prophecy was terrifying. She had to be referring to King OAD and our agreement.

I repeated her words, "You cannot give him what he seeks. The strokes were painted long ago. You will dismantle his Staff. You must or all you love will perish."

But if I did not hold up my end of the bargain, *what then?* The fate of that decision would be just as dire, would it not? The strokes were not in my favor, and I wondered what I had done to deserve this quandary. I must have displeased Chitchakor himself to be met this way.

I looked up to see I was lost. The candles had lit the way for me when entering the banquet hall, so I had not been paying close attention to the whereabouts of my chamber.

"It is this way," a sultry voice sang in the dark. I turned to see one of the Priestesses behind me.

"Thank you," I said as she brushed past me to show me the way.

We walked in silence until she stopped at a door. "Here." She stepped aside and revealed from behind her huge frame, a familiar door. I turned the knob and tried to quickly dart inside, because something inside me was ringing an alarm. This was no happenstance that she had come upon me. Before I could get out of earshot, she spoke once more. "Alliances you make now will eliminate the bloodshed you engage in later. Love will be what stops the king's rage. You are a true queen. Your sacrifice will save many."

"What sacrifice?" Was she talking about the one I had already made, by saving Spitzle and getting into this mess? *Or is there more to come?*

"There will be many before the painter is finished with this stroke." Then she was gone, as though she had vanished in a wisp of smoke.

Many more? What else is there to lose? Where will this journey lead to next?

Chapter Nineteen

I paced in my room most of the night. It did nothing but heighten the pitch of my nerves, but still I persisted. Giants slept. They actually slept—in fact they needed it in order live. I was starting to believe Malarin was being funny when he created their lineage—he'd made them so fragile. It was counterintuitive to their stature. They appeared invincible but they, in fact, needed to eat and sleep, like humans. They probably had to shit too!

Cane was the first to come to me in the morning. The knock on the door was welcome. It meant things were stirring, that we would be making progress soon or at the very least develop a plan. I still had no idea how long the serum would last, how long I would be able to communicate with everyone. That added an extra layer of pressure.

"May I come in?"

"You are always welcome, wherever I am." I moved out of the entryway and he slipped inside.

"What do you make of last night's ceremony? Are High Priestesses often wrong? Do they have false visions?"

"Why would you ask such a thing?" I never considered Cane a doubter of the strokes. He seemed devoted to the existence of magic. It was part of what I loved about him, the part of him I was most akin to.

"I must know if you have ever heard of them being wrong." There was a desperation in my friend's voice I had never heard before.

"No, I have never heard of any of the prophets being wrong. Not the High Priestesses, or the Ramalans, or among our people, where we revere the Pythoness."

"She was wrong." Cane took a seat on my bed, slumped and dejected. "I do not have a son. I cannot have a son. She called me here for no reason. Now I am commanded to attend to this mission with the Niffler, when I should be back on Atlantis helping prepare for the Trials."

I sat beside my giant friend. It was a strange reversal. Come to think of it, I wondered why he did not alter his size when he was in troll company. A question for another time. In that very moment, I realized I did not understand procreation within the Conduit world.

"Can Sorcey not bear a child?"

"Conduits have one opportunity to have children. It is during our consummation. If we did not conceive during our first union, the female form does not have the ability to change and therefore is incapable of carrying a baby through pregnancy."

How odd. What a strange caveat to the painter's great creation. I supposed, in a sense, it made the union all the more special and the legacy of the Conduits all the more sacred. I suddenly felt empathy for my friend. *Did he and his partner want children?* What a terrible tragedy. We all had our tribulations to bear.

"I did not know. I am sorry." Right or wrong, it was how I felt. After all, it was the birth of my grandchild that had brought me here. Building a family was an honor every creature should get to experience if they wished to.

"Do not pity me and Sorcey. We have lived rich lives without a child. When we had the opportunity to strategize conceiving, we left it to the strokes. But that is it. The strokes were not in our favor. The Priestess said I would have a son, and that is impossible."

We were back to where we started. "Perhaps you will adopt?"

Cane looked at me but said nothing. I wished I could read minds in that moment. Then the door opened and the empress stood in front of us, bare-breasted and seemingly agitated.

"The Niffler is awake. The interrogation will begin, and it has been said that you two must be present." With that she turned around and left the room, the door ajar, apparently with the assumption that we would follow.

Cane and I both rose and started off in her direction.

"Perhaps you are right, my friend," Cane conceded. "There are many ways to build a family. We may adopt."

I patted him on the shoulder.

"But what on earth are the circles?" Of that, I had not the faintest idea.

Chapter Twenty

My heart ached for the Niffler. He stood in front of a merciless tribunal, and half of them were his family. The interrogation—or trial, rather—was taking place in the bowels of the Solomon Palace, well below sea level. Adanc was here. She was magnificent. At some point the giants had built an underwater chamber that allowed her to engage with them in full view. I had never met the water creature before. She was a sight. Twice as large as a giant, so massively larger than me. She was iridescent blue. Her skin or scales—whatever she possessed—sparkled like the belly of an oyster, but with teals, blues and soft hues of greens. Her body was slender like an eel's, with over fifty fins; I lost count when she moved. Her eyes were all white with specs of deep blues. I had never seen anything the likes of her.

When she spoke her voice demanded reverence—soft and commanding at the same time. Dalinkas had used much creativity when conjuring up this phenomenal creation. Ratatoskr sat beside the window of the tank, almost as though he was on guard of his sister.

It was obvious they had an intimate connection. The empress and emperor, along with the three Priestesses, were in thrones adjacent to the window. The two royals sat a level below the perceptive eyes of the Priestesses. It was clear who was really in charge of the proceedings—those with true sight. Cane, Chaness and I were the only other witnesses in attendance.

We sat back and to the right, on a large bench. There were many more seats around us, so apparently at times many were allowed to attend the interrogations that took place down here. For all I knew, maybe it was ordinarily a performance hall. Nonetheless, today it served as a courtroom. I looked at Chaness for the third time since she had walked in but she had not bothered to make eye contact with me. There was something wrong; I could feel it. This too hurt my heart. After all, we were family, and she was endearing and kind; that much was clear.

The Niffler was in the center, chained to the floor in such a way that he was forced to be on his knees. It was degrading. He had yet to speak but I could only imagine what was going through his mind.

Emperor Juness addressed the thief first. "Niffler, you are here to answer for your crimes."

Niffler said nothing and Juness continued. "We know you have stolen the Golden Spool Of Thread."

I did not know what he was accused of taking until now but I did know a thing or two about the Golden Spool Of Thread. It was a Rittle whose gifts included the potential to create something that was impervious to all forms of magic, or the capacity to bind one soul to another, plus there was the rumor it could sew the strands of fate.

The Rittles were a rare find, not entirely lost but nearly unknown. Much time had passed since they had been laid to rest in the caves of Cataphet. There was no origin story that explained how they began to manifest on the surface. All we knew was that they now resided in the hands of various creatures. Just as I was surprised to hear the bequeathing to OAD of the Staff of Banishment, I supposed I had always assumed wherever the other Rittles resided, they were safe and meant to be there, exactly as determined by the strokes.

When I returned from my thoughts I noticed the empress was watching me. I wondered what she assessed from my reaction.

The emperor continued. "What say you in accordance to this accusation?"

The Niffler said nothing.

"By way of our code, that is an act of treason punishable by death."

The Niffler said nothing, his expression stoic.

"Being that there is only one of you in all of the strokes, we dare not exterminate one of Malarin's unique creatures. For this reason, we see only one way to hold you accountable, and that is condemning you to an eternity in solitude."

That stirred a minute reaction as the Niffler passed a sideways glance to his brother and sister, who looked unmoved. Again my heart ached for him. He seemed so misunderstood to me. I had the heart of my father when it came to misfits. *How can he not feel betrayed by his family?*

"Return the Spool and reduce your sentence to a thousand years of solitude."

Niffler laughed, a clear act of defiance. *Could he not see he was already in a terrible predicament*? There was no way out for him, and my own hope was diminishing. I needed to search for the blade. I needed his help. I couldn't wait a thousand years. My mind was racing, playing out scenarios. I needed to persuade him to comply and oblige him to me all at once. Two tasks that felt impossible at present, but there had to be a way.

"Brother," Adanc's voice echoed in her water chamber, "you have done wrong for centuries. It is time to make things right. Return the Golden Spool to its rightful owners. Grant yourself mercy."

The Niffler looked up at his sister and a flash of emotion stirred in him. "You do not even know me, sister. You know not what I have done or why I have done it. To condemn me is to condemn our creator. Or would you contest he made a mistake in the strokes? Who are you to challenge the will of Chitchakor?"

I had never regarded things in this way but the Niffler conjured up valid considerations. He was born of the strokes, the same as me or any of the creatures that wandered this planet.

The High Priestess commanded everyone's attention. "You are correct, Niffler. I see it as you do. You were created with the desire and ability to collect precious things—there is nothing that makes this good or bad, for we do not have the right to determine which strokes are virtuous, and it reasons that if the painter made you in such a way, you are perfect as you are. But this is the hour of your redemption, because what you choose today will dictate the fate of the world. I have seen it."

"This world has never done me a service. Perhaps it is time for a new fate to come forth." He snickered.

They were cornering him and he was going to respond as he always did, in the way that had kept him safe, by retreating and licking his wounds. Only this time it would be in a cell. This was disastrous. If we were able to get him to disclose the whereabouts of his treasury, it would be likely that the vastness of it all would take centuries to comb through and find what we were looking for. I did not have time for that chore and I would wager that neither did the giants. They were going about this all wrong, but there seemed there was nothing I could do.

I could tell by his reaction to his sister and his friendship with my father that he did not wish to play out his existence alone. That was the bargaining chip. How could they not see that?

Ratatoskr spoke next. "You are a fool, and a desolate one at that. You can spout vindications for your behaviors but it will still leave you alone."

He loved my father, he mourned him; I saw it with my very own eyes. The Niffler didn't desire an eternity of solitude—that would be such a cruel sentence. I couldn't allow it to happen. "I will stand with him!" I shouted as I got to my feet.

"You will stand with him for what?" the empress demanded. "This is not your trial."

"I will stand with him and his character." The stares upon me said it all; I was insane. And perhaps I was, but I could not persecute a creature I knew was wounded and worthy of an opportunity that was never given to him. And that was before I factored in my need of his help. My father was the best judge of character I knew; if he trusted the Niffler, then I knew he saw his value and true nature. And if my father thought the Niffler made a good friend and ally, I would be a fool to disregard his judgment.

"And how do you suppose you will do that?" the empress sneered.

"The Niffler will escort us to his treasury. I will personally take responsibility for him. If he attempts escape, I will make the capture. If he performs any further trickery, I will hold him accountable."

The emperor interrupted me. "You are far too small to wrangle the beast."

"I will go with her," Chaness' voice trilled behind me.

The emperor looked at his wife but did not contest.

"And if he escapes?" the empress challenged looking straight at me. "You both will be executed for his crimes?"

The emperor nudged his wife, not wanting to publicly question her but clearly opposed to her inclusion of the princess.

"Yes. I will see to his punishment," I said. "There will be no need for Princess Chaness to suffer consequences. I will face his sentence." Everyone stirred in their seats and I saw an intrigued and mischievous look glint in the Niffler's eyes. What was worse was the look of opportunity in the empress' gaze. Her aura lit up with excitement. "But he has to take us to the treasury. If he fails to do this, I will order all trolls, until the day of his capture, to hunt him down and see to it that he spends the rest of eternity in a cell."

The Niffler turned away from me. What that meant, I did not know. The empress stood and looked to her Priestesses. "Is this as you wish?"

Have I fallen directly into a trap? I did not like being toyed with. There were too many moving parts here but there was no way they would have known I would offer to stand with him.

"All is in order with the tapestry of fate."

The tapestry of fate?

CHAPTER TWENTY-ONE

"Are you sure about this decision?" Cane asked as we walked back to our rooms.

"No, of course not. But my father thought him a friend. You know how good a judge of character he was. Besides, I need his help just as much as the giants need their Golden Spool back." I sighed.

"Those are all things to consider. What, may I ask, do you need of him?"

I hesitated. *Did Cane need to know my predicament?* "I have reason to believe he may have a blade that belongs to OAD, the king of the powries."

"I see. And you are dear friends with the king?"

"I owe him a big favor, and this is how he has chosen to collect my debt."

"And if the Niffler doesn't have it?"

"Then I surely have done something to provoke the strokes."

Chaness came around the corner. Her face reflected excitement, and it occurred to me that she probably had not spent much time outside the Solomon Islands. Perhaps she had never left this place. What a sad life for a troll—rather, a half-troll. We loved to travel. It was part of our nature.

"When do you think we will leave?" I sensed eagerness in her voice.

"As soon as your empress is ready. I must see to my shuttle, and if it suits the Niffler, we may use it to get part of the way to his treasury."

"And if it doesn't?" She looked at me expectantly. Apparently I was now leading this mission.

"Then we will travel as a Niffler does."

"How is that?"

I just shook my head.

Several hours later the empress was ready. What took her so long was beyond me.

"Meet us at the palace gates. I will escort the Niffler from his cell to your charge," the empress announced, then flitted off. Chaness led the way to the now-familiar entrance. Moments later Dafnee appeared with a chained and gagged Niffler in toe. He was being dragged by two male giants.

"Why is he gagged? Why are his legs bound? He doesn't need to be dragged," I protested.

"Doesn't he? Would you have him get away?"

The giants dropped him off at my feet. "Give me the key, empress. The Niffler deserves the respect of walking by himself and the capacity to speak."

The empress rolled her eyes. "It's your life." And she threw the keys at me.

"Cane, would you mind?" He knelt down with me and we quickly removed the excessive restraints. The Niffler said nothing when I pulled the gag out of his mouth. He just looked at me inquisitively.

"Can we maneuver the straps more into a harness?"

"Indeed." Cane began to make the appropriate adjustments. In a matter of minutes Cane was able to create something much more suitable for the Niffler and significantly more dignified.

Chaness took the lead once Cane fastened the lock on the harness that stretched across his chest and behind his back. He would be hard-pressed to wriggle out of it.

"After you, empress." I gestured with my hand and she pushed past all of us to lead the way. I wondered if she even knew where we were going.

Chapter Twenty-Two

It took us no time at all to get back to my shuttle. For such a large caravan, we moved quickly. It helped that the empress had a shortcut that led out of the palace and spit us out practically on top of the shuttle line. Apparently, she knew exactly where we were going.

Trolls could sense their shuttles; they were an extension of us in more ways than their looks. A bit of our being went into them, almost like animating our children.

"We are just above it. How should we proceed getting into the line? Without collapsing it altogether, of course."

The Niffler broke his silence. "I have a tunnel just to the left, here. It enters into the shuttle line. It is how I found you—and your father, for that matter."

Dafnee came to her own conclusions very quickly. "It is also how you infiltrated the palace, isn't it?"

He did not have to respond for her to confirm her suspicions.

"We have scoured these tunnels for your entrance point. Where is it?" She looked around. We all did, expecting a large hole.

"I am not just a thief or a rodent. I possess magics as well. How do you suppose I have permeated so many places that appeared impermeable?" There did seem to be something on his side. "As I said before, the painter made me this way."

He took a few steps and Chaness pulled back on his chains. "Well, I must show you, mustn't I?"

I nodded at her and she gave lead. His large nose investigated the ground until he found what he was looking for. He moved so fast I could not quite make out what he did. It was as though he shimmied his whiskers in an exceptional way. The dust around him stirred, spiraling into the air and dissolving into nothing, exposing a cavernous hole.

"What did you do there?" Dafnee demanded.

"I am taking you to my treasury, not sharing my secrets, Empress," he hissed.

"We will have this tunnel fortified," she announced, as though any of us doubted that.

"After you, Empress." The Niffler just chortled. She stoically led the way and I had to give her credit for her fearlessness. Dafnee was not one to entertain reservations.

One by one, we followed. The tunnel was steep but easily traversed.

"Niffler, can I transport us part of the way if not all of the way through the lines—perhaps save us time?" I was hopeful I could speed up our mission.

"No," he said plainly. "There are no troll lines that can carry us any closer to my sacred space, I can assure you."

That was disappointing but not at all surprising.

In no time at all we were in my shuttle line but something was different. The damage had been repaired, which could only mean one thing. Tazzle knew I was here. My stomach knotted. She must be worried.

"Stay here," I instructed as I ran ahead. There was a note just inside the hatch.

I read it quickly.

My Queen,

Your daughter charged us with the task of finding you in regards to your extended absence. When we discovered your shuttle abandoned and in a dismantled line we feared the worst. Princess Tazzle is prepared to storm the Solomon Islands should we not hear from you soon. Please contact us, let us know your state.

Your devoted servant and friend,
Goutel

Below her signature, in less formal font, it read,

I will never forgive myself if something has happened to you on this errand. Please come home.

I opened the door and rushed over to my wall of tolls. I grabbed the first thing that was catalogued as communication magic. Of course, I didn't know exactly how it worked. I shook the contents into my hand. It was a small origami swan.

"What in the strokes do I do with you?"

Instantly, it flew from my palm and fluttered about in front of me, repeating my words in lyrical form.

Dammit, did I waste the gift on my question?

I spoke again. "Daughter, Princess Tazzle, no need to worry. I am sorry that you found my shuttle in such a way. I ran into a friend of my father's who needs my assistance. I will be home shortly. Tell Goutel all is well, no cause for alarms—or arms."

The paper swan repeated, "What in the strokes do I do with you? Daughter, Princess Tazzle, no need to worry. I am sorry that you found my shuttle in such a state. I ran into a friend of my father's who needs my assistance. I will be home shortly. Tell Goutel all is well, no cause for alarms or arms."

Well, it wasn't perfect, but it would get the message across. But how did I send it?

"You write the name on the paper." Cane's voice startled me. He had shrunk and entered the shuttle without me noticing. "It's Kitsune magic. They use it to send the messages to their would-be lovers. Is everything okay?"

"My daughter is worried. She is likely to start a war with the giants if I don't get this message to her."

"Well, that would be unfortunate indeed. Do you have a pen?"

I swiped one up from a neighboring shelf. Gingerly, I reached for the delicately folded bird, put it against the wall and quickly scribbled Princess Tazzle of the trolls on the paper. When I let it go, it disappeared.

Suddenly there was a scuffle outside. *What now?*

Dafnee shouted above the noise, "You will let go of me."

"Where is our queen?" the familiar voice of Goutel demanded. "Surrender her to us immediately."

Cane and I rushed out to find twenty of my strongest she-trolls armed and ready to demand answers.

"I am here. I am safe." Immediately they put down their weapons and Goutel rushed over. Before taking me in her arms for a hug, she paused and composed herself, always vigilant about appearances. But I was not nearly as worried about what my most loyal people thought of me hugging my closest friend. I pulled her in.

"You are okay?"

"I am."

"What is this?" Dafnee asked in what I suspected she thought was a respectful tone but which came off as shrill and combative. It did not help that neither of the parties could understand each other.

"Upon finding my shuttle abandoned, naturally, my people worried. It isn't an ambush, I assure you." I looked to my guard and realized that they were completely captivated by the sight of Chaness, who was, in turn, sizing them up in her own way. Now seemed as good a time as any for introductions. "This is Empress Dafnee, Princess Chaness, the Niffler and, of course, you are familiar with Cane."

No one had taken their eyes off the princess, and now Goutel also stared in wild wonder. I cleared my throat and only then got everyone's attention. "This is Goutel, my trusted advisor and friend, and this is our Sholl Guard, the strongest of all the she-trolls among us." They each bowed in accordance.

Goutel leaned in and whispered, "You are certain you are okay?"

It was a loaded question but for the time being I was okay, and that was all that mattered. There were a million scenarios that could lead to various outcomes that would end terribly for me but none I could explain now, and none I desired to drag my friend into. Tazzle would need her wisdom if I did not survive this mission. So I answered her with as much reassurance as I could.

"No one here will harm me." I hoped my eyes gave her solace. It was not the entire truth but some things were better left unsaid.

"I am going with you," Goutel said it with such confidence that I doubted even Dafnee would object.

Chapter Twenty-Three

Dafnee in fact said nothing in response to Goutel's assertion. I, however, wished to object, but not here, in front of an audience.

"Very well," I agreed while I calculated how I would send Goutel on her way. "Come with me to collect some tolls from my shuttle and then you may excuse the guard."

She promptly followed me in. Once out of earshot, I spoke plainly. It was true that the empress couldn't understand us, but Cane and the Niffler could.

"I need you to go with the guard."

"Absolutely not. You are either safe enough that you needn't any help or you are in trouble and cannot express it, and I need to be with you."

"I wish it were that simple." I collected a few bottles and put them in the sack Goutel had packed for me a couple of days ago.

"Why do you wear your crown? You hate it. There must be a reason you are out of character." She was so observant, my friend.

"Sometimes I wish you were more daft."

"Do not avoid my question."

"Because some power only responds to power."

"You mean that giant female thing? How do you speak giant?"

"That is the empress Dafnee of the giants, and I took a serum. I have no idea how long the serum will last, and this is wasting time." I pointed to my translation shelf. "See if there is anything there that may help me in the future with communicating when this serum finally wears off."

Goutel quickly acquiesced. "And the enormous troll, what is it?"

"Her name is Chaness. She is the offspring of the troll Xieleo and the giant Prince Kaness. She is a princess among the giants, and as far as I can tell she is kind and eager to help." Before she asked, I thought I would explain the Niffler. "And the Niffler is the rodent. You were correct in your assumptions that he would be found here, where he once met my father."

"Why do you have this entourage and where are we intending to go?"

Her inclusion was not lost on me. "My entourage and I are escorting the Niffler to his treasury."

"In chains?"

"What is taking so long?" Dafnee shouted into the shuttle. "Come, we haven't time for secrets."

"I must go." I put two more jars in my bag and pulled my crown off my head and put it into the sack as well before throwing it over my shoulder.

"I am going with you." Goutel was stern and I did not have the time to argue, plus a piece of me wanted her here with me anyway. So I relented.

I nodded and she took another handful of tolls and put them in her own bag. "I will release the guard and send them with a reassuring message to Tazzle." Then she was gone. I took one more glance around my shuttle and bid it goodbye for now.

Chapter Twenty-Four

I watched my shuttle disappear in the distance as we moved down a dark passage. It would be safe until we returned, especially now that the Sholl Guard and my daughter knew where it was. Goutel walked by my side. Having taken her own translation potion that she had received from a shaman many centuries earlier, she was relieved to understand and to be able to communicate with all parties present.

"How deep must we travel into the earth, Niffler?" Dafnee asked impatiently.

"I said nothing about this journey being quick."

I suspected as much. The Niffler must have thousands of tunnels; it was the only explanation for his ability to go unnoticed for so many years.

"You will take us the long way to tire us so that you may plan an escape," Dafnee argued.

"It does seem likely," I agreed with her. "But he will regret this decision, I promise him that." Ours was a tenuous alliance. I was greatly aware of the sacrifice I would be making if this mission went poorly.

"If I take you a longer way, it is because I am only trying to avoid our imminent demise."

Chaness was intrigued, as was I. "Demise? How will we be met with ill intent down here from anyone other than you?"

"Oh, sweet naive princess whom they keep locked in the mountain, ashamed of your bestiality..." Chaness instinctively pulled on his chains and he yelped involuntarily. I was happy for it. There was no need for him to be hostile, especially to Chaness. "There are things deep in this world's crust far more depraved than I."

"Be quick with it. What is down here, Niffler?" Dafnee was always impatient, but this time we were all listening, waiting for the monsters' name.

"You have no reference for them. They are creators of the magma, the stone itself. Yes, dragons manipulate the elements, but what makes the element itself? Haven't you wondered?"

"The painter, Malarin, made the lava, the hot earth and elements," Goutel said what I was thinking.

"That is nonsense only spoken by those who have not seen the Shadows of the Earth. Ethereal beings that work tirelessly to produce the flame that melts the stone. Once I believed they were the flame itself, but this is not the case. They create the flame from their shadow. Their complete absence of light generates a spark hot enough to melt all metal and stone until it bubbles up where other creatures can access it."

"And they are volatile?" Chaness asked.

"Would that not seem obvious? Of course, I have never approached one. Why would I challenge such a beast?"

"You're a coward," Dafnee asserted. "You tell stories of monsters and shadows in the night."

"If you do not believe me, Empress, perhaps I can introduce you?"

"It is best that we avoid these creatures, Niffler. Take us however we must to avoid them." I did not need to see one first hand to have a healthy fear.

"I second Queen Peozleo," Cane concurred. Goutel didn't have to say anything for me to know how she felt. Given the opportunity, I was sure the empress felt the same, whether she wanted to admit it or not.

"Very well. I will take you the safest way possible. It will take two full days, without rest."

"I must rest," Dafnee contested. "My body will demand it."

Chaness elaborated, "She will actually fall asleep after twenty hours of consciousness. I can carry you, Empress," she quickly offered.

"What will we do with the Niffler?"

"I can handle him," Cane volunteered. "At the very least, I can match the princess' size."

"Two full days, then," the Niffler repeated.

"Two full days?" I heard Cane mutter. I felt bad for him. I knew he had other engagements. "Does that mean we will need two full days to return?"

"Possibly, or if the current is in our favor, we may find a much swifter way."

"The current?" Goutel asked.

"It will make sense in due time, troll."

Chaness pulled on his chains again. This time he muffled the pain better but the point was made and I appreciated the Princess for it. I did not know when we would have time to connect one-on-one, but I would make it happen before we said a final farewell. There were things to discover about this dear one. There were words to be exchanged.

Chapter Twenty-Five

We walked in relative silence, and every once in a while, the Niffler would perform one of his spells to expose a different direction. I never looked to see if they closed back up, but I assumed they did.

All of the sudden the empress dropped to the ground, rattling the tunnel so hard that some of the walls appeared to crack from the weight. We all stood still, making certain we would not be crushed by the earth. After some long, suspenseful moments, we determined it must be safe enough to move.

"She has fallen asleep," the princess said, handing me the chains that bound Niffler. I, in turn, handed them off to Cane, who was quickly growing in size to accommodate for the Niffler's potential escape.

"She was serious about needing her rest," Goutel observed.

"It is a shortcoming of giants, one could say." Chaness picked up the empress and slung her over her shoulder. Thank the strokes that these tunnels were vast because the Niffler himself was so large.

"They instantly fall asleep to recharge their batteries at the twentieth hour. She will be out cold, as if in an oblivion, for four hours—then, as though lightning has bolted her back to her senses, she will return to the living. The only one of our people who doesn't suffer from the exhaustion is the High Priestess. Something else fuels her entirely."

"But you do not suffer from this frailty?" I was curious.

"No, never have. I suppose that is the troll in me."

"You were telling me about your mother," I prompted, seeking knowledge that had been eating at me since we'd started this conversation during the celebration.

"She died during my birth. Not only was I enormous but her essence seemed to leave when life entered my body, or at least that was how my father described it. My mother turned to stone and I took my first breath. In so many words, I killed her."

"Oh, dear one, is that the burden you have led yourself to bear?" I wanted to hug her, console her. Of course she wouldn't understand that her mother made that sacrifice willingly. Perhaps she didn't even know she was doing it, but a male giant would not know how to give his life force to animate the trolling.

"The empress reminds me of it frequently."

"Does she?" Goutel sneered, sharing the same sentiment as me.

"She doesn't understand either. When trollings are born, a parent must give their life force to animate the child. How is it when giant offspring are born?"

"The baby builds its shape and life in the mother's womb."

"Inside?" I said, shocked.

"Yes, inside the mother, where the baby is conceived."

Goutel nearly shrieked with astonishment. "What does the father do?"

"I don't know. He gives her the seeds to build the baby."

"What a treacherous incarnation. All the weight is on the mother," Goutel said, aghast.

Cane muffled a laugh. "It is not that different from Conduits."

"Dalinkas left nothing to the man. Your men must be weaker than our male-trolls." Goutel was beyond herself with disgust. I felt the same but recognized we needed to be respectful. Not every creature could be as blessed as us trolls.

"The she-trolls form the trolling with clay. It takes years. When the form is right, our male trolls give their life force to animate the infant. Sometimes their lives are taken during the birth but it is their knowing contribution. Your mother did both to conceive you. She must have known how special you would be."

"But she gave birth to me and I animated when I left her womb and she took her final breath."

"The strokes still me in my tracks!" Goutel was going to turn to stone if this kept up. "How could this be?"

"I am an abomination. I know; they have told me for years. As soon as my father passed, each caretaker since has been disgusted with my mere presence on this earth." Chaness' voice was hollow as she spoke. She was heartbroken, and who could blame her? She believed she had killed her mother and was a burden to those left to care for her.

"You are no burden, dear princess, I assure you. You are a miracle."

What she'd said had my mind spinning. *Why would they keep her secret if they hate her existence? Why not send her out into the world to make her own way?* Unless they were afraid of what others would see in her strengths… Unless they were scared of what she could become or what she could incite.

The giants never hated the trolls. They wanted to make certain that we trolls never learned what procreating with a giant could produce—an enormous troll without the frailty of their own makeup. The empress was cruel because she was afraid of Chaness.

Chapter Twenty-Six

Once I realized the dynamics between Chaness and the empress, or rather all of the giants, I found it hard to speak. Everything that I wanted to say would only condemn the only family Chaness had ever known. *What good would that do*? Then she would feel entirely alone. No, I had to earn her trust first. Then we could navigate a different situation for her. *Maybe she will want to come live with us.*

"My Queen," Goutel interrupted my thoughts. "Does it not seem we are going in circles?"

"Why would you say that?" I looked around to see if the Niffler was close enough to hear us. I did not know his true abilities but he was several lengths ahead with Cane. Chaness was between us. I shuffled my feet a little more to create some extra noise.

"I suspected it a lap ago and I made a mark on the wall. We've just passed it again."

I took a deep breath to steady myself. It seemed unreasonable to trust the Niffler but we also had no choice. I had put myself on the line for his betterment. *Can he not honor the bargain made?*

"Are you absolutely certain?"

Goutel nodded. "But I know to challenge him will come at a cost, so let me make certain."

"How long do you estimate our lap takes?"

"It is difficult to say but it is a substantial amount of time."

This was not convenient but neither would it be convenient to confront him without proof of his deception.

"We wait."

Now I had two troubling scenarios to consider.

I was impatient. *How can I not be?* We walked in silence until the expression on Goutel's face said it all. Her suspicions were confirmed.

"Halt. Stop at once!" I said firmly.

"What is it, Queen Peozleo?" Cane was in a hurry to see this errand done. He would be very disappointed.

"The Niffler is deceiving us."

Just then, the empress woke from her slumber. "He what?!" she shouted.

Chaness startled and dropped the giant woman. I would have laughed if I wasn't so frustrated with the circumstances. As the empress brushed herself off, she scowled at Chaness, who sheepishly tried to apologize. "Never mind you," the empress scolded. "We will discuss this later. What is the Niffler up to?"

I took a deep breath, ready to argue my case. "He has us moving in circles."

"While I sleep, can nothing be managed?"

"I assure you, things have been…" I trailed off when the Niffler interrupted.

"I am leading us in circles. I must."

"Must you?" Dafnee sneered. She leaned in to do damage to the Niffler when Cane stepped in front of her.

"At the very least we can let him explain himself." Cane was always the defender of the defenseless. I appreciated that about him.

Niffler looked up at him with a bewildered reverence. In a very short amount of time, he had experienced not one but two individuals defending him. It was unfamiliar and yet I sensed it was softening him.

"We have to circle the entrance to avoid the Shadows. This is how I go undetected, how I have stayed alive all these years."

"We have been down here for hours and seen no trace of the *Shadows* you speak of," Goutel quickly pointed out.

"Because I evade them. Isn't that obvious?"

"Or they are not real and this is some ruse to keep us from your treasury," I accused.

"Is that what you really think? You live in the ground. You know there are things that go unseen, unspoken about."

There was truth in his words. Most trolls believed there were creatures unknown to us deep in the center of the world. Some believed it was the painter himself, still slaving away on his creation from the inside out. Whatever it was, it exuded energy of a different magnitude. I recollected a faint memory from my youth. I was in the catacombs of the palace. To this day I cannot say why I was there alone, but I was. I heard a noise like none I have ever heard since. It was a rustling of the earth. Not an earthquake, but the feeling as though the ground itself was antsy. When I turned around to see what was happening in the dark tunnel behind me, there was nothing. Only blackness. That was the problem. I could see in and through the dark. This was simply darkness, opaque and voluminous—then it was gone.

"You know I am right." The Niffler had watched me as I got swept away in my memories, or had he read my mind? I still did not know the magnitude of his gifts.

"This is nonsense!" Dafnee shouted, which was completely unnecessary because we could all hear exceptionally well, even if we were not standing in close proximity. "Stop stalling and take us to your lair. I command you!"

"You are not the only royal here, empress," Niffler hissed. He was right, but challenging her would only fuel her fire.

"You were sentenced by my assembly. You will answer to me." Her eyes narrowed and her shoulders rolled back. She was going to hold her ground.

"May we vote on it?" Chaness almost whispered.

"Excuse me?" Dafnee did not like multiple hands in the pot. "How dare you suggest such a thing?"

"Wait a minute." I stepped between the empress and the princess now. "I think that is a beautiful idea."

"You would."

Cane chimed in, "I do too."

Dafnee looked around, knowing she was outnumbered. Goutel would not take her side in any event. The problem was, I did not know how this vote would go. There were two foreseeable outcomes. Either we were knocking the empress down a few notches and potentially shaving off some time, or worse, inciting an enemy we knew nil about. There was nothing to be done but pray to Malarin.

"Be done with it, then." Dafnee raised her hand. "Those in favor of ending this madness and getting straight to the treasury, vote now."

Cane raised his hand and I understood his hurry. But I was surprised by Goutel's hand silently erecting behind me. When I shot her a sideways stare, she looked alarmed.

"I want out of here and he cannot be trusted." She said it to me although all could hear it.

"Very well. That is the majority. Take us to your lair now, beast."

“Wait. There are three of us,” the Niffler protested.

“A prisoner has no vote.” Dafnee pushed past him to hurry things along. I looked at my companions, knowing there was nothing else to be said. But I had a sinking feeling we had just poked a bear and awakened it from its slumber.

Chapter Twenty-Seven

The Niffler wanted to protest further but knew there was no use so, with a flick of his tail and a twitch of his long whiskers, we were suddenly falling. It was not into an abyss. It was into a trove of treasures. Light glinted off a bricolage of metals and gems, gold, silver, rubies and diamonds. It was blinding to take it all in, after hours of walking in the dark. The fall was brief and the calamitous sound of several large beings landing on the ground reverberated off the walls. Everything shook and jingled. It almost sounded like wind chimes.

"Be careful!" the Niffler shouted. He was tangled in his chains. Cane was trying to help him but they were both failing miserably.

"Unlock him, set them straight and then fasten him back up."

"Are you certain about that?" Cane looked at me skeptically.

"He is of no use to us if he cannot move. Do you think you can find anything in this cavernous collection? Because I cannot, and I do not wish to spend a lifetime trying. We need his help to find the thread and the blade," I slipped.

"A blade?" the empress quickly prompted me for more.

"As I said, I need his help too." That was all I was going to give her. Goutel looked at me nervously and I just shook my head. "Stay close to the Niffler, Goutel. I trust Cane's abilities but I don't trust the Niffler's cunning."

"Thank you, Queen." The rodent smiled at me coyly. "It is nice to know you respect me as an intelligent creature."

"I would be a fool not to, and I am no fool."

Dafnee pretended to muffle a laugh. I liked her less and less with every passing moment. "Where is the Golden Spool?"

"I will have to see where I last put it."

"Is there order to this mess?" the princess asked as she examined a pile of pearls. It was thousands upon thousands of pearls strung together, possibly an assortment of necklaces of all lengths; I could not tell for certain.

"Of course there is order to it."

I looked around at the stacks of items. Some of the piles included similar articles, like the pearls, while others were all different categories of things. Chalices, stones, tridents, wands… *How in the strokes will I know if the Niffler has the missing blade of the Staff of Banishment?*

I turned to see him at my shoulder, now properly chained and mobile. "Impressive, right?"

"If you consider stealing from others' fortune honorable, then yes, this could be an impressive collection," Goutel took the words right out of my mouth.

"You know nothing," Niffler dismissed her. I expected Goutel to rebuff him but she did not and I was grateful for it. "Tell me about this blade."

"Shouldn't you appease the empress first?" I looked over at her. She was impatiently staring after him but also seemed distracted by all the riches around her. She would look at the Niffler then pick up an object and examine it.

"Then you will have no chance to look for your item. She will wish to leave immediately."

He was right. "You want to help me?"

"I liked your father."

It wasn't an agreement but it said a lot.

"I loved him too." I truly did. He was a good king and a good father. Who knew it would be his virtue that would help deliver me from my conundrum? "It's a blade. I know little more. It is a Rittle." I didn't want to divulge further, but there was no other way. "A piece of the Staff of Banishment."

The Niffler's eyes got wide before a wave of recognition washed over him. "I cannot be sure I have that blade but I did stumble upon a bag of Rittles not long ago."

"This blade went missing fifteen hundred years ago."

"As I said, I cannot be sure. But this is the largest congregation of Rittles I have seen in over a millennia. For many generations they have been in the hands of rulers, kings, leaders and the like." He shot a glance at the empress, who was now draping herself in jewels. "It was an odd thing to come by, because no one is speaking of their absence, yet I found all but three of the Rittles in one place."

"You mean you stole them?"

"No, Queen, I found them."

"You found them? Where?"

"In the southern lands, west of here, before the white flakes stick to the earth. Outside of a settlement. They were simply there. I could feel their magic, of course, sense their value in the soil they inhabited. The only thing keeping them from being exposed was an enchanted sack, but it did little to disguise them from a seasoned hunter of treasure like me."

"What in the name of the strokes would they be doing there?"

"I don't know. But it is what prompted me to steal the Spool."

"Why?"

"Clearly no one was paying attention to the whereabouts of the Rittles. How could they be hidden in some hole in the ground and not a single word was being murmured about the theft of not one but all?"

"What was your theory?"

"They, themselves, were enchanted somehow. Cloaked."

It was a fine enough theory, but the only two other creatures I knew to have a Rittle were looking for it. OAD wanted his Staff back in order, and Dafnee wanted her Spool. "You unsuccessfully stole the Spool, OAD still has what is left of his Staff… Which was the third Rittle you intended to confiscate?"

"Why, you have it, Queen. It is your crown."

He caught me off guard. *He intended to steal from me? My crown is a Rittle?* I turned around to see that Goutel still had my bag securely on her shoulder. In it was the very item the Niffler would swipe given the chance.

"No one has ever mentioned the troll crown being a Rittle."

"Have they not? Odd, how the origin of things gets lost in the crevices of time."

"How can you be sure?" I was not convinced that he was telling me the truth. That was an epic tale he was spinning.

"I understand you wanting to dismiss it but it is the truth. I know the feel of a Rittle in my teeth, upon my skin and in my blood. I am the collector of the world's treasures. Each item vibrates differently for me, but none as beautifully as the Rittles."

"How did we trolls get the crown, then?"

He looked at me as though I had grown two heads and a beak. "Why, it was given to you, of course."

"By whom?"

He shook his head as though my questions kept getting more

outlandish by the moment. "Trolls account their histories somehow, right?"

"Stop with the insults. Of course we value our histories. Who bestowed us the crown?"

"Malarin, Chitchakor, Dalinkas himself painted in the strokes that the trolls be the keeper of the Crown of Thorns."

"The Crown of Thorns?"

CHAPTER TWENTY-EIGHT

I wanted to walk straight over and tell Goutel to be extra cautious but that would create an unnecessary spectacle. I was playing out scenarios in my mind. How could I indicate the importance of the crown without instigating a slew of questions from Goutel?

"Do you want to see the bag of Rittles or not?" the Niffler interrupted me before I could act on any of my strategies. "The Spool of Golden Thread is with the other Rittles."

Dafnee overheard him. "Take me to it, then."

"I'll take the Niffler," I said to Chaness, and she gently let go of his chains while I promptly picked them up. I wouldn't be able to hold him long if he took off, but after that exchange I felt like I didn't need to worry about him abandoning us. I hoped I was right.

"I won't be chasing after him if he flees," the empress said as she casually stepped past me.

"I wouldn't expect that of an empress."

A job better fit for a queen.

The Niffler moved slowly, navigating towers of gold and silver bars. I could see in front of us was a large chest, perfect for storing valuables one felt extremely attached to. Sure enough, that was where we were headed. Dafnee realized it too and forged ahead, putting more space between us.

"Is it in here? Is this where you have hidden it?" she demanded.

"You cannot just sift about my things," Niffler shot back.

"They are not your things. They are things you have stolen from others." She reached the chest before us and flipped the lid open. On top was the Spool of Golden Thread. Dafnee scooped it up and stuffed it in her knapsack while simultaneously examining what else was in the box. "What's in the bag, Niffler?"

"That is none of your business, Empress. You have your thread. Be away with you."

She opened her mouth to object when suddenly an avalanche of treasures slipped from the farthest wall. The noise was thunderous, so loud that I barely heard Chaness' warning. "The Shadows found us!"

I turned in time to see a black wisp of a figure emerge from the wall itself.

"Quick, grab the bag!" Niffler shouted at me. Without thinking, I darted toward the chest, shoved the empress out of the way and grabbed the mesh bag and its contents, releasing the Niffler's chains at the same time. "There is only one way out. Follow me!"

Everything was happening so quickly I was lost in the blur. "Goutel! Chaness and Cane!" The three of them were paralyzed with shock. In front of them the black shadow loomed. From its hands oozed lava. Where there should have been feet there were stumps of flame. Everything around it was beginning to melt. "We must go!"

Cane was the first to move. He took Chaness' arm and Goutel began running toward us. "Which way?"

"Down here," Niffler ordered. Then I heard him mutter under his breath. "My treasures! All of them will be lost."

I had to believe that was the truth as the smell of melted metal was palpable in the air. I could taste it in my mouth. Goutel was behind me now. "Where are we going? We are trusting the Niffler?"

"We have no other choice. He will get us out of here," I said as confidently as I could.

Dafnee was the closest on his tail. Cane and Chaness had caught up easily, with their size. It was Goutel and I who trailed behind, and the divide was getting bigger. More towers fell behind us. I was torn between looking at what was happening in our wake and terrified of knowing.

"The Shadow is not following us." Goutel apparently had decided to look. "It is occupied by the treasures."

"It wants the metal. The elements are what feed it," the Niffler explained. "But it will make quick work of my collection and we will be the last ones holding anything it may desire."

I held tighter to the bag in my hand and looked at the one over Goutel's shoulder.

"How much farther?" Cane took the words out of my mouth.

"A few more yards this way."

"Faster, beast!" Dafnee shouted. "You would see us meet our demise."

I turned around and saw that the Shadow was indeed nearly done melting the entire contents of the treasure trove. That was remarkably fast. The aura around the Shadow was hazy. It hung in the air and lingered on my palate. But something else caught my attention. There was a small dark figure at its feet. There was a second aura, another creature. I had never felt anything like its power before, sinister and focused like a projectile at us.

"Do you see it, Goutel? Can you taste that there are two beings here?"

"I am sorry. What are you asking, my Queen?"

"Here! We are at the tunnel," the Niffler interrupted us and moved quickly to the left, exposing an exit. "Go! Dive in. There isn't time for hesitation."

"You had better be leading us to safety," the empress cautioned as she was the first to enter the passage. It did occur to me that the Niffler would be happiest with her gone. *Maybe this is a trap.*

Cane ducked in next, followed by Chaness, and I hoped the empress' suspicions were wrong.

"Peozleo! The creature is coming." Goutel's voice was shaking. I pulled her around and pushed her in front of me.

"Go. I am right behind you."

She jumped in and I moved to follow her. I could feel the heat of the Shadow coming upon me. The Niffler moved so fast I barely saw him. He wiped his chains in such a fashion that they caught hold of the Shadow's right leg and it stumbled, giving me a small window of space. I secured the bag with the Rittles on my shoulder and leapt into the darkness. The Niffler was right behind me. I could feel his whiskers tickling my back. My eyes adjusted quickly and I could see we were all safely in one of the Niffler's tunnels.

"Keep moving. The Shadows can penetrate walls."

Everyone started down the passage when I felt the Niffler stop.

"What is it?" I turned to see terror on his face.

"It has me," Niffler almost whispered.

"What has you? Wait!" I shouted to the others. "The Niffler needs help."

Everyone paused but the empress. My eyes followed the chain back to the wall that now filled the space we entered the passage from. The metal links disappeared into the mass of dirt.

"Run! You have to run!"

"I can help you. Let me unlock your chains." I used my free hand to try and finagle the clasps.

"There isn't time." Suddenly the Niffler's body was slammed against the wall. I stepped towards him, determined to free him of his bondage. He had saved us. He couldn't meet his end this way. When I reached for the chains again, this time they were scalding hot. His fur began to singe. "You have to go! Take the Rittles to The Cathedral! Go!"

Then he began to scream in pain and the black wisps started to manifest in the wall behind him.

"Go!" he shouted again between guttural screams.

Tears streamed down my face. There was nothing I could do but run.

Chapter Twenty-Nine

We ran, as fast and as hard as we could. The passage was endless and we did not know how far the Shadow would follow us. Without the Niffler's guidance we had no way of knowing where we were or how to get out of his channels.

I wept for the life of a creature that was as old as time and had died in chains, chains I felt I put on him. Goutel watched me. She would steal a glance while she ran by my side. I knew she wanted to comfort me, but there was nothing to be said. We could continue on this way forever, lost in this endless tube until the Shadow finally found us.

Dafnee interrupted the lengthy silence. "We must devise a plan. I can feel my body getting tired." And then, as though on cue, she dropped to the ground.

It brought us all to a hurtling stop.

"Is she okay?" Cane leaned over her. "Has it been twenty hours? Surely it has not."

"It must be time for her slumber," Chaness reminded us all and then scooped up the empress and threw her over her shoulder. "I can carry her."

Chaness started forward again.

"Wait!" Goutel said. "Since we have stopped, let us see what we have at our disposal."

I panicked. *Was Goutel referring to the Rittles?* I did not wish to expose that I had them. But quickly I realized she meant what we had in the bag she carried.

"The queen and I brought several magics with us. There must be something that can help us manage these tunnels and find our way out."

"Excellent idea, Goutel." I patted her on the back as she took inventory. I wiped away my tears; it was time to start thinking clearly. I could grieve later. I *would* grieve later.

"What do you have?" Cane peered into Goutel's hand, where three small tokens lay.

"Do you know what these do, my Queen?"

I examined the round object first. "That is a dwarf's strength capsule." The next object I took in my hand, trying to remember who had given it to me. It was a long, spiraled strip of leather. When I rubbed it between my fingers I saw that is sparkled a pearlescent rainbow. "Brilliant!"

"What is it?" Chaness asked.

"It's the shed of a unicorn horn."

"What does it do?" Cane asked as Goutel put the other items back in the bag.

"I can make a wish with it."

"The strokes are in our favor," Cane cheered.

"For some of us," I said mournfully. Cane quickly caught my sorrow and backpedaled.

"I am so sorry, that was thoughtless of me. I only meant—"

I interrupted him. "I know. Think nothing of it."

"What will you wish for?" Chaness looked at me curiously. "For an exit?"

I was already formulating the wish in my mind when I said it out loud. "One better. I wish for all of us to be back at my shuttle."

Before anyone could blink, we were standing in front of my shuttle. It almost made the entirety of what had just happened completely surreal.

Chapter Thirty

"Come, let us get the empress home," I said as I somberly climbed into my shuttle. Where once I was concerned about its capacity, I no longer had a care. I could do difficult things. I had done difficult things today.

The magic of my shuttle proved to be up to the task. Cane reduced his size to normalcy and Chaness and the empress fit comfortably inside as the shuttle intuitively expanded. The lines near the islands were obsolete, but I would use a more antiquated method for navigation—traveler intention.

"Chaness, please tell me where on the island you would like to go." Before we'd built the lines all over the world for speedier travel, we could estimate destinations based on our travelers' intentions. This method turned out to be far less precise since often a voyager's idea of a place was vague.

"The palace gates will suffice."

Goutel came up behind me as I set the course. "You did all you could to save him."

"Did I?" was all I could say.

"You did," she assured me as she took a seat behind me and set her bag down. I glanced over at the sack I'd set beside my toll shelves. The contents felt heavier than ever now. I would honor the Niffler's final request and deposit the Rittles at The Cathedral. This mission was becoming more and more arduous and I did not even know if I had the blade I was seeking to honor my agreement with OAD.

It felt like it had been years since we made the arrangement and saved Spitzle's life. *How have things spun out of control so quickly?* Before I could put any more thought into it, we were at the palace gates.

"Cane, I will take you home as soon as we get them settled."

"Thank you, Queen Peozleo."

"Of course."

Goutel's eyes at my back were boring their own hole. Her concern was stifling. I loved her and valued her attentiveness but I needed her to stand beside me right now because we were far from being done with our errand. I turned around and met her gaze, trying to convey all of this until I could use my words. Her expression softened and I knew I had gotten through.

"I can take her in," Chaness said as the hatch opened. "You needn't concern yourself."

I pulled the Golden Spool of Thread from her knapsack to give it to whomever was prepared to take it and began to follow the princess to the gate. "I want to give you a proper goodbye. There are still words to be said between us."

Relief flashed across Chaness' face and I realized she thought I would just abandon her now that this was over.

"Goodbyes will not be necessary," a familiar female voice chimed. I looked up to see the High Priestess waiting at the gate. "We must speak, Queen Peozleo."

"Is something the matter?"

I heard the footfall of Cane and Goutel behind me as they followed us out of the shuttle to see what was going on.

"We know of the fall of the Niffler. Events have been set in motion that you must be made aware of. Please give me the Spool." I handed it over.

"What events? Can this wait?" We all stood at the gate, waiting for the Priestess to explain.

"It cannot. During the week you have been gone, much has been seen."

"A week?" Cane repeated, aghast. "It has only been a day."

"Time works differently that deep into the earth. It has been nearly seven days."

"I must go," Cane asserted.

"First you must stay and hear what has been seen. Only then can you decide to go or join the others."

"Join us for what?" Goutel's tone was also exasperated.

The High Priestess looked at my friend with what could only be interpreted as pity. I didn't like the look at all.

"High Priestess, may we pass? I wish to bring the empress to her bed chamber," Chaness asked.

"Very well, Princess. The empress will not be attending to any further travels. Please take her to her room and meet us in the court chamber." The Priestess moved and let Chaness through. "The rest of you can follow me."

She turned and began to walk slowly toward the palace. Another Priestess came out of seemingly nowhere and took the Spool, then ran off in another direction. I exchanged glances with Cane and Goutel. "I don't think we have a choice." I gestured with my hand for them to follow her.

"It appears we do not," Cane agreed and followed in line.

"I don't like this, my Queen." Goutel shook her head and then, too, followed behind Cane.

Neither do I, Goutel. Neither do I.

Chapter Thirty-One

We sat waiting for the princess to return in silence, the heavy, uncomfortable kind. The High Priestess stared at me. I read the subtlety in auras well, better than most trolls, and hers had shifted since we last met. It was tense, uneasy, and oscillated between several other emotions.

Chaness shuffled into the room. I could sense her apprehension. No one knew what to expect of this meeting, and none of us was excited about it.

The High Priestess nodded at the princess and then began. "Thank you for returning the Golden Spool of Thread. Fates have changed since we last convened. You must deposit the Rittles at The Cathedral." Her eyebrows raised in my direction. I had no reason not to. "In Cataphet's caves is where they must be held until the day of a new discovery."

"I intend to see to this immediately. If that is all, we can be on our way."

"That is not all." Her voice was laced with agitation. "Bring me the tapestry. We used what little Thread we had left to decipher as much of the future as possible. Thanks to your successful mission, we are able to complete the depiction of the next strokes. What we are seeing is disturbing, but what we've just confirmed is terrifying."

Quickly the two other Priestesses manifested from nowhere carrying a large roll of fabric. They lay the roll atop a long bar, fastened the corners, and the slightest one of them all began to pull on a chain that ran up the wall behind her. As she did, the fabric unraveled, exposing a stunning array of work. Depictions of battles and dragons, nymphs and every other creature ever painted adorned the fabric. The most captivating part was the subtle notes of gold that were woven throughout, connecting each scene that would otherwise stand alone.

"We needed the Golden Spool of Thread to complete what we had started when the Niffler stole it." The High Priestess pointed to a scene in the bottom left corner. "You sought him for your own means. To repair the Staff of Banishment and return it to King OAD." I hadn't told anyone but Goutel of that, but of course, her vision would expose my motives.

"He and I made an accord, and he is the rightful owner of the Staff."

"It makes no difference. If you return his Staff—in truth, if he even remains in charge of what he now possesses—all will be lost." She pointed to the final image on the tapestry, a circle of water.

"Why?"

"The reasoning has not been seen… yet."

My mind was racing. Goutel grabbed my arm as an expression of comfort. But all I wanted to do was brush her off. I was drowning in my own skin.

"The end of all or the giants?" Goutel asked. But it didn't matter; I would not have any part in killing anyone or anything.

"Would that matter?" Chaness asked disgustedly.

Goutel tried to repair the damage but the wound was inflicted.

"I only asked what is meant by the prophecy. You do not know what the queen has agreed to, what is at stake."

I put my hand on Goutel's fingers that still gripped my arm. "It makes no difference. I will have to find another way."

"It is not enough to ignore his request. You must collect his Staff and dismantle it," the Priestess interjected.

"How would you suppose she do that?" Goutel was ready to stand up and create further discord.

"The queen will tell OAD that she is bringing the Staff here to be reassembled. He does not possess the means to complete this task himself; that, we know for certain. We will pull it apart and send it to different corners of the earth."

"What is my part in all of this?" Cane stood, ready to excuse himself.

"You must attend to delivering the Rittles with the queen, and when the time is right, you will know where she will find the Stones. The Stones must also be laid to rest in The Cathedral."

"What Stones?"

"You know what I speak of. The Stones of Atlantis."

Cane's expression informed me that he did know what she was talking about. "The Katuan Stones are exactly where they should be."

"For now."

He shook his head in disbelief and sat down, resigned to his part in this vision. *But could I be compliant with this? Did I have a choice?*

"And I, High Priestess, what is my part to be had?"

"Dear princess, you were born for this very purpose. You hold the key to undoing this morbid fate. You will go with the queen."

Goutel and I looked at the princess, who appeared excited and something in me wanted to tell her to run, to run from it all.

Chapter Thirty-Two

The walk back to my shuttle was somber. My heart had not caught up with my head, and neither was willing to fully accept the dilemma we were now facing. I believed in the fate of the strokes. The day I'd decided to cheat Spitzle's death, I'd set things in motion that were now jeopardizing the entire world.

"What will we do?" Goutel asked in hushed tones as we stepped out of the palace.

"What we must."

"What must we do?"

"For now we must get the Rittles to The Cathedral. Let us start there." It was all I could muster. "Then we will return Cane to his home."

"My Queen, you cannot betray the powrie king. It will not go unnoticed."

Cane and Chaness were a ways behind us so I took a moment to speak to my friend plainly. "Goutel, there is nothing to be done. This is today's quandary. The strokes change with every decision made.

Right now, I am making the simple choices and praying to Malarin that by some stroke of fate the impossible decisions somehow become manageable. None of this will affect your strokes. You are innocent and pure in all of this. The painter will reward you."

"Where you go, I go. My strokes are entangled in yours. The painter knows that," Goutel asserted and stormed into the shuttle.

"Is she okay?" Chaness asked when she got close.

"As okay as can be expected."

Cane raised his eyebrows. He better understood the gravity of our situation, but even still, he could not truly grasp all the consequences, and the poor princess had spent much of her life sheltered from big burdens. It would be hard for her to comprehend the magnitude of the problems we faced. Betray a bond and suffer the consequences—not only myself but my people too—or singlehandedly contribute to the demise of all of Malarin's creatures.

When I put it that way, there was not much of a choice.

CHAPTER THIRTY-THREE

"Do you know where The Cathedral is? How long will it take to get there?" Cane asked impatiently.

"It is not that simple. The Cathedral moves every few thousand years. It is governed by different rules than any other strokes you have encountered. I have only been there once myself."

"Different rules?" Chaness was captivated. "There are rules?"

"Not rules but guidelines you can count on for the most part. For example, you can generally assume a large construct will stay where it was erected. The Cathedral is the home of the last raw, untethered strokes and a very powerful and temperamental dragon."

"What does that mean for our mission?" Goutel was worrying enough for all of us.

"It is fortunate that I have met Cataphet once before. It will give her some pause before she acts too rashly."

"Rashly?" Cane was nearly at his limit; that was becoming obvious. He wanted to get home to his wife and the responsibilities for his people he'd left unattended. I could understand that, but I needed him present.

Chaness touched my arm to get my attention. "What did Goutel say? It sounded like gibberish."

"What?" Then in dawned on me. Goutel's shamanic toll must have worn off. I heard her just fine, as did Cane. But now she could no longer communicate with the princess. This was terrible timing.

I turned to face Goutel. "I think your magics have worn off. Can you please see if there is anything over there that you can use?" I pointed in the direction of my tolls. The translation serum simultaneously let them hear my intended words—for Goutel in trollish, and the princess heard giant. Luckily I could still bridge our communication, but for how long—I still did not know. This serum had been very effective so far. I could only hope it stayed that way. It was not wise to mix magics. There were many accounts of terrible outcomes from that sort of corruption. So I couldn't implement a different communication charm until the serum ran out.

I continued while Goutel searched for a solution. "Cataphet is a rarity, literally the first dragon ever made. She was granted the ability to command all of the elements—earth, wind, water and fire. She and The Cathedral share in a special, symbiotic relationship. They are nearly one and the same—they have been together for so long. Cataphet was scorned by one of her very first companions. She doesn't care for any of the other creatures the painter animated, least of all Conduits."

"Why Conduits?" Cane demanded.

"It is a long story, but in short, the one she would do anything for broke her heart. It doesn't matter. You must be here, according to the Priestess, and I will keep you safe." I intended to keep us all safe.

"So how will we do this?" The princess was back on track and I nodded in appreciation.

"I found something!" Goutel interjected. "A communication tether. Looks like it is nymph quality."

"It is worth a shot."

Goutel took the contents from the jar and walked over to Chaness while I explained that Goutel was binding their communication. Chaness watched expectantly while Goutel tied a purple ribbon around first Chaness' finger and then about Goutel's own thumb. I saw the wisps of magic move between them.

"That isn't nice," Goutel snarled at the princess.

"What?" I said, ready to mediate.

"Chaness just said I tie a worthless bow."

I hadn't heard that. "Princess, did you just insult Goutel's ability to tie a bow?"

"I didn't say that. I only thought it," Chaness sheepishly admitted.

"By the strokes, can either of you understand your verbal communication?"

They both shook their heads.

Cane chuckled, understanding where I was going. "You'd better mind your thoughts, then."

Goutel was mortified. Chaness was a little slower to catch what was happening.

"It would appear you two will be communicating through your thoughts. Please be mindful."

"This is going to be a nightmare," Goutel confirmed what I knew she felt. "But it is all we have for now."

"She can hear my thoughts?" Chaness smiled. "This is amazing!"

"Just be aware of the intrusion and keep the peace."

They both nodded and I continued strategizing.

"First we must locate The Cathedral. I have the fortunate advantage of knowing where strange occurrences are happening along the shuttle lines. That is usually an indicator of some obscure magics present." Goutel read my mind and quickly uncovered the shuttle map she'd sent me, which showed the Niffler's last known location. I took a deep breath, pushing back the urge to grieve his sudden loss—there would be time later. Goutel spread the line grid out. It was vast, spanning the globe.

"Wow," Chaness whispered. "You go to all these places?"

"I have been to most of them."

Goutel was all business. I liked her when she shifted into this gear. "Look, we have three likely locations." She pointed at the first one. "Here our lines have been destroyed three times in the last three hundred years." Her finger went to the next one. "This one is closest to Listy. We haven't been able to conjure new lines there for centuries." She crossed her arm and glared at the last one. "And no one knows what to make of that black hole. Something keeps that land barren."

"Let's start here," I pointed at the first one. "We are closest."

"Plus, you're avoiding your daughter, because you know if we pass through those lines just above Listy, she's going to come find you."

I darted a sour glance at Goutel. She was right. She always was.

Chapter Thirty-Four

"You knew that location was going to be vacant. Your grandparents reported they thought it was an ancient dwarf city years ago," Goutel said.

"Will you stop?" I turned to her, exasperated. "Of course I don't want to disturb Tazzle. She's a new mom. She has enough on her plate without me pulling her into this mess I am in."

"We are in," she corrected.

"Yes, we," Chaness added.

Cane was the least happy about our circumstances, and his disappointment that we were not successful in our first attempt was clear. But he also agreed. "It would seem we are a team." He was choosing to speak in giant for Chaness' comfort. Goutel was content with not being privy to all that was said. Besides, she got the translation in the princess' thoughts.

"Then let us get this over with."

"How do you know she will see us passing through?" Chaness was like a beacon, glimmering and shining as she learned of every new thing she could.

"There is a power grid that keeps tabs on all shuttles, but especially the royalty."

"Will I be able to have a shuttle? I could carry so many travelers." It warmed my heart to know that she was spending time envisioning a life with the trolls.

"I think that would be brilliant."

"She's here," Goutel announced just as my shuttle screeched to a halt.

"How long will this take?" Cane looked around for my daughter to manifest, but at the very least she would have to knock. No sooner did the thought cross my mind than a rapping was heard at the hatch. I opened it slowly and there she was, with my granddaughter strapped to her back.

"Do you want to tell me what is going on? You were going to skirt the city and not explain yourself. You are a queen mother." Tazzle pushed her way past me and only then realized I wasn't alone. "I'm sorry," she whispered. "I would never disrespect you in front of guests."

Tazzle's eyes stayed fixed on Chaness once she saw her. The princess was hard to miss.

"I know you wouldn't." I made playful eyes at my all-too-alert granddaughter, Fetzle. She was already so much bigger than when I left. "She grows more beautiful and stronger every day." I brushed the trolling's head gently as I introduced the others. "Tazzle is my daughter and Princess of Listy. You know Goutel." Goutel waved sheepishly. "This is Cane Kraus. You two have met on the occasion. And this, my dear daughter, is our kin, Princess Chaness of the giants. Her mother was a troll and her father a prince of his people."

The ever-diplomatic daughter of mine put on the charm. It was one of the qualities that would make her a successful queen. She had one hell of a stone face. "It is a pleasure to meet you, Princess

Chaness." She nodded, as was the custom. "May I introduce my daughter, Princess Fetzle." Tazzle turned to present the child.

"Princess Chaness doesn't speak trollish yet." I smiled at her and, from the look on her face, I knew Goutel had translated the exchange.

"She has grown substantially," Cane observed.

"Trollings, especially she-trolls, grow very rapidly." Tazzle pulled the baby to her bosom and smiled down at her. "Her father's life-force propels her growth."

"How is Spitzle?" I asked.

"Well, he is charged with many duties in your absence—and your absence." She gestured to Goutel. "And while I care for this little one, no less."

"My errands are nearly done." I tried to put on as good a face as I could.

"Are they? Really?" She turned to Goutel for the answer. "I expected better from you." She shook her head shamelessly at my dear friend.

"Really, Princess. We have to drop off a package at The Cathedral, then see Cane home." He nodded enthusiastically. "Then we'll be returning something to the Solomon Islands."

Goutel was good, better than me at simplifying our agenda. I wondered how many times she had used this tactic on me.

"How did all of this nonsense come about and why didn't you tell me your happenings sooner?" I knew my daughter wouldn't take a simple explanation.

"This has all unfolded rather quickly, my dear, and I only wished to let you rest after birthing Fetzle. Goutel's appearance has been helpful but I am sorry it has put further weight on your shoulders. Let me leave her here, to assist."

She shot me a death stare. I wanted to keep her safe and out of harm's way. I also wished to take any burdens off my daughter. It would be best for all.

"No way. Whatever you are doing, you're always safer with Goutel there. We can take care of ourselves."

Goutel's shoulders relaxed and she nodded in agreement. "I concur, Princess. I will help move the queen along."

"I know you will." My daughter turned to leave. "I suppose the sooner I leave you to it the quicker you will be home to hold this little one." I smiled at my darling granddaughter, who cooed in her mother's arms. "It was a pleasure to meet you, Princess."

Chaness smiled and nodded.

I hoped these two could carry on joyously. Chaness could use a friend like my Tazzle.

"Cane, we will see you on the next occasion."

"Princess."

"I have something for you, my Queen." She pulled a small rolled parchment from the baby's sling. "The Pythoness sends one of her cryptic messages." She handed me the scroll. "I read it. It makes no sense. They never do."

My hands shook as I unrolled the parchment. In her harsh script, it read…

He cannot have the Dirk of Inverness. The Priestess weaves the truth.

The jeweled blade must end up with the woman who can hide it in plain sight with the son who will never be born. She must be present for the destruction. There is no other way.

"Does it make sense to you?" Tazzle asked casually as she got ready to close the hatch.

What could I say that wouldn't leave her fraught with worry? "That we are on the right path."

"Great. Then we will have you home shortly." My loving daughter smiled as she disappeared behind the door.

"What did it really say?" Goutel asked immediately.

"She confirmed the king must not get his Staff back. And..." I looked to Cane. "You may play more of a part here than we yet know."

"Why would you say that?" It was clear that was the last thing he wanted right now.

"Because once again there is mention of a son."

He threw his hands up and found a seat.

Chapter Thirty-Five

I slowed my shuttle to a crawl as we approached. Whatever anomaly was creating the disturbance in the shuttle lines, whether The Cathedral or otherwise, should be approached with caution. After being witness and nearly being killed by a Shadow, I reasoned there were things in this world that held mystery and should be feared.

"Can you sense what it is?" Chaness asked.

"No."

"Is the force short-circuiting the shuttle line?" Goutel looked at me from across the space. "That is what has been reported by the other shuttles—disfunction in the line."

"No."

"Perhaps we should go faster," Cane suggested.

"No." I was using my senses to feel what was beyond the walls of my shuttle. Suddenly I felt something above us. It was large, pressing, and by the taste of its aura, ancient. Before I could warn the others, the shuttle was pulled into something like a vacuum. "Hold on!"

The shuttle shook and vibrated ferociously. Chaness closed her eyes tightly, Goutel took hold of my arm, and Cane put his head in his hands where he sat. Everything rattled around us and there was a pressure in the air that I had not felt before. Then it just stopped.

"What was that?" Chaness opened her eyes and looked around.

"I do not know, Princess, but I suspect we will find out shortly."

"It will come back?"

"More likely that whatever it is has just arrived."

"Rather you arrived here," a loud baritone voice reverberated off the walls. "What brings you to The Cathedral, Queen Peozleo?"

Goutel and I could understand the voice because we were created at nearly the same time as the originals. We were the last of the world's creatures to speak dragonian, a knowing passed down through our lineage. Cane and the princess couldn't even hear it; they only felt the vibration. "Cataphet?"

That got the other two's attention.

"The dragon is here? The original is with us?" Cane looked around.

"My other companions cannot hear you."

"I know that."

"Do you have anything to remedy that?"

"Yes, but I will not be doing any such magics today. Why are you here, Queen?"

I shook my head at Chaness and Cane. Both of them looked deflated. Goutel just looked uncomfortable.

"I come to deposit the Rittles in The Cathedral."

"Why do you have the Rittles and why would you bring them here?"

Did I explain that it was the Niffler's last request? Or that it was ordained by several prophets, or better yet, I could let her know that if I did not do this, I would be destroying the world. I quickly decided on the simplest explanation. "The Niffler gave them to me and this is where he said they should go."

"The Niffler gave up a valuable thing? Why would he volunteer that?" Cataphet laughed gently. "I have never known him to be generous with anything."

"You knew him well?" I was now very sad to be the one to have to tell her.

"We have run into one another from time to time, on the rare occasion spending longer periods together to soften the burden and boredom of an eternity alone."

"Then I regret to have to inform you that he is gone. Met his demise at the hands of a Shadow."

"What? Why would he poke the beasts? They only ever attack when provoked. He knew that; I told him it myself." Suddenly my shuttle disappeared and we were all in a large cavernous hall. A striking window stained with greens and golds was the only source of light. Colors bounced off the walls in an enchanting way. I turned around to see Cataphet in all her grandeur coiled up and waiting for an explanation.

Chaness unwilling shrieked.

"Excuse the princess, Cataphet. She has never left the giants' palace in the Solomon Islands." Everyone else had the right mind not to speak. The large black dragon made even Chaness look small. Cataphet's scales shimmered with gold flecks. Her eyes were golden hazel-green like the window. I was happy I had met her once before; otherwise I, too, would be stunned into silence at the sight of her.

"Tell me of my friend."

I recalled the story, every gruesome detail. Chaness teared up when I described the rodent's sacrifice. I had to fight back the tears as well. Goutel stood stone-like during the entire interaction and I was starting to grow concerned for her mental health. Cane listened while simultaneously looking around at the magnificence of The Cathedral.

"So he would have you leave them here, in the largest haven in the painter's creation. It makes sense, I suppose," Cataphet agreed. "They were here once before and still they found their way into the world."

"How did you lose sight of them?" The moment I asked the question I wished I had framed it differently. Less accusatory.

Thankfully she laughed. "Queen, I assure you that the Rittles have a mind of their own. Do not mistake them, as many do, as tokens to be desired. There is much more to them than meets the eye."

"As it is with most things." I agreed. "So you will store them safely?" I picked up the bag and slung it over my shoulder.

"I will. Come with me." Then we were gone, the dragon and I, in the depths of The Cathedral caves. I could smell it in the air. Taste the dirt on my tongue. It was familiar and felt like home. I liked it. "Put them in here." A door exposed itself in front of me and I did what I was told, placing the items on shelves in the space. It was an odd assortment of things, from crystal balls to swords. I would have never known their power by the looks of them, but the feel of them on my skin gave it away. The bag was nearly empty when I pulled out a bejeweled blade. I knew exactly what it was.

Cataphet was outside the room but watching my every move. When I held the blade in my hand, she hissed. "How do you come to have only part of the Staff of Banishment? It is cursed! That should not stay here."

"The blade must end up in the hands of another."

"Why? Why must it be separate from its parts? Who dismantled it to begin with?"

I explained what I knew and that King OAD had the rest of the Staff, that the giants and two seers I had encountered confirmed that he could not restore his Staff, and that to even try would bring about the washing of the great canvas in the River Tins—the end of all life.

"There is a blood on it that soils the soul." She took in a deep whiff of the air around me. "Alas, it will return not in your hand. That blade has a destiny that is yet to be written in stone."

"Do you see the name of the woman who will carry its burden?"

"You know the name, Queen Peozleo. Even I can see these strands of fate have already been laid out for you."

"To the woman who can hide it in plain sight with the son who could never be born," I repeated the prophecy.

"The very one. Sorcey."

I shook my head because it was becoming very clear that Cane and his dear wife Sorcey were as ensnared in this treacherous path of saving our world as I was, and I wondered if I was responsible.

"But first you must get the king's Staff and dismantle it further, as you were directed to do."

A moment of resentment washed over me. *What right does an original who chose to hide away in a magical Cathedral have, telling me how to conduct myself?* All I wished to do was save my family. As though she could read my mind, Cataphet interrupted my thoughts.

"We all play a role. There is more to be expected of me and The Cathedral. In fact, I sense you have more to say."

Did I? "Oh, yes, there may come a time I have to bring the Katuan Stones here for safekeeping."

Cataphet cocked her head inquisitively. "That is a very odd coincidence." Then she shook her head gently. "There are no coincidences."

Chapter Thirty-Six

Cataphet and I returned to the great hall. Cane was going on about his wonderment at The Cathedral.

"The entire Katuanak Arena could fit in here. What this must look like on the surface!"

"You can tell the Conduit it looks like nothing." I tried to listen to both conversations while I took from Goutel's shoulder the bag that held my crown and I slipped the Dirk of Inverness into it. "The land we dwell in now is rich with power and a tinge of darkness that will later evolve into something none of us can imagine. But that won't be for many thousands of years. Perhaps then I will return with The Cathedral. It will serve as an even better, more powerful energy source."

"What is taking place here?"

"The slow but steady manifestation of what I like to refer to as voodoo."

Voodoo—that was a silly name.

"You will see, this land will serve to be magical like no other. It is where the world ends."

"I trust you, Cataphet. Any land that can harbor The Cathedral is destined for something uniquely commanding." I turned to the others. "We have done what we can here. Let us get you home, Cane."

He looked so happy I thought he might jump out of his skin. It dawned on me I didn't know where my shuttle was. Before I could ask, we were back in the familiar space and I let out a deep breath. Goutel moved to my side.

"Are you okay?"

Cataphet's voice interrupted our exchange. "Take this coin. It will provide much support when the Stones require transport. Give it to the Conduit, request he say something of consequence to you three times, and you will hear his call. Which I dare say will not be long from now." A small round medallion engraved with symbols appeared in my palm. "The queen of the trolls will always be welcome here. No invitation necessary. No key be employed. No obstacle will deter her. And before your reign is through, I will see you again, dear queen."

"Until we meet again," I said aloud and then commanded my shuttle to make haste to Atlantis.

CHAPTER THIRTY-SEVEN

Cane could barely contain himself. He quickly shook Chaness' hand and said goodbye to Goutel with a rushed embrace, and then we were at the surface of Atlantis in a small wood near Balto Beach.

Cane glanced around when we manifested in the trunk of the tree. "I cannot wait to see Sorcey. I just want to hold her in my arms."

He started toward the meadow that separated the wood and the beach. I had not spent much time on the island but enough to know the general geography.

"Cane, I will need to bring your wife with me."

He looked at me, aghast.

"There is nothing to be done. I need you to call on Sorcey." I knelt down to let him see my own anguish in what I was about to do. "I have no choice, you know I have no choice, and it has become very clear that Sorcey has a role to play in all of this as well."

Defeated, he just looked past me. I wanted to hug him, to tell him it would all be all right. But I could not. It would be a lie and I had more integrity than that. More importantly, my friend deserved more than that.

"I must go get the Staff from King OAD under the guise that I will return it in one piece. Sorcey needn't be present for that but I will be back through here today to escort her down to the Solomon Islands where she will receive the Dirk of Inverness."

"Why must she go with you? Would she not be safer here? You can just return with the Dirk."

I shook my head. "Cataphet confirmed the seer's vision." He knew as well as I did that according to the Pythoness, she had to be present at the dismantle. We cannot choose to believe some of what was said and not all of what is required."

"Very well, I will be back here with my wife. Please hurry."

"Of course."

"And..." Cane paused. "Please take care of her."

"With my life." He turned to walk away. "Cane, please take this. Because it stands to reason someday I will need to transport the Katuan Stones to The Cathedral." I tossed him the small medallion Cataphet had given to me. "Say my name three times and I will arrive. No matter where you are."

With that, I whispered to the marble OAD had given me, telling him of our arrival, threw it in the air then dissolved back into my shuttle.

Chapter Thirty-Eight

I paced side to side while Chaness and Goutel looked at me with wary stares.

"Goutel, you do not have to do this. You were not named in any of the visions."

"You will not try and dissuade me," she shot back without hesitation. "My place has always been beside you. You are my queen, my friend and my life. Serving you has been the greatest achievement of my existence and I do not intend to stop that when you are in a time of need."

I'd tried.

"Very well, then. It is time to see the king." My stomach lurched with the thought of it. This would not end well. It could not end well. Going back on one's word was dastardly, the lowest of all deceit. If the king did not take retribution, I would still have to live with myself. *But how can I live with myself if my actions result in the death of all?*

"My Queen?" Goutel's voice trembled slightly. "We will be okay."

I had been standing there, dazed, while my two companions watched me, sensing all of my fears, no less. That was not the way of a queen. I quickly rolled my shoulders back, relaxed my face and put the shuttle in motion. Seconds later we arrived at the gates of the powrie habitation of Hault.

We stepped out of the shuttle and I was shocked at what I saw. I had only been here once before, and as my memory served, it was more of a village. This was no village. This was a fortress. *What has caused him to build such a place?*

It was ominous. The bones of thousands of creatures constructed the menacing wall—the wall that kept some monsters out but more monsters in. In moments we would be in the belly of the beast, and what then? *Will OAD see right through me, suspect that we are about to betray him? Will he kill us right here and now? Could I blame him if he did?*

A small door opened at the base of the gate, too small for any of us to get through, and a brutish-looking powrie with bright red eyes and thick black hair poked his head out.

"What?"

"The king is expecting me." I took another deep breath and tasted the sourness of resentment coming off the powrie. "Tell him Queen Peozleo is here with her promise fulfilled."

He ducked back in, slammed the door and left us sitting there, unaware of what to expect next.

"What is behind the wall?" Chaness asked.

Goutel answered her both internally and aloud, for my benefit. "The powries are not known for their hospitality."

"What are they known for?"

Goutel passed me a sideways glance as I answered. "Nothing that should concern you, Princess. We will be in and out and on our way back to the Islands before you know it."

I appreciated Goutel's discretion with Chaness. That was the last thing we needed—more fear.

The large gate began to slowly open. I could hear the mechanical cogs that operated it turning. On the other side stood an army of powries. Their population was larger than I had imagined. I wondered how powries reproduced. However it was, it was quick and abundant.

"Follow me," a larger, more commanding powrie demanded once the gate was entirely open. Thankfully the princess could fit, at least inside the city walls. I doubted she could join us in the king's castle. The three of us moved at a leisurely pace behind the army. *Why did he have an army greet us? Is he flexing his muscle, ensuring I cooperate?* I looked back at Chaness and it occurred to me how she must look to the king—like a threat, no doubt. She could take out most of this legion on her own. Little did they know that she was more likely to cower than ever stir up a fight.

The army came to a halt in front of us, then gently spread, exposing a narrow walk. I looked ahead to see it must be the king approaching. Beyond him were many more soldiers. *Is he preparing for a war?*

The numbers made me uneasy, very uneasy. Amongst the trolls, we had a few elite warriors—the Sholls—for no particular reason except that some she-trolls seemed naturally adept to combat. It was a discipline they enjoyed, and so chose the path of our Master Kioz, a troll who studied under the great cranes of the east.

But nothing like this. Not even remotely like this militia OAD had built. Goutel stood very close to me, sizing the situation up as well. I wished I could read her thoughts like Chaness could, or have her read mine and assuage my fears. We should have taken such magics before entering. I scolded myself for not strategizing better. Then I reminded my inner critic that it was not wise to blend magics and I was still under the influence. I knew we were entering a perilous situation, but perhaps didn't know how perilous. I would do better. I would never leave my people so vulnerable again, and I would see to it that Tazzle would also learn from my mistake.

"Queen Peozleo, welcome." The king was nearly to us. He spread his arms wide—his Staff in his right hand. "This is impressive, is it not? I command over ten thousand powries with only a thought."

I wanted to shudder at that notion, not rejoice. *Why does he need to command thousands of creatures, and only with a mere thought?* As though on cue, he moved and the entire population shifted their heads to only look at him. It was as though he was the head of a very large snake. I did not like it at all.

"You have completed your task?"

"I have." I nodded toward Goutel, who reached in the bag and handed me the Dirk of Inverness.

OAD's eyes lit up, glowing a fiery red. The power was so close. It surged through him; I could see it.

"Give it to me." I hesitated, not sure how to navigate this next part, only what I had rehearsed in my head. I handed him the blade.

"Do you have a way to secure it back onto the Staff?"

He was crazed with joy, not hearing me over his own exuberance, tossing the blade up and down—feeling the weight of it in his hand. It was my only card to play. I had to hope he had no way of securing it, as the High Priestess had foretold.

"What did you say?" he asked after a long moment.

"Have you a way to secure the blade back onto the Staff?"

The gravity of my question sank in. I watched it transform his expression. "Have you? How would you know how to do such a thing?" The accusation was in the question. I shouldn't, unless I had something to do with the extraction to begin with.

Chaness felt the tension and she decided to intervene. "My name is Princess Chaness, King OAD. It's a pleasure to meet you." A proper king would have made introductions first, I thought as she continued. “I am half-giant, half-troll but I have lived my life with my kin in the Solomon Islands.”

King OAD looked extremely perturbed by her interruption but did his best to be polite and listen, all the while still admiring his blade. I did not know if he understood or spoke the giant tongue.

“The Niffler who stole your blade also stole from my people. When the queen helped us recover our treasure, the High Priestess warned the queen that you may have difficulty repairing the Staff. I trust my High Priestess with my life.”

Rolling his eyes dramatically but not contesting her, he looked down at the two parts. It seemed obvious that he at the very least understood giant, but he chose to reply in trollish. “We will see.” He turned around and panic surged through me. *How can we recover the Staff and dismantle it if he walks away right now?* “You three will wait here while I take the Staff of Banishment to my mason. If he confirms your suspicions, we will have to reach another accord, Queen Peozleo.” Then, under his breath, he added, “Because we powries will never convene with the filth of giants.”

And just like that, the king was engulfed by his army and we had nothing to do but trust and wait.

CHAPTER THIRTY-NINE

We sat there for hours. Red eyes' stares hammered into us like tiny beady nails. When the silence was disturbed by a fierce roar, relief shot through me. I knew he could not reassemble the Staff. *We will have our chance!* I tried not to express my allaying of angst visibly but Chaness was not very discrete.

"I told him."

"Shhhh!" Goutel scolded.

"Now is not the time." I winked at her and the furrow in her brow relaxed. She meant well. Quickly the mood of the yard shifted and the beady eyes followed the wave of soldiers moving out of the way and straight for us.

"Your Priestess was right, halfling!" The king slammed the Staff hard into the dirt. "We do not possess a strong enough adhesive to see to the Staff's reconstruction. Tell me, what is it that you possess that may do better?" The king didn't know the princess didn't understand trollish.

Goutel did not hesitate. "They have the Golden Spool of Thread."

"That will help them repair my Staff?"

"It weaves the strokes of fate. Certainly it can mend your weapon," I concluded.

King OAD closed his eyes, frustration, anger and disdain washing through his aura and all about him. "Did you suspect that the one place that could fix my Staff would be the one place a powrie dare not go?"

"How could I? I had no idea. You sent me after the Niffler." This was ludicrous, all of it. Everything that had led me to this moment. It had to be in the strokes because there was no other way to explain it. "Besides, giants don't particularly care for trolls. Visiting them would not be my first course of action." I hoped my words didn't wound Chaness, because she truly was the exception.

OAD pulled the Dirk out from behind his back. "You will see my Staff returned to me or our bargain was not met." His eyes bore hot into my skin. "There are grave consequences for crossing a king."

I would not be intimidated, I could not be intimidated because I knew what was coming next—potential war. "Do not think the trespass of a queen will pass by unnoticed, King OAD. Some of us do not need numbers to provoke intimidation."

My two counterparts stood up a little straighter by my side.

"Be that as it may, I will not let you depart here without leaving something of value behind." The next thing that happened was so quick, I had no time to process it before it was already done. "Seize her."

A swarm of powries leapt onto Goutel, stringing her up before I could move. Before the princess could move.

"No! Release her or we will not perform this task! Release her now!" I cried. "Goutel!"

Tears streamed down my face. *How will I ever get her back?* There was no bargain to be made. "Release her. This is not part of our accord. There is no need for hostages."

"I feel differently." He handed me the blade and the Staff. "I am trusting you with my very life force. You hold everything hostage."

"Goutel..."

"I will be okay. Just be safe. Take care of the princess." Her words were meant for Tazzle; I knew that and she knew that.

"I will be back for you."

She just shook her head, her final silent plea for me to save the world and leave her here to suffer the consequences of my betrayal. I could not do that. I would not do that.

Chapter Forty

We were escorted back to my shuttle. Tears streamed down my face. I was defeated. Goutel had been virtually sentenced to death in front of me. My dearest friend, my family—if not by blood, by right. We climbed in and the hatch closed.

"We will get her back." Chaness was crying too; I had not even noticed. "I told her, in our heads, that we would get her back."

I did not have words to comfort her, I did not have words to comfort myself, and I saw no way this would end with Goutel returned to me safely. We both knew it when we'd said goodbye.

"We will get her back," Chaness repeated.

It dawned on me. "Can you communicate with her now?"

Chaness shook her head. "No. Her voice drifted away a short distance back."

No words would balm the rawness of the grief I felt. No promise could reassure me of our victory on any front. But one thing was for certain, the strokes were not in our favor on this day. Nonetheless, Malarin knew better than me or any other creature how the strokes of fate blended to create the world we lived in. I would never be the one to challenge it, although if given the chance, I would choose to change it.

"We must get to Sorcey Kraus. From there it will be in the hands of the giants to finish what they have started."

"You are giving up on her?"

"Never, but we are already dedicated to this outcome. Either way, Goutel's life depends on it."

I directed my shuttle toward the island of Atlantis.

Cane and Sorcey were exactly where I had asked him to be, under the arbor of the trees near Balto Beach. They both looked the worse for wear.

"I will be back shortly, my love." Sorcey kissed him. "Do all you can to stop the Trials."

"I promise you I will. I will stop the Trials no matter what it takes."

Sorcey's face was tear stained and raw. "I love you. We will return quickly."

I wanted to reassure her but I couldn't.

"I am ready, Queen Peozleo." She stepped toward me and let go of Cane's hand. As we drifted away I could hear him say "I love you" again. We manifested in the shuttle immediately after. Chaness approached Sorcey, and I realized that, of course, they had a friendship. The Krauses had spent a lot of time with the giants.

"Princess Chaness, it warms my heart to see you."

"I missed you, Sorcey. It has been so long." The pair exchanged a loving glance but could not embrace due to Chaness' size.

"We must be on our way." I designated the gates of the palace as our destination and my shuttle lurched forward. I caught Sorcey and straightened her up when the movement threatened to topple her over. She was still crying. "I will get you home safely, I assure you."

"It is not this fated mission. It is my ignorance that put others in danger that breaks my heart."

"You would never put anyone in danger on purpose."

Chaness just listened to our exchange in silence.

"I was warned. We were warned by the Ramalan Kassandra. The Trials will end in destruction but we did not believe her because she saw me and Cane bearing a child—a son. He was gone when the prophecy was shared. If only he were there, we would have taken different action." She put her head in her hands and wept.

She hadn't believed the prophecy, just as Cane hadn't. "Sorcey, from what I understand, you could not have known. Cane didn't believe the High Priestess either."

She wiped away the tears. "Perhaps, but we may never know, and many may die because of my decisions. Now I must see to this fated ritual to stop the end of the strokes, but what of those whom I hold dearest? What will become of them while I am off with you?"

I wanted to comfort her. In many ways I felt her pain. But there were no words, because I did not know how long this would take, and we were both committed to seeing it through.

"Let us pray for the safety of our loved ones." And with that, all three of us prayed with all our might just as the shuttle pulled into its destination.

Chapter Forty-One

The High Priestess and Empress Dafnee stood awaiting our arrival. Something around the islands must warn them of a strangers' approach. It made me wonder once more how the Niffler got through. Something we would never know.

We stepped out of my shuttle. The empress quickly came over to Sorcey—clearly the only one who deserved a greeting.

"Sorcey, it is a pleasure to see you again. I wish it was under better circumstances," the giant woman's voice boomed. I hadn't missed that voice in her absence.

"Thank you, Empress. The pleasure is mine." Sorcey did a wonderful job of keeping it together considering the circumstances.

"You have it." The High Priestess came to my side.

"I do. Would you like it now?"

"No, no need. We will need you present at the ceremony."

Apparently my job was never through. "They have Goutel," I said.

"I know."

Rage flashed through me. "Did you always know? That he would take her hostage?" I stopped walking and looked up at the Priestess. I could feel Chaness at my back.

"Yes. But she will not die by his hand. He will bring her here to bargain."

"But they can't come here. Why can't they come here?" My voice cracked. I heard what she said but I couldn't believe it. She'd set us all up to die. She could not be trusted.

"Adanc, the sister of Ratatoskr, and the Niffler. She patrols these waters, and the powries won't go deep into the earth. They were not created to. They lose powers in the depths."

"What? Why?"

"Adanc loved the giants ever since our first emperor. She loves the princess." The High Priestess glanced back at Chaness, who looked lost in thought. "Loves her very much."

"That's not what I meant. Why do the powries avoid the depths? OAD said the power of all powries lies within his Staff. That it was gifted to him upon his inception."

"He tells the truth. The Staff of Banishment was given to him when he was born from the blood of the brother Tindle—when Fih stabbed him."

I shook my head, not understanding the correlation. "He *is* the Staff?"

"No, he is the result of bloodshed. Powrie strength comes from blood staining the earth. The Staff is the ultimate symbol of bloodshed, brother murdering brother… That is the energy that created the king and all who follow him."

"So the Staff feeds him, and so does violence."

"Yes, Queen."

I'd thought as much from what Goutel and OAD himself had told me at the ceremony back in Listy. "Blood only seeps so far into the soil, so they must stay close to remain strong." She nodded as I followed the train of my thoughts. "Do they multiply from the savagery as well?"

"I believe so."

"So without the Staff of Banishment, they will rely on violence alone for their power and their posterity? They have to satiate their thirst for blood somehow."

Her face was pensive and tight as she affirmed my assessment with another nod.

"Priestess, you are inciting a war."

"You are but forgetting one thing." I shook my head in disbelief. "Something has been collecting the Rittles. Something incited the Shadow elementals."

"The Niffler. He is gone."

"We both know it was not the workings of the Niffler. He was cunning but not capable, nor malicious in this way."

"Then who?"

"Or rather what?" she corrected. "Whatever it was, it dismantled the Staff of Banishment directly under its keeper's nose without causing disruption."

I thought about the militia OAD had built and the walls. Of course, it all made sense now. He would never lose his Staff again.

The Priestess continued. "We will require two more Rittles to accomplish a similar but less efficient feat. That is a creature we must put a stop to. A powerful, destructive force."

Two more Rittles… But I returned them all…

"Now come. As I said, we will need you."

My crown…

CHAPTER FORTY-TWO

Once again we were down in the court. Adanc was present too, her large viewing window exposed and full of vibrant blue water. Chaness had been extremely quiet after having heard the Priestess' confessions. I worried for her. The only solace I had was that I believed what the Priestess had said—that Goutel would not die by OAD's hand. We may have a war to fight when we were through but that would all be easier to traverse with her by my side. And if I didn't make it, Tazzle would need her guidance. But Goutel… She had to survive.

"Why must Sorcey be here?" I asked the High Priestess as we waited for the empress and Sorcey to arrive.

"She must learn an invisibility enchantment that only I can give her and only she can pass down."

"Where will the other pieces go? Will you keep them?"

"No, certainly not. We will be charged with safeguarding the wasted Rittles."

My crown will be a wasted Rittle.

"If they are powerless, why do they need safekeeping?"

"Make no mistake, they will not be powerless. They will be the obstruction that ensures the Staff cannot be reassembled. It will take all the strength they have to maintain the force of it all."

I considered what she said. My crown wouldn't be wasted, only diverting the power elsewhere. That was a comfort.

"When the time is right, the giants will return the Crown of Thorns to your rightful heir—only the next true queen."

I wanted to argue with her but the truth was I never much cared for the crown. Knowing it was a Rittle bestowed to the trolls and I was the one losing it felt defeating. But at the cost of saving the world, they could have it.

The empress entered the room and the High Priestess left my side for the center of the circular floor. Four more Priestesses followed her. Sorcey took a seat between me and Dafnee, and I looked across the room to see the still forlorn Chaness. I would find her after this and we would talk. We needed each other more than ever. I still had not gotten a chance to invite her to join us in Listy, not formally—I would, and that would surely raise her spirits.

"Let us begin." All five Priestesses sang in unison. I knew that was my cue to provide the Staff, the Dirk and my crown. Two more Priestesses entered through an adjacent door, holding the Golden Spool of Thread.

The empress stood up to object.

"You will sit down. We all sacrifice on this day," the chorus sang, and the usually feisty empress obeyed. The pressure in the center of the room was heavy, similar to the sensation of humidity but dry. "Leave them."

I did as I was told and sat back down. The High Priestess took the Dirk and the Staff in her hands, one in each. The Golden Spool of Thread was handed off to a second Priestess, and my crown, the Crown of Thorns, was held up by a third. They danced in an inner circle chanting words too quickly for me to decipher or perhaps in a language that not even magic could decode. The remaining four Priestesses danced around them in the opposite direction. The chanting got louder and the air in the room pulsated with intentions that felt foreign to me. Faster and louder it grew, and I wondered where they had learned of this ritual, a ritual that would break the second bond of the Staff of Banishment. I would ask the High Priestess.

I listened and watched. The room suddenly appeared foggy and my skin felt hot. I glanced around to see if anyone else was suffering from the odd sensation. I could see that Sorcey was uncomfortable in her seat. I hoped she would be okay. I had the urge to go to her when all of a sudden the three Priestesses in the center stopped, their bodies elevated from the ground and rising. Each of their arms held the objects tightly, their knuckles white. The outer circle resumed the chant, picking up where their sisters had left off, raising the pitch, and the sensations infiltrated my body again.

I needed to protect Sorcey. I looked over to see her itching her arm vigorously. Before I could move, the chanting stopped. The bodies rose higher. They hit the ceiling then burst into ash, sparkling iridescent ash. The three Rittles hurtled to the floor, making a calamitous sound. I saw that indeed the second blade was now removed from the Staff and the Staff itself appeared to be folding in upon itself. But even stranger was the waft of wind that was carrying a billow of ash directly to Sorcey. Whispers in the air, the familiar voice of the High Priestess, travelled to Sorcey's ear. I immediately understood what was happening. The High Priestess was sharing her final gift. This was why Sorcey had to be here.

Everyone seemed to come out of the magical daze all at once. Getting to their feet, the other Priestesses began to weep openly. Sifting through the sprinkle of ash that surrounded us all, I went to pick up my crown. It was no longer mine, at least not how I knew it to be. A remaining Priestess came over to me and handed me the Dirk of Inverness, and in return took my crown.

"Thank you for your sacrifice," she said.

"Thank you," was all I could think to say. Jarred from what had just happened, I looked around for Sorcey, who was busy consoling the empress. I needed to check on Chaness. My eyes scanned the room. There would be no missing her, yet she was nowhere to be found.

Chapter Forty-Three

Sorcey appeared at my side. "We must go. I must get back to my husband, back to Atlantis, before it is too late."

"Have you seen the princess?" I continued to scan the room.

"No. She could not have gone far. But Queen Peozleo, I must go."

"Yes, of course." I needed to get Sorcey to safety before the king realized what was done, if he did not already. We ran to my shuttle. I carried Sorcey so we could get there faster. We were almost to my shuttle when the empress' voice caught my attention.

"Will you leave us to fend off King OAD on our own, Queen Peozleo? That is fitting of a troll."

I turned on her, anger boiling over inside me. "You are an ignorant woman. The lowest of the trolls has more honor than you will ever know. I will be back. And when I return with my army, I expect an apology." Then I ducked into my shuttle and shot us straight to Atlantis.

I escorted Sorcey to the very spot I had picked her up from.

"Something is coming. I know it's something bigger than we can possibly imagine. You must be prepared."

"Of course, my dear queen. I will do my best." Sorcey corrected herself, "Cane and I will do our best. What will become of your people?"

"I will figure something out. The Rittles are secure in The Cathedral and the Dirk of Inverness is yours for safekeeping." I handed her the weapon.

"Indeed, we will keep it safe, Queen. Thank you for entrusting us with this task."

"I would never impose this type of burden on you. This, I am afraid, is written entirely by the strokes." I wanted to say more but there was nothing words could do for either of us now. Sorcey had her own problems to deal with and I needed to collect every capable she-troll for what was to come. So I left and said a silent prayer to Malarin, asking him to deliver my friends from any ill fate.

Chapter Forty-Four

I pushed my shuttle harder than I ever had before. Something was nagging at me about the princess' absence. *Where could she have gone?* Without saying goodbye? That was not like Chaness. I didn't trust the empress to tell her I would return, that I hadn't just abandoned her. Then there was the pressing issue of when the king would present himself with Goutel. I trusted the High Priestess' vision because I had to. Because it was the only thing that kept me from being entirely swept away by grief.

My shuttle pulled into its dock in Listy moments later, and my beloved daughter was there to greet me. When the hatch opened she immediately could recognize something was wrong.

"What? What is it? Where is Goutel?" She was holding Fetzle in her arms. I walked over to them as composed as I could manage. I brushed the little one's forehead. She was so precious, so dear to me already.

"My little Fetzle, you will be a great queen someday."

"Mother." Tazzle took my hand in hers. "What has happened to Goutel?"

I turned to the male-troll who stood closest to my daughter. "Can you please take my granddaughter and alert the captain of the Sholls that I need an audience with her immediately. Tell her to meet me in the courtyard."

"Yes, my Queen." Tazzle did not hesitate. She handed off Fetzle, kissing her cheek before bringing all of her attention back to me.

"There isn't time to tell you all that has happened. Goutel needs us."

"Where is she, Mother?"

"I made a deal with King OAD to save Spitzle and I would not change my choice. I want to make that clear. I would always choose you, choose my family. I have no regrets in this regard."

"This has to do with your arrangement? We're in trouble because of your sacrifice for us?"

"None of this is your fault. This was always my decision and my burden, but things spun out of control quickly and as the strokes would have it, the world's fate was tied to the accord I made with the king. I could not hold up my end of the arrangement and he has taken Goutel as collateral. He will soon find out what was done, if he hasn't some sense already. I must believe that he already knows what we have done."

"What did you do?"

"Instead of returning his Staff, the epicenter of his power, we destroyed it."

Tazzle gasped. "Why? Why would you do that? If he knows, surely he has already killed her." Tazzle's knees started to give and I swept her up in my arms.

"He has not, but he will, or will attempt to at least, and we must be there to stop him."

"How do you know for certain?"

"The High Priestess of the giants told me before she sacrificed herself to dismantle the Staff, because she knew as I do that it was the only way to honor the strokes. There are things happening around us, terrible things, and this was the only way to prevent the annihilation of our world. It was foretold."

"By Chitchakor's strokes." Her voice was faint, distant, as she processed the impossible situation we were in.

"You see, dear daughter, this was never about you and Spitzle. The strokes were grander. There is so much more to say, but we do not have the time now. We must collect an army of she-trolls and travel to the Solomon Islands. Because I have witnessed the militia the powrie king has accumulated and it will destroy the giants if we are not there to help in this war. And when he has finished with them he will come for me—for Listy."

Tazzle's face was a mixture of a million emotions until it wasn't. She looked me in the eyes, all fear erased from her expression. "We will end this war before it has a chance to begin."

This was my daughter, this was the queen I knew she would always be.

CHAPTER FORTY-FIVE

I looked around at the army we had assembled, immensely proud of the she-trolls who had volunteered to stand by my side, to stand by Tazzle's side—to save Goutel. She needed to know how loved she truly was, by so many. Trolls who would risk their lives, risk never seeing their families again, to stand up with their queen.

We did not have many trained fighters. Trolls didn't fight. But after this, I realized that would need to change. I could never let my people be blindsided again. We would be prepared—we would be feared, a force to be reckoned with and not to be crossed.

"We are ready, Mother. We have over four thousand strong she-trolls. The captain of the Sholl force has introduced them to some basic tactics, should this lead to a battle."

I wanted to reassure her that it wouldn't go that far but we both knew I couldn't so I didn't. I turned my attention to the masses that stood in front of me, ready to mobilize and stand beside the giants.

"Today you woke up in this beautiful city and now we find ourselves defending it. You are the brave souls, the dedicated trolls who know what we have here is worth protecting. Never before have we trolls been called to violence. We have chosen peace, and it hurts my heart to be driven to these measures. But I promise you this: Never again will we be caught off-guard. Today we will make such a mark on this world that never again will we be challenged. When we make ourselves seen tonight, we will ensure the legacy of our trollings and their trollings' trollings, because today we show the world why they will revere and respect the trolls!"

The congregation in front of me roared with solidarity and I had to fight back tears.

"We stand together! Are you with me?"

Again it erupted, and I knew it was our moment to seize the fate of the strokes.

Chapter Forty-Six

Emperor Juness met me and Tazzle at the giants' palace west gate. His eyes widened when he saw our numbers.

"Queen Peozleo, it will be an honor to stand beside you and your army."

"Where is your empress?" I had never seen him without her and it appeared obvious to me that she was the leader between the two of them.

"We disagreed and I decided it was time for her to step back and let me handle all battle strategy."

That was a relief, one I had not expected. "And your army?" I looked around. Aside from a dozen men, he was alone.

"This is it."

"Pardon?"

"Over the last few generations our army has diminished and there hasn't been a need to enlist soldiers, especially with Adanc's protection."

I couldn't believe what I was hearing. "Are you telling me these are all the willing men you have to fight the powrie force?"

"Worse. Many have fled."

I was grateful my daughter could not understand what the emperor was saying. This would not sit well with her. It did not sit well with me.

"I know how it looks, but—"

I interrupted. "It looks like they have been poorly led." I leaned in and whispered in his ear, knowing I was walking a fine line between being honest and hurtful. "That can be rectified when we are victors here tonight. It may be time for the empress to take a permanent step back, don't you think?" I wanted him to catch my drift and he appeared to.

"I certainly see the need for reform," he agreed. "I assure you that things will change here in the Solomon Islands. Starting with the tone in which we discuss our friends the trolls from here on out and for generations to come."

That brought a warmth to my heart in an otherwise devastating situation. Some relationships, at least, would be forever mended. I nodded.

"Where shall we set up our defenses?" Tazzle brought us back to the real task at hand.

I reiterated the question to Juness.

"Yes, of course, let us start by meeting with our greatest ally, Adanc."

"Come. You will meet Adanc," I said to her.

"Who is Adanc?" Tazzle looked at me as we followed the emperor into the palace.

I gestured to the troops to stand by. "An impressive ally to have."

Chapter Forty-Seven

We had a good strategy. The troops were in place. So I took the time to ask the emperor the question that had been nagging at me.

"Where is Princess Chaness?"

"She must be with the women and children—and the empress, of course."

"Do you know this? Did you see her going into the vault beneath the islands?"

"No, I'm afraid I did not. I can only assume as much."

"We must confirm it."

"Where else would she have gone, Queen Peozleo? She has no other home, no other family. She has spent no time anywhere else in the world."

"She does have other family." I tried to stay calm but struggled not to fire an onslaught of accusations of how badly they had treated the princess, and no one worse than his wife.

"That was careless of me to say. Forgive me. But I am sure she is with the empress. You will see when we are able to bring them back to surface."

He was not going to budge on this but my gut said there was something wrong. She was missing.

"Do you want me to send someone down there, Mother? We can get eyes on her so you can be present with us here," Tazzle suggested. I was grateful the communication serum was still fast at work. It meant that although she could not understand giant, she could understand me. Unfortunately, it also meant that I could not participate in any of the magics we had concocted to fortify our skin for the battle or the various other advantages that were conjured.

I shook off my misgivings. "I am present, dear. Sorry for worrying you. We need to keep all of our resources exactly where they are."

A moment later Adanc's carrier appeared at the entrance to the lower chambers. The first powries had been spotted on the surface of the water. It was as I suspected. The king had sensed the power of his Staff dissolve and would come to find it at the only place he would know it to be—with the giants. We could not predict which way they would come—beneath the earth or by sea. Neither were advantageous for them. By sea they risked the wrath of Adanc. By land they lost power so deep below the earth's surface. The Solomon Islands gave us great advantages in the fight.

The sunlight burned my eyes when we emerged from the giant tunnels. The cluster of islands were generally covered by dense forest, all but the shoreline. White sands traced the land where it touched the sea. It was attractive scenery if you preferred to live upon the earth, which I did not.

Tazzle saw them first. "They have her with them." She pointed at the approaching fleet, and in the center of it all was my dear friend Goutel. I swallowed the lump in my throat and the urge to just take to the sea and rescue her.

Moments later a hawk flew above our heads, dropping a small

rolled parchment into the emperor's hands. He quickly unrolled it and read it aloud.

You will meet my demands or I will destroy you all, starting with the she-troll.

Tell Adanc to stand down.

Return to me my Staff in one piece.

There will be no exceptions or there will be no survivors.

As the emperor read, I watched as more and more ships, at least a hundred powries apiece, filled the horizon. But where was the king? He was nowhere to be seen. I rolled the marble he had given me in between my thumb and finger.

"Mother, there must be over thousand ships. We are gravely outnumbered."

I just kept repeating the High Priestess' words in my head. Goutel would not die by the king's hand.

A disturbance on the water and one of the ships capsized. Powries were not known to be particularly good swimmers. They flailed about as the closest vessel took them aboard.

King OAD's voice trailed on the wind. "Tell the water beast to stand down!" I perched forward as I saw him manifest in his flame at my friend's side and draw a knife to Goutel's neck.

"Tell her to stand down!" I demanded of her sentry.

He shook his head. "It isn't her. She is awaiting the signal."

Another boat went under. I shot a menacing stare at the emperor. "What is afoot here? We had an agreement to work together."

"It isn't us, Queen Peozleo. Giants cannot effectively swim."

I turned to my daughter. "Ours?"

She shook her head. Unlike giants, trolls were extremely graceful and fast in the water. Faster than anyone would consider based on our size. It was one of the other advantages we hoped would win this battle for us.

The king pierced Goutel's skin with the blade. A warning wound.

"It is not us!" I threw the marble into the air and shouted into the wind.

But how would he believe me? There were no whitecaps on the water. It was an eerily calm day on the sea.

"If you do not stand down, I will kill her in front of you, Peozleo!"

I stepped forward again when I saw three ships simultaneously go down. He would surely kill her now. So I shouted the order. It was time to attack or she would be gone. I would lose her, and I could not lose her.

"Now!"

As I did, the king began to dig the blade into Goutel's skin. I flew off the shoreline and into the water but an enormous wave pushed me back—Chaness' huge frame darted out of the water with the agility of a troll. The princess reached onto the ship that contained the king and his captive. Chaness first went for OAD but he disappeared in his flame, so she took Goutel in her arms and dove back into the water.

Chapter Forty-Eight

"Take her!" Chaness yelled as she came up to lay Goutel on the shoreline. My friend was chained with fae rope, a lot of it, and gagged with elvish wool. The wool multiplied as you pulled on it and the rope was nearly impossible to cut.

Goutel's eyes streamed with tears. "I told you I would come back for you." I pulled her in close.

"There isn't time for this, Mother," Tazzle said as she too knelt down beside us and pulled us both in close to her chest.

"Queen Peozleo!" I looked up to see the emperor. "They have been seen in the tunnels. They will breach the palace."

"Tazzle, get her to safety. Give Adanc the order. No mercy. Ready our troops at the gate!"

I got to my feet, searching for the ship that held the king. If I killed him, I would end this. "Mother, do not go after him. You are the least armed by enchantments."

"You have made me the proudest mother and queen anyone could ever ask for. Honor me and never again let our city be victim to unpreparedness. And when the time is right, you will escort the stones of Atlantis to The Cathedral. Goutel will assist you."

Goutel's eyes got wide and Tazzle gripped my arm so hard I could barely break free.

I scanned the horizon of boats until a flurry of flame caught my attention. The king had reappeared on his ship. All I needed to do was cut off the head of the snake. "This is the job of a queen." I said it more to myself.

I turned and dove back into the water before the tears came, before the doubts took me over. I needed to end this and keep my family safe, my trolliage safe. I saw no other way.

CHAPTER FORTY-NINE

Once in the water I saw what was really happening. We had the strokes in our favor. The powries could not swim as we did. They floundered, and that gave my army and Adanc an upper hand. The sea creature was already ravaging the fleet. The princess was powerful in the water as well. I came up to the water's surface to ascertain where OAD's ship was. It was not where I had last seen it. Perhaps it had already been sunk.

Ducking back underwater, I saw several powries swimming toward the shores of islands. "We have to keep them in the water!" I shouted, knowing anyone within earshot would heed my order. Immediately the focus of my soldiers divided. Some stayed in the water while others swam to the land.

I boarded the closest ship. Two armed powries came at me brandishing swords. I easily ducked and threw the first one overboard while the second came at me from behind. His blade hit my back hard, nearly piercing my skin—my knees buckled. I swung my large right arm back behind him, knocking him onto the bow of the deck.

He crawled to get out of my reach. As I stepped forward I picked up his sword, striking hard and fast, cutting his head clean off.

I looked up to see the battle had hit the sand, and the monstrous thing I feared the most transpired. A mob of powries jumped on one of the Sholl guards. She did her best to defend herself but it wasn't enough and her comrades could not get to her fast enough.

When troll blood was spilt and stained the sands, a coursing and rippling occurred in the carnage. Up sprouted four new powries, adolescent in size and feverishly bloodthirsty. We could not bring this fight to the land. They would multiply and swarm us all—there would be no survivors.

My eyes searched the shoreline for my daughter, to the place where I last saw her and Goutel. Tazzle had my dear friend over her shoulder and they were climbing up the mountain. In a matter of moments they would be able to enter the side tunnel that led straight to the vault deep beneath the islands, where Goutel would be safe with the giant women and children. But before they could, a flurry of powries bubbled out of the palace.

There were too many. We could only win this in the water. Our blood did not multiply their forces in the water. The princess and Adanc were still managing the straggler powries. I had lost sight of the king's vessel once more. The chaos on the decks of the ships around me made it impossible to distinguish between him or any other powrie in the fight.

Tazzle was surrounded. Two giants appeared at her side and were doing their best to fend off the mob. The Sholls were being brutalized on the beaches below, unable to reach them—barely able to fight off the ever-growing number of powries sprung from their own blood. I needed to get back to my daughter.

I swam back to the shore, reaching for the first powrie I could get my hands on and ripping their head clean off. Their green blood spewed everywhere. Immediately the earth vibrated under my feet—two small powries shot out of the blood. *They can duplicate in their own blood?* This was worse than I'd thought.

The emperor was being swarmed upon as if by ants onto honey. I turned to help him before I would scale the mountain to reach my family.

Then I felt the heat of his flame before he spoke. "Peozleo!"

He was behind me. I turned to see OAD on land and only a few yards away.

"I will kill you with my own bear hands. The blood that spills from your veins will double the size of my army, and that army will murder your legacy." The king was wielding a gigantic sword, one that looked too big for his body but that gave him the advantage of a longer reach.

I pulled two daggers from my belt. "There is nothing to be done," I reasoned, knowing nothing would stop his bloodthirst for revenge, and a part of me couldn't blame him. I only wished to save my family. "The Staff had to be destroyed to save the world. If we hadn't done it, we would all be washed away regardless. This fight is futile."

"Futile." He spat as he approached. "Futile is trusting a troll. Futile is choosing compassion for lesser beings when you know you are the superior creation. Never again will I open my doors to the filth of this world. No troll, nor giant, nor hobgoblin alike will make a mockery of me and my generosity again." He swung at me. I jumped back.

"I was wrong. But wrong or not, fate brought us here and I couldn't see the end of the world."

He swung again and I ducked, barely missing the strike this time, feeling the coolness of the blade graze my back.

"You cannot burn down the whole world. What will be left?"

His red eyes grew crazed with rage. "I have no desire to see the world burn only to immerse myself in the blood of my enemies. I will see every troll become fertilizer for my powries." He leaned in, ready to land a blow, just as I heard a scream that chilled my bones. It was Tazzle. I knew that voice anywhere.

Something came over me. I charged. His blade pierced my right thigh because he hadn't expected it. I fell on top of him. The blade scraped my bone but I persisted. I got my knife to his neck. If I drew blood, more powries would rise. I only needed to seize him in to stop this. My leg gushed, and with every drop, my blood fed the earth that sprouted more.

He laughed a wicked laugh, knowing my conundrum.

"Just let them live," I whispered in his ear. "Let my family live."

"Never. Unless your blood can feed my power for an eternity, you will always be beholden."

I looked up to see Tazzle fighting with everything she had, doing everything she knew how to do to save Goutel. My attention was divided when suddenly a colossal disruption at the water's edge had us both turning to see what was happening. It was Chaness, clawing through a sea of enemy soldiers to get to me, with a mob of powries on her back. Even in the water, where she was wounded, they would materialize. Something about her giant origin made her blood fertile no matter where it was shed.

It was enough of a distraction that the king got hold of his blade still in my leg and twisted. I rolled off him onto the ground in pain. Chaness yelled my name, watching on with her own horror while trying to save herself.

OAD bolted on top of me, knocking the daggers out of my hands. He would win. There was nothing left to do. I turned my head to meet Chaness' big, beautiful, kind eyes.

"I love you," I whispered and she reciprocated. The king raised his sword to take his final blow but something in Chaness snapped. She shot out of the water and took hold of the king in her enormous hands. He stabbed at her face but she kept her grip tight, pulling him back into the water with her—saving my life.

I scrambled to my feet to see another fatal blow to the princess' beautiful face, and she sank into the deep, dark depths, holding tightly to the king's torso, not allowing him to break free.

I leapt into the water but they sank so fast I couldn't catch up. I searched the sea for any sign of Adanc. Surely she would come to the princess' aid. The water beast was far in the distance, annihilating what was left of the powrie fleet.

"Adanc! Adanc!" I cried but she could not hear me over the screams of her enemies.

"Queen!" The emperor's voice was weak. "My men and I will secure the shore, drive them back into the water. Save your daughter."

Tazzle screamed again. I looked up. She was surrounded. Torn between my daughter and the princess, I made the impossible decision and climbed the mountain to help Tazzle and Goutel. Just as I made it to them, the bloodthirsty frenzy stopped. The powrie army dropped their weapons and, as though in a hypnotic trance, just walked back into the tunnels. Tazzle grabbed me with her shaking, bloody arm.

"Mother, what are they doing? What trickery is this?" My daughter's voice was weak, trembling.

I held her and watched in disbelief as the swarm subsided, mindlessly retreating.

"Chaness cut off the head of the snake." I looked down at the emperor rising among his men and my trolls who had fallen. He was bloody but still alive. "The princess sacrificed herself to save us all."

Goutel began thrashing about in her chains, unable to shout through her gag. I pulled her in close. She resisted, pushing and pulling as though she was in a fit. I understood her pain. I couldn't believe what had just happened.

The High Priestess' words rang in my head. She had told Princess Chaness she was the key to it all. She knew all along that it would be the princess who would save the world. The princess no one even knew existed, mistreated by her own people. It was she who changed the strands of fate.

EPILOGUE

Dear Tazzle,

I hope that someday you can forgive me for what I am about to tell you. Truth be told, I have never forgiven myself.

You will always remember the day that Princess Chaness saved us all from certain demise at the hand of King OAD on the shores of the Solomon Islands. That day was one that forever united the giants and the trolls in both our grief and in blood shed. Even Empress Dafnee wept for the princess and kissed the hands of your mother, humbled by her own misjudgments. Adanc and Ratatoskr wailed with all the survivors, lamenting the greatest hero we all have ever known. None were more heartbroken than me or your mother. I still weep.

The prophecies of the High Priestess and Pythoness were re-painted in the strokes. The end of the whole world was averted by the sacrifice of those the world had not entirely accepted. Both the Niffler and Chaness had never been fully embraced. The queen was forever haunted by the High Priestess' words to the princess the day before the battle. She told her that her part was always fated to save the strokes.

What you may not know is that after we picked up the pieces and collected our wounded and dead, your mother was dispatched to another duty she promised to fulfill. She spoke of it on the shore where you saved me.

How she had the strength to meet every challenge ever presented to her is beyond me. Nevertheless, bloody and brokenhearted, she fulfilled yet another promise to a friend on that day. Cane and Sorcey Kraus called on her to bring the Katuan Stones to the caves of The Cathedral by order of the original Cataphet.

The Trials had ended in destruction just as the Conduit Kassandra had predicted. As Malarin would have it, Cane and Sorcey were deceived by the notion that they may never conceive. Time will tell how this plays out in our world, but one thing was for sure—all the other visions were realized. It seems likely that their strokes are still in the process of creation. How their fates will paint the destiny to follow will astound us all.

The day of the battle, the queen arduously, collected as many Stones as she could from the ocean floor. At the same time she saved as many Conduits as she could from the wreckage of the Trials' destruction. I could not be there for any of it. It took several weeks for us to find the magic that could unbind me from my chains and gag. It was an excruciating time for a million reasons, but none more than the secret I am about to tell you.

As I stand here, certain the day has come for me to take to stone, I have only one real regret, one true betrayal. When Princess Chaness and I needed to find a way to communicate, we shared in a nymph ribbon bond. We could read each other's thoughts. On the day she saved us I could hear all that went on in her head.

She was certain she would never belong anywhere, that she would always be the beast that no one desired around. As she witnessed the love your mother had for you, for the trolliage, it overwhelmed her and she decided that she would do anything to preserve it.

Here is my treason, as plain as day…

As the princess fell to the floor of the ocean, I heard her process. She did not die that day; instead, she made a deal with the devil. Her blood, her life, her essence for ours. She chose to be captive, she chose to be his life force for all of eternity. I could not tell your mother on that day, and by the time I had the capacity to use my words I didn't want to watch your mother's heart rip back open. Worse yet, I knew she would spend the rest of her life chasing the princess, at the expense of another war. Princess Chaness deserved all of this and so much more. But I couldn't do it. I didn't do it.

Now she lives her days in a prison, feeding her blood for our peace. I cannot bear dying without telling you the truth. You must tell the creature Adanc what I write here on these pages. She loves the princess and will seek her release. She has more soul than I will ever possess.

Forgive me. The cost of peace was the price of a beautiful creature. I conceded to her last request of me to never tell your mother but I cannot die not telling you.

Always yours,
Goutel

ACKNOWLEDGMENTS

First and Foremost I have to thank my extraordinary collaborative group! These ladies are incredible individuals and an absolute force to be reckoned with as a team. Rebekah Gates, thank you for your ability to intuitively know when to take the lead, you know me better than I know myself. Darah Votaw, thank you for your excellent organization and launch strategy. Rebekah Liddle, your creative eye and prowess is exceptional.

I need to take a moment to thank my support system. I am blessed beyond measure with a community that encourages me and keeps me focused. Rachelle, you are my writing sister, my sun and the other half of two authors and a tripod. Jen, you have helped me hone my skill amongst other things...you are also great a friend. Sheryl, Kelly, Jan, Stephanie, Peggy, Krisanne and Gene, you all gave me roots and wings. I have many more people I could list here, but I know you know who you are.

My extended team is amazing as well! I need to start by giving praise and gratitude to Ella Medler, my editor. She continually stretches my abilities as a writer. Cherie Fox is my talented cover designer; she never ceases to amaze me. I am so appreciative of her creative expertise and it helps that she is an absolute pleasure to work with.

To my readers, specifically my VIP team, I am so thankful for you! You remind me on a regular basis that you need more of the Conduit world. Your enthusiasm and dedication to the series warms my heart and keeps me forging ahead.

Thank you, yes you (the person reading this) for taking the time to join me on this journey into the Conduit world.

WANT TO KNOW MORE ABOUT THE CONDUIT CHRONICLES

Take a moment to pop over to my website: https://ashleyhohenstein.com

While there you can sign up for my Readers Club and get FREE Bonus Content instantly! By enrolling in the Readers Club, you get access to a short story. This prequel to the first book *FOUND* gives Rand's perspective of what happened the night Sorcey and Cane died.

You can also get your hands on *FOUND & FORSAKEN* right now! Purchase it on Amazon.

A NOTE FROM THE AUTHOR

I want to say thank you so much for taking the time to read *THE ORIGINALS. The Conduit Chronicles* has been a dream of mine for many years. I am so excited to take you on this journey and introduce you the Conduit world.

If you would like to get the latest publication news for the next book in the series, FOREVER, please visit my website and make sure you join the READERS CLUB to get a FREE Bonus Content. Learn what Rand saw happen at the Kraus compound the night that Sorcey and Cane died. https://ashleyhohenstein.com

If you enjoyed the book, please take the time to review it on Amazon.com or Goodreads. I am so grateful that you took the time to read *THE ORIGINALS*. I would love to hear what you liked about the book.

ABOUT THE AUTHOR

Ashley Hohenstein lives abroad. Ashley had been a massage therapist and health educator for twenty years. She has owned several businesses and has found entrepreneurship to be dynamic and fulfilling. Recently Ashley closed her practice and is now writing full-time as she travels the globe. She was an avid reader at a young age and enjoyed getting lost in other worlds. Her dream has always been to become a published author. *The Conduit Chronicles* came to her on a backpacking trip through Europe. It took seven years to get the first book written and published. If you want to learn more about the author visit her website:

https://ashleyhohenstein.com

Also By Ashley Hohenstein

The Conduit Chronicles Special Edition:

Two Legendary Prequel Tales

Ashley Hohenstein

I am dedicating this special edition to my outstanding team! They have made this publication possible and together they make me a stronger woman and writer every day! You are my tribe, Beks, Rebekah and Darah, I love each of you.

A NOTE TO READERS

THE LEGENDARY PREQUEL TALES SPECIAL EDITION is the compilation of two stories that take you into the more fantastical aspects of the Conduit world long before the events of *FOUND* transpire.

I believe you can read this story as a standalone and enjoy every twist and turn but it is written to be read between Book IV, *FATED* and Book V, *FOREVER* of The Conduit Chronicles.

The two prequel tales happen simultaneously, at times the characters cross paths. I would highly suggest you read *THE ORIGINALS*, first. But if you desire to be a rebel, go ahead. I have always liked rebels. That being said, the epilogue at the end of *THE QUEEN*, does have some spoilers.

Consider yourself warned.

A Conduit Chronicles Story

GWENORA

I loved the way the ocean mist tickled the soft skin beneath my wings. I imagined that the sea herself was showering me with tiny little kisses. I swooped down a little closer to the water and dipped my feet into the surf, simultaneously stretching my wings out as far as I could expand them. Not every dragon could fly. Many of us needn't take to the skies. But I was a commander of the wind, the air we breathed, the very strokes that rustled the trees—the sky was my kingdom. I felt the most at peace in the clouds. The great Painter created me with a love for the heavens in my bones.

I directed my gaze upwards. There was an enormous cloud above me. I flapped my wings hard, propelling myself straight up, aiming for the center of the white wispy mass. My face felt the familiar cool moisture first. I inhaled through my nostrils and my lungs joyously took in the humid air.

One then two flaps kept me elevated and cloaked in the cloud. I looked ahead and saw I was not far from my destination. A small island appeared in the distance. It had been years, centuries, since I had been there. I wondered how it might have changed. As I pulled my wings in tight to my body I dove back down toward the water, exhilarated by the wind that sang in my ears while it sped by. Words only I could understand echoed in the breeze. To be an original was to be one with the strokes. Malarin formed us with immense power, like no other of his children to follow. I internally said a prayer of gratitude to my creator.

My feet were now hovering once more just above the water. A few more moments and I would be back on the island, our own little creation. Perhaps I would see an old friend there, I thought.

A smile spread across my face at the possibility. Then I saw a shadow from the corner of my eye. Before I could turn to see what it was I felt searing pain charge up my right leg and into my spine. My wings stiffened, burned and throbbed. They were pulsating. Something was wrong, very, very wrong. I tried to turn my neck as the shadow grew closer but it had also stiffened and I could not manage it. My body was dead weight now, my senses could not be conjured and my gifts were out of reach. I plummeted into the ocean waves.

Yilliana

I looked at Jolena. She was stunning in the mélange of colors of the setting sun. Her chocolate skin glistened, the perfect shade of pink on her cheeks. The kinky tendrils that shot from her scalp in every direction were as wild as she was. I loved running my fingers through her mane.

"Stop staring at me, Yilli. It is unnerving."

I squeezed her hand tighter in mine. "It is hard to take my eyes away from your glory. Chitchakor perfected the strokes when he imagined you."

Her eyes rolled dramatically. "Beauty is in the eye of the beholder."

"Well then all should behold you, my paramour."

"We have been married for nearly a thousand years; gone are your dreams of illicit affairs and trysts."

"Every day with you is new and feels like a clandestine love."

Jolena laughed so hard she had to stop walking and hold her belly. "Do you not tire of this sort of exuberance?"

"Never," I said as I kissed her full lips. She held the back of my head gently while her tongue moved firmly in my mouth, igniting all the right places. I was just about to suggest we meander back to the cottage when screaming interrupted our exchange.

"Come! Help! She is still in her fit! Something is wrong!" a man's voice carried over the crowd.

People were swarming toward the end of the road, where the path to the sea met the street walk.

"Jolena, we may be of assistance." I picked up my pace and headed toward the crowd. Jolena said nothing but I knew she was in step behind me. It was not in her nature to meddle. She preferred to keep to herself.

I pushed people out of the way as I made it to the spectacle. Most moved when they realized who I was, whispering, "It is the Alchemist. She will help," as I passed by. When I was close enough to the upset, I knew what it was about. Kassandra was convulsing and thrashing about violently. Her Atoa, Dagan, stood a few feet away attempting to contain her.

Sorcey reached the epicenter of the spectators just as I did. A skilled Healer, she would likely be better equipped to handle any injuries incurred.

"Sorcey, Yilliana, you must help. She has been at this for nearly a half hour. I have never seen the likes of this vision before," Dagan said.

Sorcey gave me a concerned look and reached for Kassandra's arm. The moment she touched her, Kassandra stiffened before wailing, folding her arms over her head, then collapsing to the cobblestones.

"Come, Yilliana, let us carry her to my home to rest," Sorcey suggested. The crowd immediately began to dissipate and my introverted partner stood back before waving me farewell and carrying on toward our cottage on the other side of the island. I nodded to Sorcey and lifted Kassandra over one arm while Sorcey took the other. "Dagan, we will bring her back after I have properly assessed her condition. Fret not, dear man. She will be in her right mind soon."

Dagan hesitated before nodding in understanding and moving off the road where he was comforted by a friendly bystander. We walked in silence, Kassandra's limp body between us.

We entered the Kraus residence a moment later. "Let us lay her here." Sorcey directed us to a wide bench with several cushions atop the surface. Once she was settled I looked around.

"Where is Cane?" Sorcey and her Atoa were never far from one another.

"He tends to an errand for the preparation of the Trials. Less than a week away, there is much to be done."

"Without question."

The 8th centennial Katuan Trials were set to take place in a few days' time. The arrivals had already begun. Hundreds of Conduits would be attending from around the world—possibly over a thousand. We had been holding the Trials here on the Island of Atlantis since the Katuanak Arena was formed eight hundred and fifty years ago. I personally attended the first Trials and took up residency here on the island thereafter. There was something glorious about this place. It held more magic than any other location in the world, or at least any other place I had ever been to. As the only Alchemist of my time, being in close proximity to the rawest forms of magic gave me additional strength and abilities I was still tapping into. Sorcey and Cane were among the original Paksyon of Conduits who performed the Covening and brought about the inception of the Trials. They were very respected and often revered among our people. I had much admiration for the Soahcoit.

"Can you fetch me a cold cloth from the ice box in the entry?" She pointed in the direction we had entered.

"Certainly." I moved quickly to assist and when I returned Sorcey was making a thorough assessment of Kassandra's body. I handed her the cloth and observed in silence.

Kassandra was a Ramalan who had the gift of sight. Unfortunately for her, Malarin painted into the strokes an inconvenient caveat for her visions. They came to her in a fit, a violent visceral episode, and only she could understand their meaning.

"She seems intact," Sorcey concluded as Kassandra's eyes shot open.

"You will have a son!" she asserted, pointing at Sorcey with a firm finger.

Sorcey and I shared a bewildered glance. That was impossible. Sorcey and Cane had not conceived upon consummation. They could not bear a child. Perhaps Kassandra had damage Sorcey could not detect.

"Kassandra, rest." Sorcey stroked her head gently with the cool cloth. "Dagan says it was an extremely volatile vision. It has you in disarray."

Kassandra sat up. "No! There is no time." She swatted at Sorcey's hand and adjusted herself where she sat, making eye contact with both of us repeatedly. "We have to abandon the Trials at once. There will be death and destruction. It is already set in motion."

Sorcey and I looked at each other, the same question lingering in both our eyes—*could this be true? Surely there had to be a mistake.*

Gwenora

W*here am I? What happened?* Panic surged through me. My vision was foggy at best. Stars twinkled around the brim of my clouded lens. I shook my head to clear it. Sharp pains radiated in every direction. I shrieked from the shock of it all.

I was wet. Sand clustered on my torso. I searched my brain for answers but there were none. I pressed harder into my memory. There was nothing. Nothing… absolutely nothing. *Who am I?* I did not even know my name. My legs felt heavy. I tried to move but it was no use; I might as well be carrying the weight of the world on my back. A large wave struck me from behind, pulled the sand out from under me, sweeping me back into the water. There was no energy to fight it and a fog of disorientation was enveloping my consciousness, making it hard to stay awake. This would be my end. Whoever I was, I was going to die here on this shore.

YILLIANA

As I walked home I considered what I would tell my partner. Sorcey and I agreed to keep the prophecy to ourselves while we sorted out what was causing Kassandra's misfiring. After all, it had to be erroneous. Conduits were peaceable. We did not harm one another. Furthermore, Kassandra had asserted her vision included Sorcey bearing a child, and that was inconceivable. I shook my misgivings. There was nothing to be done for her at present.

I opened the front door. "Jolena!" I called for her but immediately knew she was not home. I'd assumed she was returning to our house while I helped with Kassandra. Perhaps she had another task to attend to.

A piece of parchment on the chest caught my eye.

Yilli,

I was summoned to assist the Ancients cross the seas from the south. My fleet and I will be preparing our departure at the harbor. Please meet me for a farewell.

Jolena

The timing could not be more unfortunate. I wanted the comfort of my wife. We had been waiting for the call of the Ancients for weeks but there was reason to believe they had found their own means of transport to the Trials. I did not know when she had written the note but surely she would not take to the sea without saying goodbye.

I ran as fast as my feet would carry me to the harbor. As I ran I thought about Jolena's gifts. She was an Admiral. She could captain several ships at a time exclusively by herself and she had yet to ever lose a vessel to the ocean depths. Of course, it helped that I enchanted her vessels with the ability to stay afloat, but I imagined she would have maneuvered them just fine without my assistance. It was, after all, her gift. Watching her sail was magical. I had a flicker of a thought—perhaps I should join her? No, it could not be done. Sorcey needed me, Kassandra needed me—I would be better utilized here. There was a mystery to be solved and I knew Sorcey and I could uncover it.

I considered whether I should tell my wife what had happened now that she was leaving or wait until she returned, since there would be nothing for her to do while away and I had made a promise of secrecy to Sorcey. It would worry Jolena to know I was concerned, so there was only one thing to do—keep silent. The ships' masts appeared on the horizon and I picked up my pace yet again.

Jolena saw me and waved as I approached, jumping down from the bird's nest and meeting me at the dock.

"I was worried I would miss you." She pulled me in for a kiss. "The seas are ready to help me on my voyage; I can feel it in the air."

"Sorry I took my time getting back to the cottage this afternoon. I have something for you." I handed her a small conch shell on a golden chain. "I will keep mine close. We may send brief messages to one another, if only a few words, but it is something." I had made them two moons ago, when we thought she might be tending to the Ancients, but the devices had not been tested. I could only hope they would work. "Our messages carry on the wind, so be sure to whisper when the winds are in route to the north."

"You are brilliant." Jolena kissed me again.

"We will see. I have not had time to test them. This will be a good maiden voyage."

"I will mind the winds." Another kiss. "I appreciate your ingenuity, my love. We must be off. The sooner we leave the sooner we will return." Jolena referred to her fleet as her companions, although she was the only one on board. She shared a language with her ships and the ocean.

"Of course." I hesitated and Jolena saw.

"What is it? What is wrong? I will be safe. You know I will be."

It was too much to explain, too much unknown. She would be back before long and I could confide in her then, when I knew what was going on.

"Sorry. Nothing is wrong." I took her face in my hands and kissed her forehead, nose and cheeks softly. "I am just going to miss you."

"And I you."

With that she pulled back and leapt onto the starboard deck of her commanding vessel. It was beautiful. I had helped with the construction but most of it had been built by Jolena and Njord.

Njord was a Master Craftsman. He could build anything from the wood of the earth—be it fortress or vehicle, it was Njord who would see it done. Together they saw Jolena's dream realized. Each boat could hold fifty men comfortably. Her commanding ship had a cabin that gave her privacy should it be needed. Each ship had three masts and a gigantic rudder that made it agile in the water. It was impressive to see, whether they were sailing away as they did now or approaching the harbor.

"Goodbye, my beloved," I whispered as she waved on in excitement. Then she turned to tend to her mission.

I walked home in a daze, replaying the conversation from earlier. No matter how many ways Sorcey had tried to console or reassure Kassandra that all would be well, she would not have it. I was shaken to my core about the entire incident. We had no reason to believe Kassandra's sight was faulty, except that in the same breath she had foretold of Sorcey and Cane having a child—an impossibility. And now I would be alone for a while, with nothing to do but ponder the foreboding prophecy.

The road forked and I decided to follow the path to the sea. Balto Beach would clear my mind some, bring me peace, so perhaps I could come to some conclusions about what may have happened—more importantly, how I could assist.

As an Alchemist I had a variety of tools at my disposal. Enchantments, tokens and charms that could help us decipher what was malfunctioning. I suddenly felt oddly titillated by the prospect of having a challenge to solve. It was not often that there were unknowns in a world that you had roamed for nearly a thousand years. Mystery was rare and exciting. That was how I would frame this predicament, as a welcome riddle that I was up for solving.

I took the first steps onto the white sand of Balto Beach. A comforting sensation crept between my toes and along the arches of my feet, warm and soft.

The ocean lapped gently on the shore. If Jolena knew about any peril to come, she was at peace with the forecast. I reached the water's edge and walked parallel to the waves, alternating my gaze from the ocean to the sky until something caught my eye in the water. A glimpse of purple bouncing in the break. As I moved closer I realized it was a creature. No, not a creature.

An original. A dragon. I gasped.

Gwenora

My head was throbbing. I moved slightly, adjusting my neck. Immediately pain shot down my entire back and into my hind legs, making me yelp.

Something stirred around me. I had yet to open my eyes. I assessed my surroundings with my other senses and searched my memory for cognition of where I was. The last thing I remembered was sand and waves. I was on a hard surface now, the clumps of sand were gone, and a soft fabric lay upon me. My nose told me I was near the ocean still, but there were many more scents—spices, freshly tilled earth, lavender oil.

The air moved again and I knew whoever was in here with me had come closer. There was nothing to be done. I had no recognition of where I was or, strangely, who I was. My brain knew the information was there, somewhere in the recesses of my mind, but it evaded me as though it was cloaked or behind some hidden door.

I opened my eyes and in front of me, kneeling, was a woman with long, wavy, caramel hair. Her skin was sun kissed, nearly the same shade as her locks. Dark brown eyes scrutinized me. Then she smiled. "You have awoken, thank the strokes. I have been watching you for hours."

Candlelight lit the room. It was a small place, quaint in its furnishings. A few chairs, a fireplace, pillows strewn about and a large wall of bowls, spices and the like. I said nothing as I tried to move, shoving off the fabric, wincing in pain as I attempted to get to my feet. Simultaneously, I realized that I knew the nature of things, objects and general dispositions of my surroundings. Whatever was clouding my mind had not extracted all of my wits.

I could not get to my feet. I had no balance. I toppled over sending more waves of pain in every direction once more.

"You are hurt? I cannot see the wounds but you cry out in pain," the woman observed. Her voice was soft and soothing. It was endearing. *But what can be trusted? Someone has harmed me. Is that not obvious? She may be my captor.*

She stood. "Let me bring reflective glass. Show me where your wounds are. I may be of assistance." The woman hurried back. I realized I was on a table a few feet from the ground. She placed a long silver stone in front of me then waved her hand and an image appeared upon the stone.

"Where does it hurt?" She pointed at the stone, at the image. "Show me."

I looked up at her, bewildered, but something deep inside me shivered. In the stone was an image of a small purple creature with specks of silver scales sparkling through, four legs, a long tail and sharp magenta eyes. The feeling in my gut formulated into terrifying words in my mind. *There is something missing. This form has been defiled.* I—had been defiled.

I got to my feet and stepped back two paces, losing my balance again. It was as though I was used to a larger weight on either side of my torso, steadying me. I shook my head. The pain pulsated through me, constant, unforgiving, and the voice manifested again… *Something is missing.*

The woman put the stone down and I was relieved to not have to face whatever was haunting me in that glass. "I am so sorry. I did not wish to agitate you." She pulled a chair up so that she no longer needed to kneel to be at my eye level. "My name it Yilliana, dear fierce one. I would never harm you. You are to be revered, an original—a dragon."

I am a dragon? "I am a dragon?" I said aloud.

But by the look on her face I knew she could not understand the question.

I repeated myself and this time I could hear the secondary voice like an instant replay of my words. I could not say how I knew it, but I instantly understood that what she heard, if anything, was not my words.

I took a deep breath. This was going to be complicated in every way possible.

"I am afraid I know nothing of Dragonian. To me you sound as though whispers in the wind." She rubbed her forehead anxiously. "Perhaps you should not speak yet; you may be in too much pain." Yilliana reached for something I had not noticed on my hind leg. "What is this token?" The question was clearly for her own musing.

The moment she touched it, shock waves of sharp, stabbing sensations moved through every inch of my body. My head got hot from the sudden surge, then the torrent heightened to such an extraordinary amount of pain that it all went black.

YILLIANA

The original was lifeless again. *I have to do something!* I looked down at the listless body of the small purple dragon. *Dear fierce one, what in the strokes could have happened to you?* I examined the small metal anklet around its hind leg, this time careful not to touch it. I had not known dragons wore jewelry, and by the reaction I'd just experienced, I thought this particular token may be far more than it seemed.

Whatever was happening, all signs appeared to imply that this creature was in pain. I could not see the wounds, therefore I could not tend to them, but I knew someone who could. *The question is, how can I get the dragon to her?* I looked around the cottage quickly, thanking the strokes the original was dwarfish, the size of a small feline.

A leather bag caught my eye. It was not a distinguished way to travel but it would have to do. I administered several invisibility and camouflage wards. A number of new Conduits arrived on a daily basis to the island. This meant I did not know what gifts I may encounter, and something inside me told me I could not let anyone else know of the original's existence. There was subterfuge happening here and I knew not whom I could trust. Except for Sorcey. I would always be able to trust her and Cane.

I applied two more sealant enchantments and gently put the dragon in the leather sack. *Dalinkas, please forgive me. I know an original deserves the highest reverence.*

My feet could not move fast enough, and when I felt the dragon stirring around wildly in my bag, I thought I may be sick from embarrassment. There were still too many people around to interact with the original here and now. I picked up my pace. Sorcey and Cane's home was just around the east side of the arena. My hand moved to steady the sack. I was afraid someone would notice the abnormality occurring and become curious.

I turned the corner and could see the Kraus threshold. Practically sprinting to the door, I knocked as soon as it was in my reach. The iron door knocker was cool in my clammy hand, my nerves getting the better of me.

Winston answered. "Yilliana, I was just leaving. Shall I fetch Sorcey for you?" He casually moved aside, making way for me to enter the room. It felt like it had been weeks since I was here with Kassandra and Sorcey, not a day ago.

"Is she present?"

"The lady of the house is. Cane is not here, I am afraid." With that, he asked nothing further and went to fetch Sorcey. It was odd that Cane was still not home. Very rarely did the pair part ways. But in this case I was grateful to have an audience with her alone. I sighed in relief and looked inside the bag through the small opening to see the purple dragon looking up at me inquisitively. I sensed the original wished to say more but there was no insight for me to be had. Dragonian was a lost tongue, spoken only among its kind. Though I suspected the original understood me.

"Yilli." Sorcey spread her arms as she approached. "So soon I am blessed with your company. How may I assist you in these early morning hours?"

Winston stood but a few feet back. I needed the veil of secrecy for my nerves. "May I speak with you alone?"

"Certainly. Follow me." Sorcey gave a backwards glance to her friend, who quickly turned toward the door to leave. "We will converse in Cane's study. I will contact you and Lucia as soon as Cane returns," she said to him by way of parting.

Winston nodded as we moved out of sight.

We entered the large oval room. My eyes were drawn to the tapestry behind the long wooden table. It was a faction diagram beautifully woven into a mélange of color and overlapping circles, each faction jetting from the hollow center like rays of sunlight.

"It is stunning, is it not? Cane was gifted it by Tulisia. She is a brilliant artist."

"It is breathtaking," I agreed.

Sorcey pulled up two chairs and took a seat in one. "I can sense something is distressing you greatly. Is it Jolena? Is she well? I saw her fleet leave the harbor yesterday."

I shook my head, trying to clear out any fears and just dive into my dilemma. I could trust Sorcey. *I know I can trust Sorcey*, I reminded myself.

"I have something to show you." I set the sack on the table and slowly pealed back the flap, exposing the small original inside.

Sorcey gasped. "Why? Why have you captured a dragon, an original child? This is intolerable."

The dragon nervously looked up at Sorcey, aware that her reaction was of disapproval. "It is not as it seems. I found it, washed up on the shores of Balto Beach. I have done my best to nurse it back to health but there is something wrong. This token upon its ankle; it pierces the skin and will not budge. I cannot communicate with the creature and it seems unable to fend for itself. I only wish to do right by the dragon. The original is in pain. It only just woke after passing out from the agony," I quickly explained.

Sorcey's face softened. She believed me at once. Her shoulders relaxed and she took a deep breath. "You found it washed up on the shore? It is so small and does not appear to have the fins of a water commander. How could it be so far removed from land?"

I shook my head. The dragon crawled out of the bag, with every step wincing and hissing in pain. From the look on her face, Sorcey empathized with its torment as well. It was now looking warily between the two of us.

"I think it understands me. But that is no use, because I cannot comprehend, and I barely hear a sound when the dragon opens its mouth. You see it as I do, that this dear creature is in pain? We must do something," I pleaded with her.

"There is much mystery here." Sorcey looked down and reached for the metal band. This time the dragon stepped back, obviously associating its last painful episode with the trinket. Sorcey pulled back her hand. "May I touch your body, great one?"

The original looked at her skeptically. So much emotion coming from those bright eyes. Then the dragon leaned in and Sorcey took that as consent. She laid her healing hands on its back, immediately recoiling.

"I am afraid I cannot heal this creature. I felt it. The original's strokes are different from mine. But the poison that is in its blood is not so different, and I believe I can encompass it and remove it from the bloodstream so the pain is abolished temporarily." Sorcey's face grew stern. "Someone intentionally hurt this original child with poison. I believe it has something to do with this ring. We will need to figure out how to remove it, but until we do I can contain the toxin."

"How can I help?"

Sorcey looked at the dragon in response. "I must ask you to trust me. We need a needle."

I could not fathom what the original was thinking, but whatever it was, it did not show fear. It lay down. Sorcey and I exchanged glances before she ran to her chamber to retrieve the tool she would use to relieve the dragon's pain. A moment later she was back. The original lay unmoved as Sorcey pierced its thick scaly skin. A minute drop of silver liquid appeared and then, just as quickly, the wound healed itself.

"Never have I ever considered a day like today," Sorcey mumbled under her breath. "Let me help your child, dear painter," she prayed before piercing the skin again, this time not removing the needle. The dragon winced but did not cry out or move, and in front of my very eyes a clear sticky substance began to pool below the wound. Slowly at first, then much faster, until it just stopped.

Sorcey quickly removed the needle and the wound healed.

"What is that?" I looked down at the pool of gelatinous fluid.

"Troll tears," Sorcey said, disgusted.

"How in the strokes would troll tears make it into an original's blood stream? And how did you know that?" Saying it out loud, it sounded even more ludicrous.

"That is beyond me. I only know what it is because of helping the Queen Peozleo after an incident in her shuttle a century ago. It is rare and very identifiable. Trolls were created alongside the original children but we are more in their image, so I can identify with their strokes better."

The original had yet to move, then suddenly it was up on its feet, clearly feeling better, no sign of the pain it was in moments ago.

Sorcey and I hugged each other, excited for this small victory.

"You did it. I knew you could help." I laughed with relief.

"For now," Sorcey responded solemnly. "I think there is much to this anklet. We need to discover how to remove it. The question is who put it on in the first place and to what end?" Her face furrowed in disgust.

The dragon moved around limberly, stretching and shaking. I wished I knew what in the strokes was on its mind.

GWENORA

I did not know what they did to me but for the first time since I had awoken I was without pain. Still wobbly footed, I continued to feel a distinct absence about me. Though without knowing any more than that I was a dragon, it would be difficult to say what I was missing. I looked up at both of these women—they were good, sincerely compassionate beings who meant me no harm. Thank the heavens that Yilliana had found me. There was no way to speak my gratitude. Yilliana had confirmed what I'd suspected; she could not even hear me.

After their embrace and Sorcey's assertion, the two began to devise their next course of action.

Yilliana was throwing out various proposals. "In a few days' time the streets will be teaming with many more Conduits."

What was a Conduit, I wondered.

"Certainly we must find this fiend before then. It must be someone on the island."

"Must it?" Sorcey asked. "It could be any individual or creature making their way here. We already have many guests but more arrive every day. There are Pixies to consider, Water Sprites, an assortment of magical beings…" Then she paused. "But I have no idea what anyone's motive would be for harming an original." She shook her head, looking down at me with grave concern on her face. "Who would seek to hurt you, fierce little one? What must you know that you cannot tell?"

I considered her words. I knew nothing. Absolutely nothing. Not even who I was.

"What shall we do, Sorcey?" Yilliana kneeled down and put her head on the table on which I stood. I felt a pang of guilt. These two women were worried sick about my well-being. What a burden to bear. "Jolena is gone, fetching the Ancients. What shall be done? How can I keep this creature hidden and safe?"

Sorcey knelt beside her and rubbed her friend's back. "It is a burden the painter left you to shoulder. This seems to be fated in the strokes, Yilli. I will help you as best I can, asking around discreetly and making keen observations of any odd behavior. But I am also still attempting to sort out how to heal Kassandra. She has proven to be a peculiar patient."

"Of course." Yilliana looked up at Sorcey and took her hand. "I am committed to helping you with this mystery as well."

Sorcey smiled. "One challenge at a time, great Alchemist—even for you."

The two of them were close; it was very clear by their interactions and compassion. Yilliana stood and Sorcey followed. "I must get this dragon home. My cottage is the safest place for hiding it. It is in the country and I can implement many wards without detection." Yilliana met my gaze. "And I am going to devise a way to speak to you, dear one."

"If anyone can, it would be you, my friend." Sorcey took her in her arms again before addressing me. "It has been a pleasure to meet you. You are in good hands with the Alchemist, but if there is anything I can do to be of service—I will."

I hoped my eyes conveyed my appreciation.

Yilliana picked up the sack from behind me, her face once more dismayed. "This is not suitable transportation for an original." Then she perked up. "But this may help."

She waved her hands and recited several words very quickly in succession. I was not paying close enough attention to catch them. With that she opened the bag, appearing much more pleased with herself. I acquiesced. I understood why I was being hidden for my safety. But this time when I stepped in, the leather material dissolved away and it was as though I was suspended in midair. I could see everything about me.

Yilliana closed the flap and I got comfortable. "I hope this suits you better," she said as she waved her final goodbye to Sorcey and we slipped out of the house.

Voices carried on the wind, conversations, music and the thrumming of footfall. Dawn had arisen and the day was clear and crisp. Smells wafted in the air, spices. Some seemed familiar, others foreign, and the distinct pungent aroma of fish filled my nostrils.

As we approached the center of the settlement things got louder. When Yilliana turned a corner I was amazed at the sight. A huge coliseum stood in all its glory right in front of us. Around it were a variety of tents of different colors and sizes. People bustled by, stopping to look at items being displayed by the vendors. It was mesmerizing to watch them carry on.

The streets were paved with large tan stones, tightly fitted together to make them as seamless as possible. I looked around at the other buildings that lined the streets before we emerged into the crowd just ahead. The structures were two—sometimes three—stories high, with open balconies on the highest floors or rooftop terraces. Long drapes of all different colors danced in the wind. Ivy crawled up the sides of the buildings in places, creating more vibrance. The arena appeared to be at the center of it all—vast, many stories high, with arches and walkways on each level. I could not say if I had seen anything like it before now, since I could not remember, but it was very impressive.

Yilli was dodging people, trying not to bump into anyone with my transport. She was managing very successfully when a young woman came out of nowhere and hurtled into her. Yilliana stumbled two feet backwards from the impact. I fortunately did not feel a thing.

"I am so sorry, Yilliana," the woman said.

"No matter. How are you feeling today, Kassandra?" I admired Kassandra where she stood. Long golden hair that fell to the middle of her back, loose braids pulling it away from her face. She was in a violet-colored robe. Gold stitching hemmed the long sleeves. Kassandra was shorter than Yilliana and bone-thin.

"Better," she said. But then she abruptly began to convulse violently. The crowd around us moved out of the way, all but Yilliana, who stood her ground and waited for the spectacle to stop. She reached for her friend, who now looked dazed. "I am okay," Kassandra said when Yilliana's hands braced her shoulders. "It is all these new arrivals to the island. I cannot make heads or tails of any of my visions." Kassandra shook off Yilliana's embrace.

"What did you see? The same?"

"It is of no consequence. Remember, my sight is misleading me."

"Hardly. The painter has gifted you," Yilli insisted. "Things are just befuddled right now."

"My sight is faulty; is that not what we discovered yesterday?" Kassandra was not angry with Yilliana, just very distressed.

"One misguided episode cannot mean you are lost."

"Well, I saw the Rittles. All of them—found." Kassandra shook her head. "In the dark somewhere, below the earth."

Yilliana hesitated and I wondered what this vision could mean. What were the Rittles? Kassandra seemed distraught with her misguided sight. She barely lifted her head in acknowledgment.

"The Rittles have not been seen for ages," Yilli maintained. She reached for Kassandra's shoulder, to comfort or perhaps to keep her attention. "Did you see anyone, or where this dark place was?"

"No. All I see is shadow. Will I ever heal?" Kassandra shook her head then waved Yilliana on and took back to the streets. That poor woman… Yilliana would set it straight once I was safe, I was certain of it.

She pulled the bag in tighter and continued to maneuver her way through the crowd. When we got closer to the coliseum I heard a different kind of voice manifest around me. It was deep and alluring, buzzing and vibrating from within the walls. *Can Yilliana hear it? What in the world could it be?*

Just then the Alchemist got pushed against the wall and when the leather brushed against the stone I heard it loud and clear. "Gwenora, you have come home." But it was not one voice, instead a cacophony of them, joyously shouting "Gwenora".

Who is Gwenora?

YILLIANA

I practically sprinted home, afraid someone might have detected the original. Kassandra's malfunction was getting worse. I wanted to help her. I needed to help her. She was in pain; that was clear. Then a quiet but firm thought floated into my head. *What if she is not misfiring? What if there is more truth to what she is seeing than we suspect?*

I tried to shrug it off, primarily because her prophecy about the Trials also included foretelling that Sorcey and Cane would have a child, and that was impossible. I reasoned the thought away. She was having glitchy episodes. Once I could focus all of my attention on her dilemma we would fix it straight away, but the original required more of my attention for now.

I slammed the door and implemented a slew of wards before gently placing the sack on the table and letting the dragon be exposed. So many questions, even fewer answers, and the stakes appeared to be getting higher.

Communication with the original was essential. Dragonian may be a dead language but I was a great Alchemist; I could find a solution. I had to find a solution. The dragon crawled out of the bag and off the table.

"Are you hungry? Thirsty? Do dragons eat? What do they eat? Oh, dear Chitchakor, why did you see this to be my fate?" I sat down on the ground.

I was so lost in thought that I nearly jumped out of my skin when I heard the trill of the conch. I hastily got to my feet, frantically looking for the shell. "Where have I put it?" I never would have misplaced it if I was in my right mind. The gentle noise got fainter and I knew I was losing my brief connection with Jolena.

Finally I found it on the counter beside the east bay window. I pulled the conch to my ear. The voice on the other end was hers but it was growing quieter and quieter by the moment. I could barely make out the words.

"I love you, Yilli. I am midway, beyond the land mass to the west. I will return to you no later than the eve of the Trials." Her voice brought tears to my eyes. She said something else but the last bit of the message was lost on the winds of the sea, the very ones that carried the message to me. A breeze wafted through the cottage and I had a moment of confusion. The winds carried from the east. Jolena was certainly coming from the south; she would need the northern wind to carry her message to me. An ache twisted in my stomach. I brushed it off. The winds must have shifted, which would explain why her voice had trailed off.

I could not respond until the winds changed their course so that they may not lose the message traveling in the wrong direction. The winds were not in my favor at present or her message would not have been carried to me. I was feeling overwhelmed and paralyzed. This was not a feeling that overcame me often. My knees buckled and I put my face in my hands and let the tears fall, until I felt a gentle nudge on my arm. Warm smooth skin brushed up against mine. No, not skin—scales. When I looked up the original was nestled next to me in a ball, peering up at me with kind eyes. I dared not touch it, afraid I would cause it pain once more, so I just sat there and together we offered each other the best comfort we could, with our eyes.

GWENORA

Yilliana and I shared a quiet but powerful morning. We were both lost in thought. I could not articulate the words to fill the space, and she chose not to.

I wondered about the woman Kassandra and her visions. I thought about the voices calling for Gwenora, welcoming her home—*who are they, where are they and who is Gwenora?*

But most of all I wondered if I would ever discover who I was and what had happened to bring me to this state. I sat staring down at the anklet on my foot. My inner voice, the one that lives deep in the belly, repeated itself, *the key to who you are is in this token.*

Just then Yilliana entered the room. "I brought you something to eat."

The smell in the air suggested something from the sea. *Do I eat fish? Is that what dragons eat?*

"It is rockfish. One of the delicacies on the island. I garnered it from Greeden. He is an exceptional cook." Yilliana set the clay bowl of food down in front of me. I was willing to try it. *Am I hungry?*

Perhaps, since my body was still attempting to heal fully. But my sense of smell was indicating this was not what I wanted for nourishment. Yilliana sat down cross-legged on the other side of the bowl, waiting patiently for me to eat her offering. I wished that we could communicate.

My eyes shifted from her face to the fish several times, all the while my stomach growing more nauseous. Well, I would not know for certain unless I tried it. I stuck my mouth down into the basin and took a small bite of the sea creature, immediately followed by violent vomiting. The contents did not even need to hit my stomach for my body to reject them forcefully.

I projected the flakes of fish and whatever liquid was in my stomach directly into Yilliana's face.

We both sat there in shock before she started laughing hysterically. I did not feel well but her laughter was contagious and lightened the situation that could have been tense were she offended. She wiped at her cheeks with her dress. "It is safe to assume that you, my dear fierce one, do not consume the flesh of the sea. My apologies."

She was apologizing to me for my spewing food particles at her. What a gracious host. Yilliana picked up the offering and took it outside, and I was happy for it. The smell was still not sitting well with my queasy stomach. I may not know if I was hungry or what I might eat, but I knew what I would not consume—rockfish.

Yilliana returned. "You are small. Perhaps you eat birds? Or insects?"

I looked at her skeptically, afraid of what she would bring me next. The communication, between our eyes and body language, was getting better because she immediately picked up on my hesitance.

"Very well. No more experiments with your palate today."

Relief surged through me.

"The winds still are not in my favor so I can't make contact with Jolena." Her face was downtrodden. "In some moments I wish I had gone with her, but then I would not have found you and then where would you be?" Yilliana continued to talk, more to herself than to me. "I have been looking in my grimoires, searching for something that may help Kassandra with her gifts. I have yet to see anything that would give me a good foundation to work with. I may need to incant from scratch—it has been a long time since I have done that. Nor does a spell come to mind that will help me decipher your Dragonian tongue. It is in the strokes for me to generate some new magics." There was a twinkle in her eye as she spoke about creating. "I am up for the challenge."

YILLIANA

I left the dragon at home while I collected some basic ingredients for what I called a cleansing-of-the-strokes spell. There was reason to believe that Kassandra's malfunction was just a simple congestion of her strokes. Clear the congestion and the energy can go back to moving freely and fluidly. It was the best place to start. As I approached the house, I saw a piece of parchment tacked to my door. I read the note, not certain if I should be alarmed.

Yilli, I must see you at once.
Meet me near the large stables, east of the arena.
Sorcey

I entered the cottage and found where the original one lay resting. I wished I knew its name. I wished we could converse. I wondered what the dragon thought of my efforts to keep it safe. I read the note again. Sorcey would have news; that must be what this was about. I snapped my fingers and the paper went up in flames. The ashes fell to the floor.

The sun had set and the night markets would be well underway. Over three hundred Conduits had arrived by now. The streets would be busy so I grabbed my cloak and pulled the hood over my head. The dragon did not stir, only looked at me passively as I left once more. I had to assume it trusted whatever agenda I had. I walked out the door and encapsulated my home with every ward I had, ensuring the safety of the original while I crept away. I could only hope this encounter would be brief. I did not wish to be far from the dragon. I had already left twice today.

I walked briskly through the city center, around the Katuanak Arena, keeping my head down, praying that by Malarin's strokes I would remain unseen. I turned the corner to see the stables. They were dark, as expected. When I got closer I cast a small spell to detect if anyone was in the structure. Two figures were present, but one was definitely not a Conduit. *Who has Sorcey brought with her?*

I opened the gate quietly. My feet crunched on the hay that lined the floor. Horse hooves restlessly moved in the dark, keenly aware of another intruder. I approached the pair in silence. I could see their silhouettes in the shadows and quickly made out their faces.

"Yilli, thank you for joining us on such short notice. Were you followed? Do you have the dragon with you?" Sorcey asked.

I looked at the woman I did not recognize before I answered. She had long black hair. Her features were exotic. She wore very little clothes—a small piece of leather covered her breast, her belly was exposed, and several colorful sheer pieces of fabric barely concealed her lower half. Magic exuded off her. *What is she?*

"I came alone. I was not followed. Thank you for your summons. Have you news?"

"This is Molpe. She has just arrived and I asked to speak to her in private. Molpe has told me of some very alarming news. It pertains to the originals and may explain how your guest arrived on our shores."

I looked nervously between the two women. Obviously Sorcey trusted this Molpe creature, *but enough to share our quandary?*

There was no time for pleasantries. "I apologize in advance for my abruptness, but who are you and why should I trust you?"

The creature moved ever so slightly, fluidly, sensually, all at once. When she spoke her voice was soft, feminine and unusually sexy. "I understand your apprehension. It is alarming when a creature as fierce as a dragon can be manipulated. There is cause for alarm, I assure you, but not in response to me. As Sorcey said, I am Molpe, the Siren of Pleasure. I have arrived on the island to celebrate the impending Trials. My tendrils and I have travelled very far to reach the shores of Atlantis. Have you heard of my song?"

I had heard of Ligeia, the Siren of Lamentation. She thrived on the tears of the brokenhearted. I said as much. "I have heard of your sister Ligeia."

"Then you know how our gifts work. We are charged by our Siren song, empowered and nourished by our assigned emotion. My troupe and I came from the lands below the ice. We were entertaining a flock of fairies as they migrated north to the white lands. One of my tendrils engaged with a particular fae several nights in a row. He shared a story on the sixth night, one she felt compelled to relate to me. I will recount it for you now. Before I do, let me promise you, I am a creature of truth, benevolence and of love for all things painted in the strokes, but none more than the original children, because it was after them that we were created and we sisters spent many years with the dragons as our only companions. An assault on them is an assault on me."

I felt the righteousness rolling off her. I knew not the gamut of gifts at the disposal of a Siren but Molpe led me to believe that she was a sincere creature. I nodded to reassure her that I understood her conviction.

Molpe continued. "My tendril said the fae described an incident they witnessed off the shore of the eastern coastline. Their flock was flying along the bay, hovering over the shore, when an object appeared in the far-off distance. Fae do not have exceptional vision as do Conduits but they see a fair distance. The flock was surprised because the vessel seemingly manifested out of nowhere. Not a soul had seen its approach. More peculiar was what occurred next. An enormous water dragon breached into the air, missing the craft or it surely would have torn it into two. Several of the fairies were ready to come to the vessel's aid; it was that near a miss. But as the dragon moved just below the surface, thrashing and wildly stirring the water, it became apparent there was a struggle. The dragon was wrestling with something. Now the faeries were in pursuit of what was transpiring in front of them. But as they approached, the floating vessel vanished, leaving no trace of what it was or where it had gone. The water dragon floated on the waves, exhausted and befuddled. Alive, but in a sad state. The fae flock pulled the original into shallower waters and stayed guard, in the event that the mysterious object appeared again. It did not, and by nightfall the dragon was in a condition to take back to the depths. It is unfortunate that not many creatures may converse with the originals. It is their blessing and their curse. They can understand all words by all beings only to be misunderstood themselves."

I interrupted. "How do you know that?"

"We spent many moons in the same strokes. Secrets were shared in creative ways, gestures and signals. Words can sometimes be more of a hindrance than of service when it comes to communication," Molpe mused, and I could not deny the roots of wisdom in what she said. The original and I had communicated limitedly but effectively enough so far. I just wished I knew the dragon's name.

"Would you come and meet the dragon? You must be familiar with many of them. We have yet to discover a name or even what sustenance the fierce one may require."

Molpe looked warily at Sorcey before answering. "I will concede to your request but I implore you to be extremely circumspect of those around you. The originals are more powerful than any other being. For them to be made vulnerable means there are nefarious doings among us."

Sorcey met my stare. I knew she felt as I did, now more than ever, that we must get to the bottom of what happened here and who had committed this atrocity. Something deep in my soul was telling me that our future depended on it.

GWENORA

I stretched and yawned. My tail flicked back and forth giving my back a gentle rhythmic internal massage. Still, it was strange. I had a sensation that I could not expand my front legs enough—as though I was missing something. Yilliana had come and gone without saying a word but there was nothing to be said. It made me complacent and lazy.

The door in the other room opened and I heard Yilli's familiar voice. "Fierce one, it is I, your dear friend Yilliana. I hope I have not disturbed you."

I turned to see her step into the doorway and I greeted her with a nod while moving off the small bed she had made me. Two other people stood behind her. By the smell of her, I knew one was Sorcey before I saw her face. The other female looked familiar, smelled familiar, but I could not place her. She gently pushed past Yilli and Sorcey and got down on her knees to be at my level.

"Gwenora? By the strokes, could that be you?"

I cocked my head trying to make sense of the interaction. *Is that my name? Does this woman know me? Was she the voice I heard earlier this day, in the city center?* She did not sound the same.

"It is I, Molpe, the Siren of Pleasure. We spent moons together. Can you not remember?"

I stared at Molpe, unmoved by her assertions but not able to shake their familiarity.

"What has happened to you?" Tears streamed down Molpe's cheeks. No one could fake this level of torment for a stranger. *What has happened to me?*

Molpe stared at me but spoke to us all. "Gwenora is a commander of the skies. I am certain this is her—I would know those eyes anywhere—but she has no recognition of me. I can see it in her face. Her wings are gone and she has somehow reduced her size to that of a small pet. She was the size of three elephants last we met." Tears continued to pour from her eyes as she looked me over.

I was larger? I had wings? A master of the skies?

"What is this?" She reached for the metal loop around my rear leg and I instinctively stepped back, aware that it had caused me pain, terrible pain, when touched before. "Sorry, fierce one. Gwenora, what is this on your form?" She reached again and this time I did not flinch. Molpe took the ring between her two fingers, then screamed as though she had been burned. But I felt nothing. "By Chitchakor's grace, what on earth is that?"

Yilliana knelt down beside her. "I felt its magic too, although it did not burn me. What do you make of it?"

Sorcey was also hovering above me, the three of them staring at my leg then examining Molpe's singed fingers.

"I know not, but my flesh is not of Conduit flesh, it's not of formed flesh at all. I move in an energy vessel—created and sustained by pleasure. I have never experienced physical pain before. Whatever this token is, it has some part to be played in these happenings. I venture this is to blame for Gwenora's state."

Gwenora? I like this name; it has a nice ring to it. But… I had wings and was very large? I looked down at the ring. *What happened to me? And how come I can't remember it?*

YILLIANA

The three of us walked out of the house in silence. I could not speak for the other two but I was at a loss. What magic could defile a dragon, remove its wings and reduce its stature? *More importantly, why would any creature take to this task?*

"I must go," Molpe said as soon as the cool night air surrounded us.

"I will see you tomorrow at the feast," Sorcey responded as she reached for her friend.

Molpe returned the gesture but corrected Sorcey, "No, dear soul, I will take my tendrils and leave this place. It is not safe, and with magic such as this present on the island, I will not allow my tendrils to be harmed. There is one more thing you should know."

"What is that?" I asked.

"Gwenora is not just any original, she is also a Sire of the Stone. This very island was once visited by four original children. Their intention was to create. From that intent came the Katuan Stones and all the magic you feel in this land. The Katuan language is Dragonian.

They are one and the same, the only written record of the originals' language."

The air seemed to syphon from my lungs. *How have I not heard this creation tale before now?* Still, it made so much sense. The energy in this place was palpable in the air. "How did we not know this?"

"There are many histories from long before your time. You are not the first inhabitants of this place but the whispers in the wind suggest you may be the last. I must be going." With that Molpe began to dissolve right in front of my eyes.

"Wait. What do you mean we could be the last? Molpe?" Sorcey demanded. But she was gone and Sorcey and I had nothing but our fears between us. We stood there in silence, and I dreaded what I must tell Sorcey next.

"I am compelled to tell you something. I saw Kassandra yesterday when I left your home. She ran into me and slipped straight into a fit. Her vision was of the Rittles. She was still distressed. What seemed like a random episode has turned into many. Could this be related somehow? Could she be right about the destruction if the Trials proceed?"

I searched Sorcey's eyes, desperately wanting to hear her say there was no way… that it was impossible she bare a child so it was impossible that the Trials would end in death. But her gaze gave me nothing.

"I will speak with Cane when he returns. There is still great reason to believe Kassandra was somehow misguided by her gift. Consus do not carry children after they have transformed. There is something amiss in her vision. Still, we cannot disregard what Molpe hears on the wind. Keep Gwenora safe." Sorcey put her hand on my shoulder and squeezed it gently before disappearing into the night as well.

Gwenora, Sire of the Stone, Commander of the Skies and original child—I wanted to know so much more but was happy to have a name.

GWENORA

Yilliana and I spoke through the night, until the sun rose in the east. Well, I say spoke but in truth it was she speaking while I listened. She explained what Molpe told her about Gwenora—that was me—being Sire of the Stones. There was no way to explain it to Yilliana but this revelation had me wondering if it was the siren I had heard call me by this name yesterday.

I was grateful that Yilli also taught me the basic gesture for yes and no, a simple nod or head shake. It gave me some semblance of acknowledgement and participation. She also explained in depth about this world—the world of the Conduits. Yilliana described a peaceable community of individuals with extraordinary powers. Gifts that manifested when they met their Atoa, essentially their other half. Once the pair consummated they became nearly invincible and stopped aging physically. The whole interaction felt familiar, as though I knew of these peoples in a distant memory but it was too far out of reach to grab hold of the knowledge. I wondered if dragons came in pairs too. *Is my other half looking for me?*

Yilliana paced and spoke of every Conduit she could think of that might have the ability to construct a device that could ensnare a dragon. I knew none of their names—I did not even know for sure that Gwenora was in fact my name—but talking about this through the whole of the night seemed to bring peace to Yilli as she spilled all of her fears and postulations out of her head and into words.

She lay on the ground beside me now. "Gwenora—that is what I will call you. I promise you, we will get to the bottom of this. We will right this wrong. No creature should be harmed and I will not see you befall any more attacks," she said with conviction. "Who in the strokes would attempt the capture of not one, but two originals? And you, you are an exceptional prize, Sire of the Stones. The Stones speak Dragonian! Never in my wildest…" Her voice trailed off. Then she sat up. "I do not speak Dragonian but the Stones do. I cannot communicate with the Stones but they have a written language. Why did I not think of this sooner!" She jumped to her feet. "Come! I may have a solution to our communication conundrum."

Yilli grabbed the satchel she had enchanted for me from its hook, placed it on the floor for me to hop into, and quickly swept us out the door. The city center was as busy as it had ever been. Yilliana had said there were seven hundred and sixty-two Conduits in attendance so far. Shortly it would be the entire world's population.

As soon as we were close enough to make out the bustle of feet, I began to hear the voices in my head, "Gwenora, you are home. You have returned."

This has to be the Stones, right? I was their Sire. They had to be calling to me. The voices grew louder and louder. When we reached the arena Yilli slipped into one of the entrances. Suddenly the voices took over. My head was pounding from the pressure of it all.

"Enough!" I shouted.

Everything went silent. Eerily silent. The Stones listened to my command. That settled it. I had to be Sire of the Stones.

"Hello? Can you understand me?" I asked as Yilliana still traversed the halls of the arena; where she was going, I could not say.

The cacophony returned in my head. I could not discern what was being said.

"Is there a leader among you? I need only one to converse with. The rest must be silent."

Once more it went mute. I waited patiently to see what would happen next.

A deep, melodic voice filled my ears. It had an echo to it. It was neither masculine nor feminine. "No leader among us, since we were all created from one form. Welcome home, Sire."

"Home?"

But before the Stones could respond, Yilliana's pursuit was interrupted and it drew my attention.

"Yilliana, you are here to watch the combat practice on this day? We have missed your presence." It was a man's voice, cool and collected.

I addressed the Stones, "One moment, please."

"Apollo, I have missed participating in these preliminary festivities."

I looked up at the man with jet-black hair. His eyes were a rich auburn brown, he had high cheekbones and a charming smile.

"What keeps you and Jolena?"

"Jolena, I am afraid, had an errand on the sea, helping some friends pass the ocean safely and swiftly. She should be home very soon." Yilliana put her hand on the flap of the bag, as though to make sure it would stay closed. "With her absence there is much to be done around our grounds. It has kept me busy. Alas, I will not miss the Trials."

"One would hope not. What brings you to the arena if not to engage in the merriment?"

"Sorcey had asked me to confirm the podium is in good working order. I have an incantation to amplify the sound."

"Of course she would demand the great Alchemist's support. Busy are those who hold great gifts. We should all be so lucky as to have your charms."

Yilliana bowed slightly. "It is an honor to be regarded so highly but certainly any Conduit with your gifts would be highly praised as well."

"You flatter me. I simply receive what is shared. I must be off." He moved around us gracefully. "Too bad you will not be watching the events this morning. I am challenging Aphrodite to a duel."

"May the strokes be in your favor."

Yilliana continued walking in the opposite direction of Apollo and I returned to my conversation with the Stones. "I lived here with you?"

"For hundreds of years," the Stones replied. "You created us. We owe you our lives."

"How, then, is it that I do not remember any of this?"

"We do not know, but there is a great fog around you, stifling your strokes."

"How can I eradicate this fog?"

"Again, we do not know. The Alchemist may be able to help. She is very powerful and extremely kind."

"Yilliana does seem virtuous. But what can she do and how can I communicate what you have shared?"

Just then Yilliana stopped in front of a small door, round and made of wood. She placed her hand on the center and it softly swung open. The chamber was dark but I could see there were remnants of a structure inside.

"She enters the tomb," the Stones chorused.

"What is the tomb?" I asked as Yilliana got on her knees and began sweeping the floor with her hand.

"It has happened once or twice that during the Trials a stone is marred or a stage destroyed. The remnants are stored here, so that one day they may be absorbed back into our being. It takes many hundreds of years, but as a living stone, we are able to integrate all of our parts."

I suddenly knew what Yilliana was doing. She was brilliant. "As your creator, may I ask a favor?"

"Anything," the voice purred with adoration.

"May we have a volunteer, a piece of the wreckage that would be willing to stay with me and help me communicate?"

There was a buzzing around us. Yilliana felt it too. The entire arena was shaking.

She put her hand on the bag. "Gwenora, I may have insulted the Stones. I was looking for an errant piece. Forgive me. I may have just led us to our doom."

I wanted to reassure her that if we were to meet our fate, it was both of our doing, but there was nothing to do but wait.

The Stones spoke louder, attempting to resound over the buzz. "We have a volunteer." Just then the shaking stopped and it got deathly quiet, all but for the soft sound of a rock tumbling toward us.

I watched on as Yilliana picked it up and got to her feet. Instinctively, she understood what had happened. She put the Stone in the satchel with me. I quickly hugged it, knowing in my heart that this was a sacrifice from what could only be described as my children.

"Thank you," I whispered. I knew the Stones heard me although they made no reply.

YILLIANA

My heart was pounding, I thought it might jump clear out of my chest, and for the first time in a long time I was glad I was not mortal. I got back to the house as quickly as I could without creating a spectacle. As soon as we walked through the door I reinstated the wards and opened the sack to let Gwenora out with the stolen Stone.

The original stepped gingerly out of the bag before turning around and taking the Stone in her mouth then placing it on the floor at my feet. I was shaking and decided to ask the only question I could think of.

"Can you speak to these Stones?"

Gwenora nodded.

"Are we in trouble? For taking this Stone?"

Gwenora shook her head.

I let my shoulders relax. *Thank the strokes.* "May I pick it up?"

Gwenora nodded once more.

I picked up the Stone and examined it in my hand. There was

nothing particularly remarkable about it. It did not even have any of the Katuan markings. To the naked eye, it was simply a rock. The Stone fit into the palm of my hand perfectly. I accomplished the first step I required to build a bridge of communication with Gwenora. Now I would need to think long and hard about how to proceed next. I needed to create a bond between the two of us and I was certain that this small Stone would be the foundation.

GWENORA

Yilliana kept herself busy. She explained that she was going to create an incantation that would allow us to communicate. I saw her determination but sensed her doubt. *Who am I to know the undertaking she is being met with?* I was no Alchemist.

Instead I focused my attention on the Stone. It was also nice to have someone—or something, rather—to talk to.

"Do you have a name?"

"A name? I am a Katuan Stone."

"But you volunteered, so that must make you your own entity. Are you still part of the whole?"

"Yes."

"So you are still one with the arena?"

"No."

I could tell this was going to take some fleshing out. We spoke the same language but perhaps did not understand the same context of the language.

"Can you still access the unity of the Stones at the arena? It was apparent you all operated as one."

"No. When I volunteered I was severed from the whole. I will no longer be able to integrate back into the Katuanak Arena."

"Was that frightening?" The Stone sounded indifferent, but it was a living thing, was it not?

"Frightening? You are one of our creators. When the call came, I knew you would refine me into something even better."

That was a lot of pressure but I trusted Yilliana. I could trust her with this Stone. *What will her incantation include?* It occurred to me that I had no idea what her intentions were for this child of mine. *Perhaps she intends to pummel it into dust?* My heart sank at the thought of it. *What is to happen next?*

YILLIANA

I combed through my scrolls. Anything I had ever created was on this parchment. Nothing had surfaced that would lend me any insight into what I was attempting to do. I needed to somehow bridge the communication between Gwenora, the Stone and me. The trouble was, they both spoke Dragonian, therefore the tie between them would be simple. It was I who needed a vessel to translate the word written by the Stone.

It seemed to me that I was more likely to be able to pull the language from an object created by the originals than the original. There were imprinted gifts on the Stone, like Haven magic. If I could dissect it or interject it into something else, I could interfere with the signal, reflect it and utilize another vehicle to translate it. This would be the most complicated incantation I had ever performed.

My concentration broke when I felt someone approaching my wards. "Gwenora," I said quietly and she immediately knew to slip into the sack. A moment later Sorcey appeared in my doorway. I could have guessed it would be her but it did not feel like a good time to assume anything after Molpe's warning and hasty departure. Sorcey entered the cottage and shut the door, fastening the lock.

"I am sorry to call upon you without warning. Less than a week until the Trials begin, the streets are swarming with visitors already. It has been difficult to vet everyone, but I have two who have caught my eye—Apollo and Hephaestus." She said the names in hushed tones.

Sorcey had my full attention. I'd only seen Apollo earlier today, at the arena. Could he have been following me? "Why say you that these men alarm your senses?"

"Apollo has been extremely antsy, uneasy, and has asked about you and Jolena on multiple occasions." The hair stood up on the back of my neck.

"And Hephaestus?"

"He has not left his shop for days. He will not be bothered, not by any would-be Champion or visitor. He slaves away, because his fires have not stopped burning. You can see it from his chimney stacks." Sorcey looked around until she found the bag that Gwenora was peeking out of and put her hand down to coax the dragon out. Gwenora crawled out and into Sorcey's waiting arms. She walked back toward me and continued. "And does this trinket not look like a creation manufactured by the Vulcan and artisan?"

Sorcey was right; the metalwork did look like that of someone of Hephaestus' caliber. It seemed very likely indeed that he could have something to do with this crime. I rubbed my head, really beginning to wish I had confided in Jolena about the original before she took to this errand. At her current speed, by the time she returned the Trials would be upon us.

"What has Cane said about canceling the Trials? What does he think about Kassandra's visions?" I asked.

Sorcey put Gwenora down before she answered. Her pause had me worried. "Cane has not returned."

"Where is he? Absent this close to the Trials?"

"He was summoned by the Giants. We assumed it would be a short visitation. Their High Priestess indicated he needed to be present for an important ceremony. If he had known he would be gone this long, I assure you he would have reconsidered."

"What should we do?" This was terrible timing for his absence.

"For now, we wait. We cannot stop the arrivals, and the Opening Ceremony will have to commence in order for the Directorate to be chosen. Our only hope is to convene them before the first Trial. We have other matters that require our attention." Sorcey looked back down at Gwenora. "Indeed, it is possible that if we solve the riddle of who harmed our fierce friend, then perhaps we also prevent them from harming another in the Trials."

"I follow that reasoning," I agreed, because it was hard to imagine there was more than one foul plot underfoot here. They must be connected. "When can you expect Cane to return?"

Sorcey shrugged and the frightened look in her eyes stopped me from pressing her any further. She was scared and did not wish to consider that something had happened to Cane.

"What are you working on here?" Sorcey asked, realizing I was studying my previous works.

I nervously walked over to the sack and pulled out the Katuan Stone shard, not certain how Sorcey would feel about my thievery. "I am trying to devise an incantation that can allow me to communicate with Gwenora. She must know something that can assist us."

"Is that a Katuan remnant? Did you steal it? Is that why the whole island trembled?"

I cleared my throat. "I took it, yes, but I think it was given to me." I explained how, as I searched on the floor, this stone had literally rolled into my hands.

Sorcey shook her head in disbelief. "Well, what is done is done. I fear what more Kassandra may see with her sight. Misguided or not, it is unnerving."

"Because I took the Stone?" I nervously played with it in my palm.

"Perhaps, or because we have a Conduit among us who would hurt another creature, bend it to their will. For what reason, we do not know. But it is subjecting those of us with the highest integrity and good at heart to choose actions that are not of our normal rectitude. This concerns me and we would be fools to not be curious how this may affect the strokes."

GWENORA

"Who was that?" the Stone asked. "I have seen her before."

That was curious. The Stone had seen Sorcey before. "How have you seen her? Her name is Sorcey. She is a confidant of Yilliana's. We can trust her."

"I believe we can, too. We Stones weigh those who enter the arena. Sorcey has been weighed and is very virtuous. I am fond of her."

That was validation that Sorcey could be trusted if ever I heard it. I wished that Yilliana could have witnessed the Stone's assessment of her friend. I turned to see Yilli combing through her scrolls again, reading every symbol. A moment later she squealed and I jumped.

"By the strokes—ever in our favor! I found it!" Yilliana shrieked with delight again. "It is a start, a bridge between creatures—Conduit and bear. I used it eight hundred years ago. I had forgotten about its inception. Jolena and I were in the white circle, where the white bears roam freely. Jolena, as curious as she has always been, wished to speak to the white bears. It was a wondrous time. They took us in as their family." Yilliana looked down at us and it pulled her back from her memories into the present. "We will need two bridges and a vessel to carry the translation, because your strokes are different from mine. But it is possible. I know I have a spell here somewhere that will funnel the strokes into a channel we can translate."

Her enthusiasm was contagious. We would be able to communicate soon. But I still did not know what that meant for the Stone. I looked over at the small rock and hoped for the very best.

"Have you decided on a name for yourself, Child?" I asked it.

"I have."

"Be quick with it. What have you decided?" I insisted.

"Sorcerer, like the virtuous one."

"The Sorcerer Stone. I like that very much." I nodded in approval.

YILLIANA

It was hard to believe there could be any more Conduits arriving for the Trials, but it would seem more had overnight. I thought back to the last games, a hundred years prior. There were fewer than six hundred Conduits present, and that was nearly the world's entire population of Consu that year. There had to be double, possibly triple that in attendance today. It was wondrous, and if I had not been in such a state, I would have reveled in meeting all of the new Consus. This was not the time, however. I needed to focus on the pressing issues at hand, which could possibly save many of these Conduits' lives.

If I could communicate with Gwenora, then perhaps we could decipher who her attacker may be. Once we exposed the deviant, we could bring them to justice and discover why they were conducting themselves in this manner. To hurt any of the painter's creatures was deplorable, but to incapacitate an original was unfathomable. There had to be answers and consequences.

I was lost in thought. Perhaps that was why I did not notice

Apollo watching me from across the street. I reached down to where the sack should be at my side before remembering I had left Gwenora at home within my wards. She was safe. I sighed with relief. Once Apollo realized I saw him, he approached.

"Good day, Yilliana. Still I see your Atoa is absent. Where may she be? Attending to her errand?"

"Yes, Apollo. I am afraid so. It pains me to say she continues to be preoccupied." It really did. I wanted her home to assist me with this debacle.

"She is of the upmost caliber, your wife. I dare say Shatki would have no part in being away from me for so long as to help another."

"Odd, because I have yet to see her here with you. Where is your lovely partner?"

"Flitting about but not far, I assure you. She is the queen of conversation; surely she has taken up with an old acquaintance. Although it is harder to find old acquaintances in this mob, is it not? We are swarming with new blood. Where do they all come from?" Apollo looked around at the bobbing heads and I thought I saw a flash of disdain on his face.

"This disturbs you? New friends, more of our kind?"

"Disturbs? No, not at all. It irritates me like an itch to be scratched. Have you ever wondered, great Alchemist, does the insurgence of our population dilute our powers? Surely there is only so much magic in the strokes. As we grow in populace, it seems likely that the pool of power is further diminished. Of course, you are the great Alchemist, the only one of her generation. That must mean you are immune."

"I am not certain I follow your train of thought, Apollo," I interrupted him. "You think the appearance of more Consus takes from you? As though the strokes are in scarcity and not abundance? Why does that concern you?"

He waved me off. "Never bother. It is a silly thought. One that should most definitely be dismissed."

"Curious, though, do you believe that that power—this pool you speak of—includes all of Malarin's magical creatures?" The moment I said it out loud I realized it may have been too close to the mark. But it lent motive to his potential involvement in the mistreating of the originals. Dragons were the most powerful of us all. Dispatch or weaken them and the pool would be greatly enriched, thus increasing Apollo's perceived power.

"As I said, dear Yilliana, it's a fool's thought."

But his eyes said more. Frightfully more.

"Have you been keeping my husband occupied, great Alchemist?" Shatki's voice rang over the crowd. Her warm smile moved into view and pulled me away from the eerie exchange with Apollo. Like Apollo, Shatki had black hair. Hers was wildly curly, and today it was stacked on her head. She wore a silk robe that swept over one shoulder. The rest of her body was exposed. Her warm tan skin shone in the sunlight. Shatki embodied the feminine, curvy, sultry, deep and warm. Her gift was to empower the feminine spirit in all of us. Qualities like sensuality, receiving, magnetism, darkness and destruction, so that rebirth must take place. I liked her very much.

"It was me distracting him from your side. My apologies."

She pulled me in for an embrace. "Nonsense. I would be lost and found by your side as well, given the chance. There is so much wisdom within you. Where is your beloved Jolena?" Shatki looked around.

"Off. She is to be home soon with more guests. Can you imagine that—more guests?" I gestured around with my hands, slipping a sideways glance at Apollo as I said it.

"By the strokes, you sound like my husband." Shatki swooped her arm through his. "He keeps moaning about the vastness of it all. I find it exciting! Speaking of exciting, Walthrup is challenging Dracula to a duel. We must attend. Will you join us, Yilliana?"

"I wish I could."

Apollo answered for me, "More matters to attend to."

"Always." I smiled at them both.

"Well, then let us keep you no longer. Show me the way, dear wife," Apollo asked her, but the look on his face left me uneasy. "Until we meet again."

Then they were gone, lost in the crowd moving toward the arena.

GWENORA

Sorcerer was effortless to talk too. Of course, the Stone did not elaborate unless you asked an intended question, but all inquiries were promptly and simply addressed. Perhaps that was because Sorcerer was not bombarded by emotions. There was little sentiment behind the responses, only facts.

"Have you had a favorite Champion?"

"Yes."

"Who might that be and why?"

"I much preferred the Ramalan Aurora in the last Trials. She has very talented sight, can see far and wide and was a very useful offensive strategist for her Katan, always knowing the other team's moves a fraction faster than they could formulate an alternative plan. That was all Katans but the Quitsee. Noll is a powerful Amplifier. He partnered with the magnificent Shield Freida, and together they were able to disguise their actions from the Ramalan. It made for a tense Transformation Trial."

I was going to ask more when a faint bell began to ring. It was the conch shell. I ran around the cottage until I found it. Uncertain what to do next, I mimicked what Yilli did the one and only time I had heard the noise before. I put my head to the opening and listened.

A soft voice, barely audible, came through. "I hope you are safe, Yilli. The winds have not been in your favor to reach me. I have arrived on the southern landmass and will be returning north soon. You are with me in my soul. We will be together soon." Then the voice was gone.

I would remember Jolena's message and retell these sweet words when I could communicate with Yilliana—I hoped that would be soon.

Sorcerer said nothing while I had ran about. I wondered if the Stone had its own questions, but it did not ask so I did not share.

"Where were we?" I said as I returned to my seat beside Sorcerer.

"My favorite Champion."

"Of course."

Inquiries were interrupted once more when I heard footfall coming toward us. It was not the familiar gait of Yilliana or Sorcey. I took Sorcerer in my mouth and swiftly crept into the bag for hiding. There was a rattle on the knob. The caller did not knock or make their presence known. When the lock held tight, a shadow moved toward the window. I could not see their face, only form. They tried to unfasten the latch on the window but it stayed intact. One by one, they moved to each window attempting entry, but to no avail. Would they continue to seek entrance or would they give up after the initial failure? Another rattle of the knob, this time more forcefully. I feared this would-be intruder was not easily swayed.

YILLIANA

I looked at Hephaestus' shop from across the street. The windows were boarded up. Sorcey was correct in asserting that something was definitely going on. Over the last four hundred years that Hephaestus has resided on the island, he had never once closed his welding shop. I studied the list in my hand. It was more inconvenient than ever at this juncture because I needed something from him—two small inscribed metal plates.

The incantation I desired required the decals; I had no other choice. I crossed the street and knocked on the large wooden door. There was no answer. I pounded harder with the second knock. I heard the sound of shuffling feet inside—several feet, in fact.

"One moment!" Hephaestus' deep voice demanded.

I waited impatiently. The sound of multiple locks being unfastened let me know that he was intending to open the door. *Why does anyone need so many privacy measures? Is he hiding something?* I thought about my own home; that was why I had taken extra precautions.

The short round man stuck his head out. "Who calls on me?"

"Sorry to disturb you, Hephaestus. One could assume you are busy based on the state of your shop but I am afraid I am in a bind and cannot go anywhere else for assistance. Your craftsmanship is necessary for me to complete a very important incantation. One I must insist be done before the Opening Ceremony."

"Yilliana. This is not in your form, to call on me with haste. What has you riled?"

I had anticipated he might ask what I was working on. "It is gift for the Champions."

"That is not customary."

"No, it is not, but it came to me in a dream orchestrated by the strokes and I would be a fool to ignore the painter's will."

"That would make me a fool for not assisting you, and I dare say I am no fool either." Hephaestus looked over his shoulder once more before opening the door wide enough for me to enter. I quickly slipped inside and he briskly locked the door behind me. His shop was dark with the windows boarded. I saw perfectly fine in the dark, as did he, but it was dreary.

"What project do I interrupt?"

He looked at me in such a way that I became aware I was overstepping my bounds. "Something commissioned by an old dear friend, and they have asked for my confidences."

"Of course. I would never think to intrude."

But Hephaestus' eye roll suggested I already was. He walked toward a small table where he took a seat on a high stool. "Show me this undertaking."

I walked over slowly, attempting an assessment of the room whilst not exposing my curiosity. Never had I sleuthed on a friend, and I was gravely underqualified. I pulled out the scroll I had drawn the concept on, a blueprint of what I needed. Hephaestus never took his eyes off me, limiting my ability to take in my surroundings. When I reached the table, I unrolled the scroll. "The work is simple enough for a man of your expertise. I need two of these, flat and roughly the diameter of a small sand dollar."

He examined the sketch. "What are these markings?"

I had hoped they were an adequate bridge; the finished product would be two metal decals that conveyed and translated the Kata symbols and Dragonian into a format I could understand. "They are bridges, knots between different energy vessels."

"What two vessels are you entangling?"

"It is an incantation that enhances the Katan camaraderie."

He did not hide his skepticism. "Why would the painter want you to interfere with the Katans?"

"That is not for me to know."

Hephaestus paused and I wondered if he intended to share something of his own but then thought the better of it. "We do not always know why we are called to do the things we must. I understand this well. I have been compelled to things I may never have reason for, things that scare me."

"What scares you?" I tried to make eye contact with him but he kept his eyes from view.

"There are many things that can scare us. Today is not the day to discuss them." Hephaestus took the parchment, rolled it up and placed it in his belt. "I will complete this task. Come to me at first light. It will be done."

"I am grateful," I assured him as he stood and moved toward the door. I got another quick glance around the shop, and something caught my attention out of the corner of my eye. Low to the ground, movement, long hair—I could not make out what it was.

"Be on your way, great Alchemist, and leave me to it," Hephaestus said as he unlocked and opened the door. I scanned the far wall again but did not see anything out of the ordinary this time. *Are my eyes playing tricks on me?* He interrupted my thoughts, "By the strokes, be on your way, Yilli."

"Again, I am grateful," I repeated as he shut the door behind me and established the locks once more.

GWENORA

Yilliana was still out collecting whatever it was that she needed for the incantation. Whoever the inquisitive caller was, they had long since left and I was back to sitting across from Sorcerer.

"Do you miss your collective?"

"No. I am content to do this work. It has been centuries since I was integrated as part of the whole. A piece as small as me is not prioritized—it is far more important to keep the remnants with Kata symbols on them intact. That is our life force."

"I was one of the dragons that created you?"

"Yes, our mother Gwenora, along with Dionim, Gess and Plout."

"How is it that you came to do this, become the officiant of the Katuan Trials?"

"When this generation of Conduits came to our shores, they expressed an affinity for fellowship. They performed a Covening, unaware of our power as the children of the originals. We participated, collaborated, and the intention for the Trials was set. They named us Katuan, which means congregation in Asagi."

"What did you contribute to the Covening?"

"Multiple facets, the configuration of the Stones, the weighing of the Champions, the Directorate to ensure the rules are met with honor."

"Rules? Such as?"

"One, without question or exception, is that there is to be no taking of another's life by any soul in the arena. It will result in its complete destruction."

"The Conduits seem peaceable," I observed.

"They always start in this way, peaceful—without wanting. However, it has been witnessed across the span of time that power struggles ensue and harmony is not always preserved."

"You have witnessed several generations of Conduits?"

"We are nearly as old as you, dear original. The Conduits have lost their way many times."

"How many times have you witnessed the fall of a generation?" In that moment I wished more than anything that I could remember my own lifespan, who I was, what I had seen.

"I am not a creator, but it all moves cyclically…" Before Sorcerer could finish its thought, the front door opened and my attention was reverted to Yilliana, who appeared frazzled.

She locked the door behind her and threw her bag on the floor beside the table, then came and knelt beside us. "Sweet Gwenora, what have we been ensnared into?" She bowed her head in front of me. "I know not whom to trust." Yilliana looked up at me with tears in her eyes. "I am afraid Sorcey's suspicions of Apollo have merit."

She rolled onto her back in exasperation. "And now I must see to the Master Craftsman himself, our second suspect, Hephaestus. His skills are required to perform the incantation. Malarin's strokes are not happily met for me on this day!"

YILLIANA

I arrived back to Hephaestus' shop at first light, uncertain of what I would do to investigate my suspicions from the day before. I thought about bringing Sorcey with me but I felt that might make him a little too wary of my motivations. Alternatively, I made a risky decision. I determined I would bring Gwenora. The original had senses I could not even imagine. It would stand to reason that perhaps she could pick up on more than I could, and with the incantation I was preparing, I would be able to communicate with her and find out what she perceived during the visit. I also enchanted a small purple amethyst I would wear around my neck to record the encounter, then I could share all the information with Sorcey after the fact. It was the best I could do considering the circumstances. Still, it did not feel like enough.

Gwenora shifted in the bag at my side. I prayed to Malarin that I was not setting her up for ruin. In my other hand I fondled two discreet beads that could serve us if we needed to make a swift getaway. Each one had the ability to stupefy anyone they made contact with other than me. I took one more deep breath and rapped on the door. There was no wait time with this second visit. Immediately, I heard the locks being unfastened and seconds later Hephaestus, looking the worse for wear, was in front of me.

"Come in, quickly," he said hurriedly. I swiftly complied and slipped in the door.

"Were you successful?" I asked.

"I was. It was simpler than I thought." Hephaestus looked over his shoulder at me as he walked to an object on his work table. "What is the purpose of these tokens, really, Yilliana?"

The question caught me off guard. I stayed rooted where I was as I spoke. I had a better vantage point of the room from here. "I am sorry, what is it that you mean?"

"This is not for the Champions. They needn't enhance their camaraderie. These markings are those of the Katuan Stones. I am no inviolate. I live on this island as well."

I should have known he would recognize the Kata symbols. "Because we are on this island, I must utilize some of its original magic in the incantation." That was the best reasoning I could formulate and it was not entirely incorrect.

Hephaestus stood there unmoved and I had not the faintest idea what he may be thinking. All of the sudden I saw a blur of movement in the darkest corner of the room. I jumped, frightened by the velocity of it. Few things could startle a Conduit. We had exceptional reflexes and vision.

"By Chitchakor's strokes, what was that?" I shrieked.

"Nothing. It was nothing."

"That was not nothing." I stepped closer to the Vulcan. "What is happening here?" I was not certain if I was emboldened or just trying to avoid my own interrogation. Either way, I had already made my move.

Before he could answer, a small animal padded out from the dark.

I looked up to see Hephaestus just as alarmed as I was. “No, this is not safe,” he pleaded and got to his knees.

What on earth am I witnessing? The creature was furry all over. Long brown hair covered every inch of it. No larger than a mutt, it could indeed be a canine. Until you saw its face you wouldn’t know any different. It had the definitive features of an original. He had taken one captive. I was too late.

What shall I do now? Two dragons? “What have you done?” I shouted.

“Franky, why? Why have you exposed yourself?”

“Franky?”

The original walked directly over to my satchel and nudged it with its nose. *Oh no!* I had exposed Gwenora. Panic filled my chest. I took two steps backwards.

GWENORA

"Gwenora?" a male voice that I did not recognize asked. I hunkered down in the bag. I could see him but he could not see me. "Gwenora, I have been looking for you everywhere. Get out here straight away! It is me, Franky."

Who in the strokes is Franky? How does he know my name?

"Crikey, mate, I don't know how you're fitting in there but I can smell that it is you. Why are you hiding from me? It's putting me right out."

Franky, as he identified himself, poked me with his snout once more. Yilliana quickly stepped back. "What in the strokes, Hephaestus?"

"I can explain, Yilliana. Just take a moment." Hephaestus stepped forward and she stepped back again, the fuzzy animal following—or Franky, rather. "First, what is in your bag? The original is clearly set on it."

"What are you doing with a dragon in your shop? Did you abduct this original?" Yilliana accused. My mind was trying to catch up with what was actually taking place. *Franky is an original, like me? He knows my name? He can smell me?*

I popped my head out. Yilliana protested. "Gwenora, it is not safe."

But it was, was it not?

"Franky?" I asked, only repeating the name, still having no idea who he was.

"Aye, that is me." The hesitation in his voice implied he realized I did not truly know who he was and he now knew it.

I climbed out of the satchel the rest of the way and Franky muffled a gasp. "Malarin's strokes, what has happened to you? Where are your wings, your size? Who has done this to you?" he shouted, then threw a fierce gaze to Yilliana.

I glanced up at Yilliana, who still looked terrified. Hephaestus' expression was undoubtably that of bewilderment, and Franky was disgusted, angry and ready to attack.

"I do not know what happened to me," I meekly replied. "I am afraid I also do not know who you are or who I am. But this woman saved me, so do not be cross with her."

Franky softened his stance. Where there was rage there was now sadness. He came over and nuzzled into my shoulder. "Oh, Gwenora." Sobs vibrated his chest. "I am so sorry I was not there to protect you." Franky nuzzled in closer. "This is all my fault."

"You know what has happened to me?" I asked. "You knew I would be targeted?"

Franky shook his head. "I just know I should have been with you. We knew there had been attacks on our kin."

Yilliana interrupted our conversation, although she would have no idea that was what she was doing. "What is this? Are you safe, Gwenora?"

I nodded. Although I supposed I did not know for certain that I was in fact safe, Franky appeared to be a friend and not a captive of this Conduit.

Immediately she turned to Hephaestus. “Explain,” she demanded, but this time her voice was less shaky, more inquisitive.

Hephaestus’ own shoulders relaxed before he responded, “Very well. We must talk. Come. Let me make you some tea.”

YILLIANA

I was still shaking, anxious to understand what Hephaestus was doing with an original in his company as I am sure he was of me. The kettle screamed and he quickly poured both of us water over our loose leaves. Once he was satisfied with how long they had steeped he brought them over to where I sat upon a stool in the corner of the shop.

I looked on at the two dragons standing close together across the room. I knew they must be conversing. I wished now more than ever that I could understand the originals' language.

"His name is Franky. He is an earthen dragon. An original Commander of the Earth beneath our feet. I first met him in the southern continents. Celsi and I were traveling, looking for a new frontier to settle into. We stumbled across the Black Rock Forest. I could feel the strange magic vibrating in the soil but I had no idea it was emanating from an original. He approached us on our second day and beckoned us into the depth of his caves. In there was a room that held strange magic indeed. I could understand Dragonian within its walls. Every word he spoke, I understood without question."

"Do you understand him still?" I asked, desperately hoping the answer would be yes.

"No. Sadly, it is only in that room that you can understand the originals' language. Now he only comes to me as a deep hiss. But when he shares his flesh, I can see things—understand his intentions, sense his needs. He and I share a bond that allows us to communicate without words."

"His flesh?" I tried not to look disgusted.

"Yes, his scales. When I ingest them, we connect on a deeper level of intuitive communication. Similar to telepathy."

"Then I must eat Gwenora's scales? How in the strokes will I get her to concede to that?" I looked down at her.

"I am afraid it is not that simple. I do not know the rules, but Celsi senses nothing when she partakes."

My hopes were instantly shattered. I would find another way. "Why is he here?"

"I know not, but he brought this for me to build." Hephaestus took hold of a parchment that was in his reach. "He brought it with him and laid it at my feet. Celsi is collecting the rest of the needed elements required to construct it."

"What is it?"

"It is beyond me to figure out, but when an original demands your services, you acquiesce without question."

I nodded in agreement.

"How have you acquainted yourself with your small dragon?"

"I found her. Washed up on the shores of Balto Beach."

"You know it is a female? She communicates with you?"

"No, certainly not. The Siren knew of her. Gwenora is her name—Commander of the Skies and Sire of the Stones."

"But she has no wings."

"Something terrible has happened to her. The Siren said as much. Her wings are gone and her size greatly diminished."

"By the strokes of Dalinkas, who could do such a thing?"

I shook my head solemnly.

"Who would want to do such a thing?"

"It is troublesome. What motives could a creature have to attack and defile an original?"

"Only the worst kind, I am afraid." We were in agreement and I was reminded that Hephaestus may have more to offer. "You see that anklet on her hind leg?"

He nodded.

"It is enchanted or poisoned, something heinous of the sort. Do you recognize its craftsmanship?"

Hephaestus walked over and knelt down. Gwenora waited patiently for him to examine the trinket before he concluded he did not recognize it.

"Never seen anything of the like. Have you tried to remove it?" he asked.

"It appeared to hurt her when toyed with, until…" I stopped myself, not wanting to expose that Sorcey also knew of the dragon's presence. "Recently, now, it seems benign."

"That is a clever defense," Hephaestus observed, ignoring my hesitation.

"I agree, so whoever devised it was clever and cruel."

Hephaestus took his seat beside me once more. "What shall we do? Are these decals intended to help free her?"

"I hope to create a bridge to be able to communicate with her. With all dragons."

Hephaestus' eyes got big.

"I must finish this task. But Hephaestus, it is dangerous. We have to keep them safe."

We both looked at the originals. I could not say what he was feeling. All I knew was that I was afraid.

GWENORA

"Is this true? You were found on the shores of Atlantis?" Franky's eyes conveyed his concern overtly.

"Yes, without knowing who I am or what I am. Only wearing this trinket and without my wings."

"Or your stature," he added. "The Siren identified you then fled?"

"Yes. She also spoke of another dragon nearly captured."

"This is bad, very bad, Gwenora. I had heard of two attempted abductions before arriving in Atlantis. It is why I came. When we last spoke you expressed a desire to visit your island, your creation. I heard that it was now inhabited. I only wished to ensure it was a safe place to be. I was relieved to find my mate Hephaestus here."

"So you did not come to bring him what he now works on?"

"No. What he works on is a device to find you. To find all dragons—a map with dragon stone."

"Does he make maps? He appears to be a metal worker," I noted as I admired his assortment of constructs.

"He is a metal Vulcan, an Elemental who can draw metal from

the earth and bend it to his will. With his will come certain properties. There is no other like him in existence." Franky puffed up his chest with pride. "I trained him in many things while we spent years in my caves. He has consumed my scales. That bonds us."

"Scales?" I looked at him skeptically.

Franky shook vigorously. "This is not fur, only the painter's unique interpretation of scales."

I sniffed the locks; they certainly smelled like fur.

"How did you know to have him consume your scales? Does it enable him to understand you?" I was starting to get excited, thinking this could resolve my communication problem with Yilliana. I would happily share my flesh if it meant we could converse.

"I was once told an Elemental of an original's same variety can communicate with us by sharing flesh. She is not an Elemental of air." He nodded in Yilliana's direction. "But she is special. You are lucky she found you, Gwenora."

I nodded. "She is trying to use a Katuan Stone to create something we can communicate through."

"Is that so? Is that part of what she had Hephaestus create?"

"It is," I admitted.

"May I see it?"

I walked over to her and nudged at her pocket where I thought she put the item the Vulcan had handed her upon our arrival.

"What, Gwenora? What is it?" A silly question that we both knew I could not answer, so I nudged her again with my nose. She felt in her pocket and pulled out not one but two small delicate metal plates. Franky came over and examined them.

"These may work to bridge the lines but she needs something more. I have some ideas. I will need to modify these with Hephaestus' help. Can you indicate that to her somehow?"

"I will do my best." I thought about how I could get my message across.

"She trusts you. I know you can find a way," Franky said as he turned to get the attention of Hephaestus.

"Franky?"

He paused and looked at me with his deep chocolate eyes, and I saw the same look that had my curiosity piqued. "Are we lovers? Why are you helping me? Why were you looking for me?"

His eyes softened even more. "We have been lovers, friends and dear companions over the span of many years. I would do anything for you, Gwenora. When I learned of the attacks, I had to make certain you were safe." He moved closer to me and brushed the side of his face to mine. "I should have acted sooner. Now we need all hands on deck to discover what has happened to you and how we may rectify it. I will not let you down again."

YILLIANA

My mind was racing in all directions as I left Hephaestus' company. I wanted to speak to Jolena. I wanted to hear the tenderness and assurance in her voice. I needed her home. It had been a few days since her last message. I needed to tell her of what was happening. She was wise and courageous; she would know what to do next.

Between Hephaestus and Gwenora, I was able to decipher that Franky had modifications he wished to make to my incantation. I knew better than to neglect an original's wisdom, so I conceded and left the medallions at the shop with the agreement that I would return tomorrow to retrieve them.

I was anxious to complete this spell. If all went well, I would be able to finally converse with my dear friend and we could get to the bottom of her attack. I was startled from my thoughts by a familiar voice.

"Yilliana, you are as lovely as ever one could be." Esther stood in front of me with her Atoa by her side. I instinctively put my hand over Gwenora in the bag.

"Esther." I bowed slightly. "Yanni, how wonderful it is to see you both. When did you arrive?"

"Only yesterday. I thought we would be the last. Alas, my father tells me Jolena is still out at sea collecting ever more Consus to join us." Esther looked around at the moving bodies and I wondered if she felt as Apollo did, that the growing numbers were troublesome.

"Jolena is to arrive home very soon with the Ancients, no less."

Yanni's eyes widened. "How many will attend?"

"That, I do not know."

Another familiar voice rang behind me. "The great Alchemist, you bless us with your presence." My nerves heightened to a pitch. *Will my shielded sack be able to hide Gwenora from our most powerful Ramalan?* I turned to face her. If I had failed, then surely Aurora would already know what I was carrying.

"Dearest Aurora." She met my greeting with a genuine smile. "It has been eighty years or more since last we spoke. How have your strokes faired?"

We embraced and she held me long and hard. Was that for a reading, I wondered.

"I have missed the island and its inhabitants but Cadmael and I have been traveling in the southern lands before the ice and have met a pleasant people there. A clan of hobgoblins." Aurora's face lit up. "Come. You three must meet him. I brought an ambassador to watch the Trials."

Esther and Yanni practically pushed me along as they eagerly moved in the direction that Aurora redirected to. The Ramalan sashayed through the crowd. Conduits parted at her approach; she was greatly revered. In the distance I spotted her Atoa Cadmael. His dark brown hair shone in the sunlight, streaks of auburn throughout. His skin was caramel and his build was brawny, with big arms stemming from a large muscular chest. I had always liked him. He was kind and often remembered the most considerate details.

His toothy smile got larger when he spotted us. "Come, come—meet Clive!" Cadmael's deep voice cheered. A small hooded being turned to face us.

Truthfully, I had never met a hobgoblin before and, had I not carried an original in my bag, I would have been much more excited. But as it was, I was feeling very exposed. There was no telling what abilities Clive had. *Can he detect the dragon?*

Cadmael pushed past his wife and gave me a welcoming embrace. "You will be fascinated by Clive," he roared in my ear, at the same time addressing Yanni and Esther. "Great to see you two as well."

I felt him shake hands with the Soahcoit behind me before pulling away and giving me another toothy grin. Esther and Yanni were still at my back, now peering over my shoulder. The hobgoblin Clive was petite in stature, with pale green skin, long black hair and elongated fingers, but the most striking feature was his large mouth that framed frightening teeth.

We all waited for Clive to say something but he did not. Aurora interrupted the silence. "Clive does not speak a language we can understand, although he and I have developed our own bond."

"That, they have," Cadmael agreed. "Clive is all too eager to assist Aurora with anything she may desire. Takes the burden off me." He laughed. "Yanni, I can introduce you to Clive's clan. Perhaps one will take to your astounding partner—ease your burden."

Yanni chuckled but it was more out of obligation than sincere amusement. Esther's eyes narrowed as though she was sizing up the creature. "How is it that you two communicate, Aurora?"

Aurora looked at Clive before she answered, I wondered if she was getting his approval. "Hobgoblins have a slight gift of sight. We can articulate each other's desires through a series of minute clips within our vision."

My mouth slacked open as I attempted to grasp what she was saying. I needed clarity. "You are saying that as the strokes would have it, you two can project an intention into the future just far enough to see each other's intended move or desire?"

"You have mastered what I have been trying to explain to my husband in mere moments, great Alchemist. Yes, that is indeed what I am saying."

"She astounds me," Cadmael said before bellowing with laughter. "I am afraid I do not have that same effect on her."

Aurora smiled at him affectionately. "Nonsense." She brushed his cheek with her hand.

Just then I felt Gwenora move at my side. The realization that I was in the presence of not one but two skilled Ramalans made me faint with worry.

"This has been amazing. Clive, it has been a pleasure." I bowed toward him then quickly addressed the rest of them, "I must be going. I am afraid I have much to attend to in Jolena's absence."

Esther, Yanni, Aurora and even Clive's eyes seemed to graze over me suspiciously but Cadmael cheerily bid me adieu. I sped off, praying to Chitchakor that I was in the company of friends and, more importantly, that Gwenora remained undiscovered.

GWENORA

There was something very strange about the creature Clive. The energy around him tugged at me. I felt an odd pull coming off his person. *Are all hobgoblins this way?* It left me uneasy. I was happy when Yilliana left the exchange. She hurriedly made her way through the crowd this time, keeping her head down so as not to make eye contact and strike up another conversation.

We turned a corner and approached the large lot of land Yilliana called home, most of which was covered in a well-tended garden. Yilliana grew many of her own herbs for her spells; she had told me as much. The sack did not allow for the wind to touch my skin and I realized something in my soul yearned for the breeze, ached for it.

The cottage was exactly how it had been when we left but as we approached Yilliana slowed down. She was sensing something that I could not. Sorcey came from around the back side of the house, and immediately Yilli's posture relaxed.

"Sorcey, you scared me."

"My apologies. That was not my intention. I have news. Can we step inside?"

"Of course." Yilliana waved her hand and a soft light amplified, then dissolved away. I had come to realize these were her wards being disarmed. "After you." Yilliana gestured with her hand for Sorcey to open the door. We stepped inside and she reinstated the wards. She set the bag down on the table beside Sorcerer. I crawled out and greeted the Stone.

"We have much to discuss, Sorcerer. But first, I would like to listen to Sorcey's news." Sorcerer said nothing.

"What news have you?"

"I sought the counsel of the Ramalan Aurora. She only arrived yesterday."

"Yes, I saw her today. She has brought a hobgoblin with her."

"Curious. She did not make introductions."

"Aurora did not insist on you meeting Clive?" Yilliana asked.

"No, she made no mention to me. Does that seem odd?"

"Perhaps not. I just assumed the hobgoblin would be with her. No matter. You were saying?"

"I asked Aurora to use her sight to verify what Kassandra saw—she could not." Sorcey smiled, a warm and encouraging smile. "I think this confirms that her gift is faulty—between Aurora's assurance and Kassandra's obvious mistaken prophecy of Cane and me with child, it seems likely there is simply a malfunction and that the Trials can go on."

Yilliana did not say anything right away.

"What has you worried still?" Sorcey prodded.

"Something does not feel right…" But before she could finish the conch began to chime. "One moment, Sorcey. It is my beloved Jolena." Yilliana darted for the shell and took it to her ear.

I could hear the message. Was that because I had exceptional hearing or could Sorcey hear it too, I wondered.

"Yilli, we make our return. I will arrive with thirty Ancients just before sundown tomorrow, just in time for the Opening Ceremony.

I miss your voice. We will be together soon." Yilliana put the conch down, tears streaming down he cheeks.

Sorcey rushed over to her friend. "What is it? Is she well?"

"Yes, all is fine. Hearing her voice flooded my already brimming emotions—I dare say that this whole mess has taken its toll on me."

Sorcey pulled her in and rubbed her back. I wanted to say something to assuage her fears. The bridge could not be done fast enough. After a long heartfelt moment, the two ladies pulled away.

"Where are you with the incantation?"

"Close. Hephaestus has to make some alterations to the decals." Yilliana paused and I wondered if she was going to tell Sorcey about Franky. "I do not believe he is responsible for Gwenora's capture."

"How can you be certain?"

Yilliana looked down at me then met Sorcey's inquisitive stare. "He has been very helpful and explained that he is working on a piece for a friend that requires the upmost discretion."

"Is that not good reason to wonder what he is producing?"

"It could be, but I examined his shop thoroughly and it gave me no reason to believe he was hiding nefarious undertakings."

I was relieved that she kept Franky's existence a secret. I trusted Sorcey, but with all that was happening, the less others knew the better.

"I trust you. You have a keen eye for deception," Sorcey observed. "Then we are left with Apollo, or some other fiend who is far better at subterfuge than I am at investigation."

"So it would seem," Yilliana agreed. "I pick up the decals at first light. It will take me very little time to assemble the bridge once I get these final components." They both turned and looked at me. "Hopefully the original has the answers."

But I did not have answers. Only I and Sorcerer knew that. I looked at the Stone, my creation, and hoped that the incantation would not harm it.

Yilliana

I watched Sorcey leave, waved her on from my stoop. I tried to feel better about the Trials but something was not sitting well in my soul. *What could make a Conduit's gift go haywire and why?* Mostly I wanted to help her. This business with Gwenora felt more pressing, so I had not a moment to evaluate how I may assist Kassandra. I could only hope that the bridge would solve this dilemma and then I could move onto the next mystery—helping Kassandra remedy her sight. Just then the wind changed course and delight surged through me. The strokes were in my favor. I could send Jolena a message.

I ran inside and took hold of the shell, bringing it to my mouth. "I have received your messages, my love. Only now have the winds moved in your direction. I love you! I needed you home! Travel swift and safe. Your beloved awaits." Then the message was gone and for the first time in days I felt a true moment of peace. Jolena would be home soon and by then I will have already performed my incantation. Gwenora and I would communicate and get to the bottom of her attack.

I shut the door and walked over to my worktable. On a rolled-up piece of parchment I had sketched my intentions for the enchantment. I looked to the left of the scroll where the leather-bound journal lay. I had folded and pressed over a hundred sheets of paper in its binding. On the leather I burned several casting symbols, overlapping and in every direction. I hoped there were enough to create a strong fetter between the languages. The metal decals would be the melding of the Kata symbols and Asagi. I had no way of knowing what the Katuan words I transcribed were but I'd chosen the Asagi words very purposefully. Routinet, Lasteea, Hinuhal. Between the three meanings, I felt I'd built in a formidable bridge.

I looked down at Gwenora, who had hardly taken her eyes off me since my outburst. I wondered what on earth she could be thinking. "I am looking at my work so far. Let me show you." She jumped into my arms when I leaned down. "This is the vessel we will use. These castings will build the energy and facilitate the tether between the Stone and the decals, which I hope will complete the translation. I used three words from each language. I dare not say what I borrowed from Dragonian but from Asagi I wrote Routinet, which means deep understanding; Lasteea, which means a connection deeper than love; and Hinuhal, which means all of the strokes." I shook my head, realizing she must already know all of this. "My apologies, fierce one. I forget you know all languages."

Gwenora leaned into me. She was so precious, so compassionate. We needed to know who harmed her. I felt the token on her hind leg. She did not flinch and I was grateful for it. Whatever poison had been administered initially seemed to have decreased in potency, but there was no telling how long this would last. It dangled from her back leg loosely but with no clasp, an unending ring.

"How did this mechanism attach to you?" I wondered out loud. "There is no explanation for it."

A rap at the door startled me. I set Gwenora down. She quickly grabbed the Stone with her mouth and hurried into the sack. I picked it up and put it on the hook beside the door, where it would appear most unremarkable.

"Who calls?" I asked as I removed many of my wards and unfastened the locks.

"It is I, Apollo."

"And I, Shatki."

I rolled my eyes. *What is this visit pertaining to?* It was getting harder to suspect anyone else of dubious behavior. Apollo was growing increasingly more intrusive. Smiling as warmly as I could, I opened the door.

"To what do I owe this pleasure?"

"I am concerned," Shatki spat as she pushed past me into my home. This was not characteristic of her nature. "We should all be concerned."

Apollo entered far more meekly but clearly in support of his wife, or at least in attendance. I watched to see if he looked around more than one would expect but he did not. His eyes only moved between me and his wife, lingering on Shatki far longer than I.

"I am sorry, Shatki. What has you riled? I would love to serve you in any way I can."

She came over to me and took my hands in hers. "See, Apollo? I knew the Alchemist would understand." Shatki shot her husband a knowing glance before making eye contact with me, her eyes pleading for something—for what, I did not know. "There is a fiend among us, a frightful foe, hidden in plain sight—as a guest of the Trials, no less."

She had my full attention. *Can she know who attacked Gwenora? It has to be what she is referring to, right?*

"Come, sit. I can tell you are in a rage. I wish to listen." I ushered her over to a bench in the large common space of our cottage. Not knowing what was coming next, I desired to have some support beneath me as well.

Shatki did not argue and Apollo followed in silence. We sat, I in the middle of the pair.

"Who is this fiend and what is their crime? I will help you in every way I can," I repeated. Shatki put her head on my chest and began to cry. When she was done, she met my gaze once more.

"There is a hobgoblin on the island." I tried to mask my disappointment. We could not be talking about the same injustice; Clive had only just arrived. With the Ramalan, no less—who would certainly see any maleficence. I listened as she continued. "I know hobgoblins. They deal in dark magic. The painter lost control of the strokes when they were created. They are distorted and without conscience."

"When have you dealt with hobgoblins? How do you know such things?"

Shatki was shaking as she told her story. "It was moons ago, when I was a little girl. Our village was in the Satpura Mountain range during those days. My parents looked after a small settlement of Conduits, no more than four Soahcoit. It was a beautiful place to grow into a woman, until the hobgoblins came."

I looked over my shoulder at Apollo, who continued to watch his wife intently. He had obviously already heard this story.

"Night had fallen and the Unconsu children had just been put to bed. I woke to the noises first—screams, terrifying screams. My mother darted into my tent and told me to remain quiet, go unseen. I listened as she fled back into the night. Suddenly all the screams were choked off. It became dead silent. Not even the crickets dared chirp. The terror was suffocating me. I had to know what was happening. I poked my head out from under the tent hide."

Shatki shook her head as though to dislodge what she saw in her mind. "My parents and all the Consus were lying on their backs, each with a hobgoblin upon their chest, siphoning life from their inert bodies. I saw my mother and father's essence being drained from them, a thick silver fog about them and inside them. No words can describe the scene, nor can I tell you how I knew what I was watching transpire. I screamed; it could not be helped. It interrupted the ritual and the Consus came to, fending off the swarm and holding them back long enough to collect us children and flee the settlement." Tears were streaming down her face uncontrollably. I held her tight and rocked her gently.

A thousand questions were bouncing around my head.

Apollo spoke. "Whatever took place did not kill Shatki's parents. They are still alive and well. But it stands to reason that hobgoblins require energy from another, either for sustenance or perhaps simply for gain—either way, they must not be trusted."

I could not argue with him nor would I discount the trauma that Shatki had endured. Her fear was too visceral for it to be rooted in untruths.

"Why would Aurora bring such a creature to the Trials?"

Neither of them answered me.

I continued. "She must not know; it is the only explanation."

Still silence between them. I waited impatiently before adding, "Could they all be depraved? Certainly, some may be of good intent."

Apollo spoke at last, "I have no desire to discover the nature of their strokes."

Gwenora

Yilliana shut the door behind her guests and slowly made her way to the hook where Sorcerer and I were suspended in the bag. I felt her hands shaking when she picked us up and set us on her worktable.

Sorcerer spoke without being prompted, unusual for the Stone. "Yilliana is upset. Hobgoblins are treacherous."

"Do you have experience with hobgoblins, Sorcerer?" I asked as I took the Stone in my mouth and crawled out of the bag.

"The collective does, yes. Many centuries ago a clan of hobgoblins landed on our shores. The Sire dragons had long since left our land. Hobgoblins began syphoning and capturing our power like a harvest in the spring. A day came when a large Stone was destroyed in a scrimmage among the clan. The collective had had enough and decided to do something about the invasion. First began the rumbling of land, then came the shower of rock. Lastly were the fissures in the earth—large enough to swallow them whole. Those who survived fled."

"How did they harvest the power? Was it gone forever?"

"No power is gone forever but rather distorted or perverted. Hobgoblins have many transformative gifts. They are Incantors by nature, bestowed with the ability to mutate the strokes, much like an Alchemist does."

Just then, Yilliana interrupted, "I feel that you two must be engaging in great exchanges without my knowing."

I nodded slightly to indicate she was correct.

"As I suspected." Yilli's voice was forlorn. She was still visibly shaken as she took a seat beside the table. "If all goes well, I will be privy to your conversations soon." She rubbed her forehead with her hand. "I do wish I could discuss what we've just learned. How much more can transpire before Chitchakor must spare me from my strokes?"

I could not say it, nor would I if I was given the opportunity, but something in my gut whispered that the worst was yet to come.

Yilliana

I paced the majority of the night, while Gwenora sat there and watched, most certainly making her own assessment of our ever-growing plight. When the first sunbeams touched the sky, we were out the house. The sky was nearly a pale blue when I knocked on Hephaestus' door. He looked even more disheveled when he answered.

"We've just finished. It was no easy task."

I swept in past him and he locked up behind me.

"Franky changed the symbols you used."

I had a feeling I had not chosen appropriate Dragonian words. I was shooting in the dark—it would have been sheer luck to get the most effective ones for the incantation to work.

"I am grateful for Franky's foresight." I bowed to the gentle original in the corner. Gwenora had already crawled from the bag and took her place beside him—confabulating, no doubt. "Is there anything else I should be aware of before I begin my work?"

Hephaestus looked at Franky warily, then back at me. "Katuan is a written language. The bridge must be in a format that considers this."

"I understand. I thought as much—the vessel is parchment."

Hephaestus pulled a small vial from the table. Inside was a dark liquid. "You will need this."

He handed it to me.

"What is it?" I examined the contents and the way they moved in the glass container. The liquid was thicker than water but not quite gelatinous.

"Dragon's blood."

I could not disguise my astonishment. "From Franky? Why?"

"It will be your ink. It has powerful properties, beyond my scope of knowledge—an intelligence of its own."

What an extraordinary gift, one I could not have acquired nor would have considered. But it made sense; I needed an element of a dragon to bridge between the Stone and the original, then the Stone to the vessel—in this case the journal. It was brilliant! "There are no words. Thank you, Franky."

"Yilliana, I have to warn you. Dragon blood has a very profound effect on Conduits. It is poisonous. Franky and I were using it while working on his assignment and he made it very clear that I need handle it with the upmost care. I know not what the consequence of exposure may be, only that it will be terrible in nature."

I nodded solemnly. His warning hit its mark; I would be supremely cautious.

"I understand. I will be extremely careful."

"Very well. Then be off. Franky and I must complete his endeavor. I wish to attend the Trials; therefore I must make haste."

I knelt down to let Gwenora back in the bag. "Will Franky be leaving after you complete his mission?" He obviously had affections for Gwenora. Certainly he would not leave her in this state.

"He has expressed a desire to see Gwenora's recovery through.

There is now a hope that by finishing this map, they may discover another original that can assist with her dilemma if you are unsuccessful."

"I see. So the project you are tending to is an object designed to find originals?"

"So it would seem." Hephaestus shrugged. "Off with you, woman. I have much to do, as do you."

GWENORA

The decals buzzed with intense energy in the bag beside me. It would have been intimidating if Franky had not described what he had imprinted into them. Beside Yilliana's contribution, the symbols for Routinet, Lasteea and Hinuhal inlaid the words Jiu, Kero and Fihi in Dragonian, which meant union, translation and connecting the broken. With my disability, I was unable to comprehend what an incantation consisted of, although it would seem I had performed one of the greatest Covenings of all time when generating the Stones of Katuanak. The decals projected the energy of the melded intentions of my dear friend Franky and the Alchemist Yilliana.

We got back to the cottage in record time.

"Gwenora, give me a moment to implement some additional wards. We must not be interrupted." Yilliana flitted about while she spoke, flicking her hands in the air and mumbling several words. I could see the strokes bending to her will. "I think I know how I will implement the original's blood," she asserted but did not bother to elaborate. When she was satisfied with her fortification, she took a deep breath then slowly approached the worktable where I stood beside the decals and Sorcerer.

I suddenly felt compelled to say something to the Stone, a farewell if that was indeed what was to take place. Sadness moved me. *What if these are the final moments of Sorcerer's consciousness? What words can instill the gratitude I have for its sacrifice?*

"Sorcerer, I need to thank you. Your courage will change the strokes forever."

"Mother, Sire of the Stones, your resolve along with the other originals' who created the collective made me who I am. We are all one decision away from an entirely different fate. That is how we were painted, divinely dependent on each other. I thank you for your courage to create something new. Whatever my strokes may morph into next, they began with you."

Sorcerer knew all along that it may be sacrificing the life force it knew. Pride replaced my sadness. Whatever my creation was, it was undoubtably inherently good. There were no more words to be said.

Yilliana placed all the constituents she had collected, including Sorcerer, in a circle on the table then reached out for me. "For your sake, dear fierce one, may you step back, take your place over there?" She picked me up, set me down on the ground and pointed toward the far corner of the room. I ran over and took a seat with the view of her and her workspace.

With one more glance over her shoulder, she said, "May the strokes be in our favor," then got to work. Yilliana moved the objects around until she was satisfied with their arrangement. The decals were now on top of the leather journal, and between them Sorcerer was placed.

Yilliana began to chant. "Routinet, Lasteea, Hinuhal." Quietly at first, then louder and louder. Sparks from the decals began to fly around the journal and swarm all around Sorcerer. A rainbow of color danced in the air, weaving in and out and through Yilliana, and back into the bridge she was creating. The chanting grew faster and her words were almost inaudible; in fact they no longer were Asagi. They were Dragonian. "Jiu, Kero, Fihi." Did she know what she was saying, I wondered.

Then she just stopped. It became eerily silent. The strokes continued to vibrate and swim around them, in a circular current. Yilliana took the dragon's blood in her hand mechanically, as though possessed. She gently removed the cork and poured the contents in its entirety onto Sorcerer. The stone said nothing. When the last drop fell, the energy of the room dissolved, the colors disappeared from the air and Yilliana let out a huge sigh.

She looked down at the journal still on the table and gasped. I ran over to see what had become of Sorcerer. Yilliana knelt down and picked me up, setting me beside her creation. The decals had fused onto the leather. Among the engraved castings and between them was the stone now transformed into a beautiful brownish-gold gem. I reached down and put my hand on the smooth, unfamiliar surface. It was stunning and shone with a glamorous glimmer.

A familiar voice rang in my ears. "I am the Sorcerer Stone."

YILLIANA

The incantation was complete. I looked down at the journal and the other constituents. The elements had all been fused and the Stone was no longer a bland shade of rock but instead a shining golden gem. Gwenora stood beside it expectantly. And then I heard it—a whisper in the wind.

"I am the Sorcerer Stone." It was a gentle and commanding voice.

I brushed the decals with my hand and electricity surged through me. I took the journal to my chest and held it tight, feeling its power. "I am Yilliana," I introduced myself properly.

The voice was louder this time. "You may call me Sorcerer."

"Sorcerer, thank you for your participation in the incantation." There was no reply so I continued. "I must know, may I speak to Gwenora?"

"You have always spoken to me. The question is, may I speak to you, dear Alchemist?"

When Gwenora saw my eyes widen with amazement she knew I had heard her. My mouth was too dry for me to speak. I was conversing with an original, with a Katuan Stone—we had bridged the languages.

GWENORA

Yilliana had accomplished the impossible. We sat on the ground of the cottage talking like old friends. As far as we could tell, she had to be holding onto the journal to understand my words. She fanned the pages and realized that the bridge was taking place in the vessel, as she had suspected. Sorcerer was translating between us. Symbols would appear on the parchment. Some would stay and others would dissolve from the pages. We both assumed the ink was Franky's donation—dragon's blood.

The excitement buzzed in the air between us, until she asked the question I knew was coming. "Tell me who did this to you, Gwenora."

"Is that my name?" I said sheepishly. "The truth of the strokes is that I do not know who did this to me, what was done or even who I am. I know in my gut that, as you have suspected, it has something to do with this object on my hind leg. But more than that, I am no more enlightened than you." I hung my head low, knowing that this had to be disappointing for Yilliana and all her efforts.

She reached down and lifted my chin. "Fret not, fierce one. We are stronger together and Jolena will help us as soon as she returns. The three of us will discover what has happened to you."

"The four of us," Sorcerer added.

We both chuckled and Yilliana corrected, "Of course, the four of us." Yilli looked outside. "The sun rises in the sky. It must be nearing noon. Today is the Opening Ceremony. We should attend. But first we must tell Hephaestus and Franky of the news. They will be delighted, I am sure."

I agreed. "We must thank them for their insights and labor."

Yilliana threw a hooded cape over her shoulders. It was emerald green and in beautiful contrast with her hair. "I must keep the bridge on me in order to hear you. Let us assume carrying it in your satchel will suffice. She stuck the journal in my bag then held it to the floor for me to climb inside, before throwing it over her shoulder.

"Can you hear me?"

"As though you were in my mind."

"When will the Ceremony begin?"

"Two hours or less. We will likely wait for the arrival of the Ancients. Which in turn means my Jolena will also be home."

I was eager to meet Yilliana's Atoa. It was apparent they cared for one another very much. Anyone Yilli could love that much would be a true friend of mine.

The streets were filled with Conduits of all shapes and sizes. Yilliana literally had to squeeze and push her way through the mob because Hephaestus' shop was directly in the city center, only feet from the arena. His threshold was in sight when a voice called out over the crowd.

"Great Alchemist!" It was Cadmael. "Where do you hurry off to on this day? Opening Ceremony Day, no less."

Yilliana turned to greet him. "One final errand before my beloved returns with the Ancients, Cadmael. Where is your other half?" Yilliana asked graciously while she searched the crowd with her eyes.

Cadmael came into my view, and by his side was the hobgoblin Clive. The creature did not move like a Conduit. His gait was more of a slink. Yilliana watched him closely. "Clive," she acknowledged.

"The Ramalan I call my own is around here somewhere. She stays busy on these occasions. Always desired by many."

"And Clive? He doesn't maintain her company? How is it that you communicate with him without her presence?"

Cadmael reached up and patted Clive on the shoulder, and I noticed a strange burn on his forearm. Welted and red around the edges, it was a crescent moon of sorts. I squinted to see it better but before I could make out any more distinctions the sleeve of his robe slipped down covering the mark. "Clive much prefers Aurora's company to mine but today she got swept away in the crowd, so he is stuck with me." Cadmael chuckled. "Poor creature did not fare well in his strokes on this day."

"Some would say otherwise," Yilliana countered before turning to leave.

I wondered if Yilli saw the mark. "Did you see his arm?"

"Yes," she mumbled.

"Sorry, what did you say, great Alchemist?" Cadmael inquired.

"Nothing. Only that I love your company."

"You are always too kind. Find me in the arena, will you?"

"I will do my best." I looked up at Clive one more time. This time his eyes were set on me, coal black with no whites to soften their stare. It was impossible for him to see me, masked in this warded bag. *Or is it?*

YILLIANA

I knocked vigorously on the familiar door. This time Hephaestus unlocked everything, took hold of my cloak and pulled me in. Celsi sat across from Franky at the large worktable. The original was hovering over a piece of parchment intently. He barely acknowledged our entrance.

"Yilliana, we are nearly done with my errand. Why have you called on me once more? Have I failed you in some way?" Hephaestus was covered in soot and his expression was that of exhaustion.

"No, Hephaestus, you have done the opposite. The incantation was a success. We can speak with the dragons," I crowed.

Franky abandoned what he was looking at, jumped down from his perch and trotted over. Celsi followed him.

"You can understand Dragonian?" Celsi asked.

"I can. So may you." I reached in the bag and handed her the journal while Franky looked up at her skeptically. Simultaneously Gwenora crawled out of the sack and took her place beside her kin. We all waited in anticipation.

"I hear nothing. Do they speak?"

I looked at Gwenora, who nodded.

"Let me see what is amiss." She handed the journal back to me and the moment it was in my grasp I heard Gwenora talking to Franky, explaining how the incantation carried out. "I can hear them plain as day." My assertion got Franky's attention.

"Is that so?" he asked.

"It is. It is nice to formally meet you, fierce one. Your assistance made this possible. I am forever grateful for your insights and contributions."

Franky's eyes got big. "By Chitchakor's will and the power of the strokes, it is so!" The two originals laughed before Franky continued. "So then you know that my dear Gwenora has no recollection of herself or her attack. With all of my faculties, I still cannot see who the perpetrator is. They must be cloaked in strong magic. Hope is not lost; I have an idea." Franky trotted back over to the table and the contents he had been examining. "Come, see what Hephaestus has helped me concoct."

I walked over and looked down at the parchment. Hephaestus and Celsi stayed put, whispering between each other. I made it a point not to eavesdrop, instead focusing all of my attention on Franky and his proposal. On the table was a map. Atop the map was a small black stone.

"This is a device I am coining the Naewena Atlas. The stone is dragon stone. The ink is a medley of my blood, Valerian root, Anise seeds and cedar leaf. Together they can identify the whereabouts of any original in the world. I began its construction in order to find Gwenora." He looked at her with longing eyes before continuing. "Now I suspect it will serve to help me find one of the greatest of our kin, Cataphet. She resides in The Cathedral, the last place in the world containing the first strokes. Because of this she grows in strength and ability more than any other. With the original strokes she can project the abilities of all dragons, earth, wind, fire and water alike. She will know how to remedy Gwenora, to set her free and discover the culprit behind the recent attacks."

It sounded like a likely solution, although I wondered how long an undertaking as this would take. *Will Gwenora need to leave? Will she be safe?*

"Have you found her? Is she far?"

Franky hung his head a little lower. "As of yet, her whereabouts have not presented themselves. I made a mistake when creating the Atlas. It would seem that I cannot dictate which original I would like to find. The Cathedral which shelters Cataphet is elusive and will require I do further investigation. I'm afraid I will need to venture off the island to see where she may be."

"Curious; is there something I can do to assist the detection?"

"Dragon magic is powerful. Until Gwenora's plight I had never seen our powers go checked. I am afraid your assistance would fall on an occluded front. If I knew how others could influence our magic, I would be able to provide a solution for Gwenora's misfortune. Alas, I am at a lost and helpless." He turned to her once more. "I am sorry."

"Please do not apologize again," she insisted.

Franky sighed. "I will do my best."

It was a sweet moment that I hated to interrupt, but there was still more to be said on the matter. "Will you take Gwenora with you?"

"I have considered it but I think not. You have kept her safe, hidden for this long. That is our top priority. I will return with answers and a remedy."

"When will you leave?" Gwenora asked.

"Straight away. There is no time to waste."

GWENORA

It was all happening so quickly now. I should be happy. I would have answers soon. But something continued to ache in my belly like rotten fish. We were missing a crucial piece of the puzzle and it was not simply the identity of my would-be assassin.

"Franky." He paused what he was doing. I looked around to see that the three Conduits in our presence were distracted, discussing the upcoming Trials amongst themselves.

"Gwenora, what is it?" He padded over and nuzzled my shoulder. "You can tell me."

"Something is not right."

"Of course, there is much to be desired here. Your state is the first thing we must rectify. I understand your unease."

"No, I feel something deeper, something bigger. How long will you be gone?" I locked eyes with him. My soul was familiar with his. Even without my memories, I knew he was rooted in my being. "I am scared."

"There are so many unknowns right now. But one thing I have

learned to be true with all my strokes, in all my years: it all circles back around. We never really lose one another. Just as the River Tins flows in an unending circle, so do all our strokes. I will be back, we will right this wrong, and you and I can share in many more adventures together. I love you, Gwenora."

I wanted to say the words but I could not. My heart knew them to be true but my mind still wanted to protest that I did not know this creature. So I stayed silent.

Yilliana approached cautiously. She had politely put down the Sorcerer Stone bridge so she could not eavesdrop when she recognized it was an intimate moment.

"Are you ready, Gwenora?"

I nodded and looked back at Franky, who once again gave me an assured wink. I wanted to believe him. I had no reason not to, aside from this feeling…

YILLIANA

Everything was coming together. Jolena would be home soon, Franky would return with a solution to Gwenora's plight, and we would bring her attacker to justice.

But when I turned the corner and saw Kassandra pacing in front of my door, I was caught off guard, reminded that she was still in anguish, and although we had no reason to believe her vision held truth, I had promised to help and had yet to see it through. I patted the sack to make sure all was well with Gwenora—she was still there, as was the bridge.

As soon as Kassandra saw me, she rushed over. "I need your help," she blurted out on her approach. "Whatever malfunction my gift is expressing is getting worse. I cannot go more than an hour without being haunted by these visions. Certainly you must have an object, an enchantment that can cure me or at the very least give me peace from these effects."

I took her by the shoulder and directed her back to my house. "Yes, I will find something, Kassandra. Come, let me pour us wine and you may retell the goings-on in your sight. Perhaps that will assist me in finding the correct suppressant."

I said suppressant because at this juncture I was not sure what was ailing her and causing the disruptive, false visions. I could not assume to cure them.

Relief surged through her and I was happy I had a distraction to help me get through the hours until Jolena returned. Kassandra sat quietly on the lounge as I moved through the house.

"Please wait here. I have a vintage I would like to share with you, it is in the back of the house." I quickly moved through the hall and into the second room that we primarily used for storage. I set down the bag gently. Gwenora and the bridge would be safest here .

I looked behind me once more before talking to the dragon. "Dear fierce one, I must tend to my friend. Please make yourself comfortable here. I will be back as soon as I can to check on you." Gwenora poked her head out of the bag as I took a bottle of wine that I knew would be tasty from the shelf and headed back toward the front house. She would be secure here; that was all that mattered. My time with Kassandra would not be long.

Kassandra was just where I had left her when I returned, still looking dazed and tired. I pulled two glasses from the shelf and poured a generous amount in each. As I took my seat beside her, I grew more concerned. Something was almost hovering about her. *Is she cursed,* I wondered.

"Tell me, how has this delusion escalated?"

Kassandra took a long sip of the wine before answering. "I do not think it is a delusion. It is so real. And the same every time. Death. So much destruction as the promise of the Stones is realized when a Conduit dies in the Trials."

"Which Trial? Which Conduit?"

"I do not see it." She bowed her head somberly.

"Is that not good reason to believe that it is not true, that perhaps a misfiring has occurred within your gift? We are peaceable. Conduits do not harm one another. It is why the Katuan Stones have allowed us to partake in the Trials each centennial."

"I know, but something changes. It is not my vision that is clouded, it is because more magic resides in these future strokes. Powers that evade my vision, cause it to appear patchy when in fact it is just unfamiliar." She lifted her face so that her eyes may meet mine. "I feel it swarming me, trying to get in, trying to translate into something I can articulate—so that not all is lost."

We sat in silence. I took another sip of my wine and considered what she was saying. *Is that the entity I feel surrounding her? The strokes are desperately trying to penetrate her, to give her foresight?*

"Say you are right. What is this magic that is too powerful for you to decipher? Atlantis is the most profoundly gifted place on this earth."

"Yes, this place is powerful and I have learned its strokes well. The only thing more potent is the mother or father of its inception—the originals."

I felt the color leave my face. *Is she just assuming or does she know something about the dragons being here?*

My voice came out as a whisper this time. "What have you seen of the originals?"

"A fierce one of the sky has fallen. She will rise and in her wake will be destruction."

Gwenora

I pulled the bridge out from the bag and placed the journal beside me. Sorcerer had not spoken since we'd returned home and I was distracted by my misgivings.

"What is the matter?" Sorcerer asked after a while, and it occurred to me that I had not noticed the Stone having empathic tendencies before the incantation, yet here it was recognizing my distress.

"Thank you, Sorcerer. I will be fine. We had many victories since last night fell, but I have concerns."

"Concerns about what?"

How do you explain a feeling that has little merit and no tangible roots? "It is hard to explain."

"Please try. I too, now, feel things."

I looked at it curiously. "You do?"

"I believe that is the word. I am stirred with emotions."

"That would be feelings," I agreed. "Something feels like it is looming in the shadows, a foreboding."

I wished the Stone had some gift of expression. Alas, that was not so. Still, it empathized. "I sense something similar."

"You do?"

"I do. But there is more…"

Then I heard the door open behind me and turned to see Yilliana standing in the shadow of the frame. She appeared withdrawn, maybe even frightened.

I maneuvered my body to face her. She seemed to stare past us—me and the Stone. Slowly, she moved into the candlelight where I could see her full countenance. It was despair.

Yilliana made her way to the chair beside the table I was atop. "We were wrong," she mumbled.

She was close enough to the bridge I asked the obvious question. "Wrong about what?"

"How could we have known?" She put her face in her hands and shook her head. "We were wrong and now there is nothing to be done."

I stepped forward and grazed her hands with my head, the only true gesture of comfort I had to give. Her cheeks were soaked with tears when she raised her head to meet my gaze.

"Kassandra saw devastation and we ignored it, dismissed it. We were wrong." She laid her head on the table and I looked on, helpless to do anything to make it right. *Wrong about what?* "How do I tell Sorcey? Because we disregarded Kassandra, all may be lost. How can we stop this? What have we done?"

Then, like a switch had been turned on, she stood up and rushed to the door. "I must go to Sorcey now. We must do what we can to make this right. Talk to the Directorate. Whatever we must do, it must be done."

YILLIANA

I needed to get to Sorcey and Cane. They would know what to do. The Opening Ceremony would take place in a matter of hours. Once the Directorate was chosen, we could plead with them, present the evidence. I was running as fast as I could. I chose to leave Gwenora and the journal back at the cottage. They would be safe there—for now.

It seemed impossible, but there were even more Consus on the island than the day before. The last of the arrivals would be on Jolena's fleet, or so it would seem. I prayed to Malarin that Sorcey or Cane was home.

Kassandra heeded my advice and went home. I said that I would call on her before tonight's Ceremony with some sort of suppressant—knowing in my heart that she had been right all along, but asserting that to her would incite panic. That panic could be the very catastrophe she saw with her sight. Then there was Gwenora. *How can I keep her safe and expose the threat?* Sorcey and Cane would know what to do. They had to.

I pounded on their door. Moments later Cane appeared in the entryway, beckoning me in. He looked extremely disheveled.

"Did I make a spectacle?" was the first thing I could think to ask.

"No. What is wrong, my friend? You are as pale as the sands on Balto Beach. Come sit down." Cane ushered me to a bench but I thought he was the one who needed to sit down. He was visibly shaking.

"Is Sorcey here?"

"No, she slipped out and will be back just before the Ceremony."

The strokes were not in my favor! "What has she told you?"

"Concerning?"

Why is he playing coy? "All of it, Cane. You must know it all." I failed at containing my exasperation.

"Yes, I know it all," he admitted. His shoulders seemed to relax slightly—relief, perhaps? "I have been trying to get someone—anyone—to listen to me. Alas, no one will."

"About Gwenora?"

"No, Yilliana, of course not. I promised Sorcey I would do everything in my power to stop the Trials. Kassandra's vision was confirmed."

"By whom? They saw the Trials end in destruction?"

"No, they saw us with child. Two separate seers have proclaimed as much, so it would seem logical to assume the rest of her vision holds merit." Cane began to pace. "I have been contacting anyone who will hear my plea but it falls on deaf ears. The Ramalan Aurora disputed the vision, and no one will consider cancelling the Trials until the Directorate is formed. Have you learned anything from Gwenora?"

"I have created a device that allows me to communicate with the original."

Cane gasped. But I could not find the patience to walk him

through that feat. "We are no closer to knowing who her attacker is, however. She has no memory. We must stop the Trials!"

"I agree and I will continue to do my best. It is Aurora's dispute of Kassandra's claim. Everyone believes her vision is faltered right now."

"Someone or something is disrupting her vision, but it is not as we thought. There is a cloud about her. Kassandra sees the truth. She saw Gwenora's attack."

Cane's face went ashen. "Then you do know who is to blame for harming the original. Who?"

"That is just it, the face of the attacker is not clear. I think that is the purpose of the cloud. Kassandra's visions are all connected and they all outline a single fate—death and destruction if the Trials go on."

"How would you have me stop this?"

"We have to gather those who will listen, prove to them that Kassandra's visions are real, not false, and then we must take action in order to save lives."

Cane shook his head. "It is not possible, great Alchemist. It cannot be proven, for to prove her reliability we would have to expose Gwenora, potentially laying her at the feet of her assassin."

His words hit me like a tidal wave. He was right. I either risked the life of the original or the lives of the Conduits I loved.

GWENORA

Yilliana had rushed out so swiftly I barely had a moment to connect the dots. My soul was stirring. Information wanted to leak to the surface, a notion in the recess of my mind—in my lost memories.

"Gwenora," Sorcerer interrupted.

"Not now. I am so close to a realization," I snapped and immediately felt the worst for it. "I am sorry, Sorcerer. What is it?"

"Something in my pages rouses. It concerns your trinket."

I looked back at my hind leg. "What? How… What does it say?"

The journal flipped open and symbols scrawled across the parchment. At the same time Sorcerer's voice, faint but distinct, spoke.

"What did you say?"

"Feworbusalee," Sorcerer repeated.

"What does that mean? How could you be speaking a language I do not understand? I thought the originals understood all the languages."

"I do not know, but it has been swelling within me for some time."

"Is it the name of the trinket?"

Sorcerer said nothing.

"Sorcerer, can you give me no insight?"

"I have none, Gwenora. The magic that courses through the bridge is separate from me. It is a mixture of original, Katuanak power and the great Alchemist's gifts—these are new strokes."

"New strokes?" It was not that the concept was entirely foreign, only that this combination was absolutely different from anything created before it. "It has its own intelligence? Wisdom?"

"It would seem," Sorcerer agreed.

"So then we must discover what these words mean and how they pertain to my state. But how?"

Yilliana

I walked back in a daze, letting the hordes push me along, too disappointed to care. All was lost and it was because I did not listen. Because I ignored the strokes. Because I thought I had control. Shame washed over me.

"Great Alchemist," Aphrodite's voice chirped. I looked up just in time to see I was about to collide with Shiva. His gargantuan form caught me off guard, then immediately filled me with hope.

"Aphrodite, Shiva!" I bowed slightly at the Ancient and he reciprocated. "Well met! Did you just arrive, Shiva?"

Aphrodite answered for him as the ambassador of the Ancients. "A few hours ago."

"Curious, is my beloved with you? Making you feel welcome?" It was the only conclusion I could make for Jolena not seeking me out immediately.

Shiva shook his head. "No, the Admiral took her fleet west for another errand."

Another errand? Jolena would never leave without telling me where she was going.

"Did she disclose where?"

"No, she has been acting most peculiar. The Admiral was several days absent of her expected arrival to Antarctica. We Ancients believed she must have had something to do for you, the great Alchemist."

I did not answer right away, not certain what to say. *Jolena was late to arrive to receive the Ancients?* She had relayed that they were unprepared when she landed. "The winds were strange. Her fleet must have met poor weather."

"Certainly," Shiva agreed, but I saw the skepticism on his face.

"Excuse me, I must meet with Kassandra. She is awaiting my call." I went to move around Shiva and Aphrodite.

"Please let her know we are all wishing her well," Aphrodite said in her authentic tone.

"I will." I smiled, trying to exude sincerity, anything but the insecurity I was genuinely feeling.

Gwenora

The minutes seemed to pass by slower than ever before. We needed Yilliana home. I knew the undertaking she was attempting was vast and complicated—potentially deadly. I wondered if the imminence of doom that I felt was from Kassandra's vision or from my own quandary. Never the matter, because the feeling was increasing in intensity and I wanted her here to help me sort through Sorcerer's discovery and what was ailing me.

I replayed the words in my head. Uncertain how to pronounce the symbols properly, I mimicked Sorcerer's pronunciation. "Feworbusalee."

Sorcerer had been silent for much time now, perhaps thinking or feeling. I heard footsteps drawing toward the house. Hope soared through me. Yilliana would know what to do with the odd language. But soon I realized there were six feet. Yilliana had only brought guests to the cottage once, and the Siren had long since left. I popped up to the window, barely peeking over the ledge. There I saw three familiar faces but not Yilli.

"We must hide," I said as I took the journal up in my mouth. "Yilliana has callers." I crawled over to the sack that lay on the floor and nestled into it for safe shelter. We had come across these three before and they had not expressed a knowing of my whereabouts in the warded bag.

We both said nothing as the trio approached. I tried to listen to hear what they needed from Yilliana but none of them spoke. That seemed odd to me. When they were just outside the door, I heard a nearly inaudible command.

"This time, we do not fail. We must enter the Alchemist's home."

Sorcerer spoke firmly, "You must go. These three have ill intent. They will find you."

"Then I will take you with me," I said.

"I will slow you down. Hurry, Gwenora, you haven't much time. One of them has vast powers. They will clear Yilliana's wards. Go! Slip out the back window. Trust me, my knowing tells me this is so."

I paused, weighing my options. Sorcerer was new to the power. Perhaps the stone was deluded. The sack had kept me hidden before. *What is different now?* But I knew in my heart something was different. There was desperation in the command—desperation meant drastic action.

"Go!" Sorcerer pleaded again. "They will not be doing anything with a journal."

"I will be back."

"Of course you will."

With that I darted out of the bag and leapt onto the back windowsill just in time to hear the familiar buzz of the wards being withdrawn from the perimeter.

Yilliana

I was even more lost. *Jolena did not hurry home to see me? What could be keeping her?* I needed her. I needed her wisdom. She would know how to navigate this terrible situation and keep everyone safe.

Kassandra's home was on the opposite side of the island to my cottage. I was out of the busy streets and in the soft meadows of the surrounding land. It was a gorgeous part of Atlantis. Rolling hills covered in long green and golden grasses. If I were not in such a state, I would have enjoyed the walk. What made it worse was that I had nothing to offer Kassandra. I could not contain or remove her sight, because it was as much a part of her as her arm or leg, and the truth was there was nothing the matter with it. It was not faulty. There was no easing her torment until we had a solution.

Dagan saw my approach and rushed out to greet me. "Great Alchemist, I am so grateful for your arrival. She is the worse for wear. Her strokes give her no relief." Dagan took my hand and led me toward his home swiftly.

We entered through the front door. Kassandra lay on a purple throw on the ground in the middle of the room. Their home was quaint, not unlike mine and Jolena's, except it was round. Dagan called it a yurt. I knelt beside her, cupping her head in my lap, while Dagan took his place at her feet.

"She's just had another fit," he informed me. "It was long and arduous. She is exhausted by all these visions. They just continue to bombard her."

I said nothing as I observed her listless form. The cloud I'd noticed earlier was thicker. It had been growing in strength. The form was more opaque in nature. I wanted to ask Dagan if he could see it but I did not wish to alarm Kassandra. *Who possesses this type of magic?* There were few Incantors on the island. Yet I had to remind myself that because of the Trials I truly had no idea how many Incantors were on Atlantis. Furthermore, because of how many new Consus there were, I had no idea what type of abilities they possessed. For the first time ever I was saddened to have so many new faces among the familiar.

"Who else has she been in contact with?" Perhaps I could narrow down my pool.

Kassandra moved slightly in my arms, adjusting herself so that her long wavy hair was no longer covering her face. Sweat kept it matted to her cheeks but I could now see her eyes—they were shut and deep dark bags framed them. Her condition was getting worse.

Dagan replied after thinking about my question. "Not many. People have heard of her condition and stayed away."

"Since the fit she had in the square… Tell me everyone who has seen her since then." This cloud I saw had formed after that episode. It was not there that day.

"You, Sorcey… Aurora came after Sorcey asked her to confirm her sight. Of course, Kassandra has been about on a rare occasion—I cannot say whom she saw then." Dagan searched his memory for any others. "Oh, and Jolena. Just before she left with her fleet. She wanted to give Kassandra her well wishes, having heard about her false vision from you."

The color drained from my face; I could feel it. I had not seen Jolena to tell her of Kassandra's state before she'd left.

Just then Kassandra began to convulse, her arms flailing, her feet flying in every direction. Foam poured from her mouth. I had never seen her visions consume her like this before. The episode went on for several minutes. I watched the cloud around her vibrate with the movements, as though it was following the frequency. When her fit finally stopped, Kassandra's eyes shot open.

"Sorcey receives the Dirk from the Queen. It will be the weapon that kills the shadow."

My head was spinning. *What did that mean? So many questions!* I could not follow where this was all going or how it was all connected.

"What Queen? Where is Sorcey? Now?"

But Kassandra had drifted off into unconsciousness from exhaustion. I tried to stir her, and when I did her arm fell from her side, pulling her pale pink robes with it and exposing her skin along her right thigh. I reached to cover her back up when I noticed a crescent welt.

"What is this mark?" I pointed to it and Dagan examined it carefully.

"I do not know. She has been thrashing about so frequently. Perhaps it is from an episode."

"Perhaps," was all I could think to say, because I did not know yet what ideas were formulating in the back of my mind. But one thing seemed certain—this was not the mark of an accident.

GWENORA

I ran, as fast as my four legs would carry me. Into the brush and out of view in case they looked outside. The shrubbery was dense and it pierced my skin as I dove into the heart of it praying for coverage. Blood trickled down my scales, warm and thick. It was almost a welcome distraction. I held my breath, not sure what I should do next. They would certainly spot me running across the open field if they decided to peer out the back windows. I was bright purple, a clear contrast to the green grass.

There was a grove of trees, not too far in the distance. I would wait until they left the cottage, then get to the grove as quickly as possible. It was all I could do. Sit and wait.

A long thorn stuck in my hind leg. It ached but I was too afraid to dislodge it. It was not a deep wound but increasingly more irritating.

Then I heard the front door open. I froze, waiting to see what they would do next. They had finished their search of the cottage. *Will they scour the grounds now?*

I heard them coming around the corner before I saw them. The hooded creature came around from the right while the other two circled around back from the left.

Still they said nothing to each other. It was eerie.

Until the brutish one interrupted the silence. "What are we doing at Yilliana's? Is she home?" He looked around, bewildered, as though he had no recollection of having just ravaged her home.

The cloaked creature calmly walked over to him.

"Clive, this is the oddest thing…" he started but then stopped immediately. I saw the welt I had noticed the other day on the Conduit's arm glow red, then fade back to a pink.

"We must find the Alchemist," Aurora asserted. Clive simply nodded. "We will search the arena then return here, to the cottage."

Then the three just walked on like nothing had happened, heading back down the path toward Balto Beach and the center of town.

I did not know where this other direction would lead me. Yilliana had never taken me to this side of the island. But one thing was for certain: I could not stay here and wait. The moment they were out of view I pulled myself from the brush, once more tearing at my skin and dislodging the thorn in my leg. Then I ran as fast as I could to the shelter of the trees.

YILLIANA

I hurried back to the Kraus house and as I did, I realized the Opening Ceremony must be drawing closer to commencement. The once-random crowd was now parading into the arena. I pushed my legs harder. Cane was stepping out of his home and into the stream of Conduits. I hurtled into him.

"I need to speak to you," I whispered on our impact.

He did not ask questions. He pulled us both back into his home and shut the door.

"Where is she, really? Where is Sorcey?" I blurted out the questions as I adjusted my cloak.

"She will be returning shortly, I assure you."

"Is she with the Queen?"

Cane did not suppress his shock. "How did you know that?"

"Kassandra. She had another vision while I was there." I was pacing as Cane looked on. "Could this Queen business have something to do with what is happening on the island, with the original attacks?"

"No. The Queen is dealing with her own troubles."

I was tempted to pry, to ask for more answers, because I believed he would tell me. But as long as it did not pertain to our dilemma, I did not have the time to get distracted. "Are you absolutely certain?"

Cane nodded.

"Kassandra's cloud has thickened. She bears a mark on her inner thigh. It is not natural. I know this because I saw a similar symbol on Cadmael's arm. I do not know its relevance but it cannot be a coincidence." I paused, because I did not want to say the last part out loud. "Jolena is acting strange. She is missing and she has not been in communication with me. I think it is all related." It felt good to put it into words.

"Was Cadmael acting odd?"

"No." I had to admit that was inconsistent with Kassandra's oddities.

"But you believe these are all related? To Gwenora's attack as well?"

"It must be." I shook my head in disbelief. "There is a powerful Incantor on Atlantis orchestrating this. It explains the marks—they must be a spell of some sort—and it explains the trinket around Gwenora's leg—it is cursed."

Cane was following me. I could tell by his expression he saw the parallel. "There are so many new Consus. How will we determine who the Incantor is?"

That was the obvious question but I thought I had the answer. "This Incantor must be very powerful. They will undoubtably be chosen to be a Champion for the Trials."

Cane's face lit up. "Brilliant! You are brilliant! We must go. Sorcey is meeting me in the arena and the Ceremony will begin soon."

"If we can stop this fiend, we will prevent the tragedy Kassandra predicted."

"Of course we will," he assured me. "Let us go."

"I must go back to my cottage first. I will leave this task to you," I conceded.

Cane paused at the door. "But..."

"I must check on Gwenora and my wife. I must know if she has returned home. I need answers for her absence. We will follow."

He did not contest further, and with that we both darted out of the house.

GWENORA

It took me longer than I would have thought to get to the grove. The trees were dense and provided me with good coverage. The whole sprint here I prayed that Sorcerer was unharmed. I regretted leaving the Stone behind. *What will I do if I found Yilliana? How can I tell her about the curious threesome?*

I collapsed by a large tree, leaning against its roots for reprieve. Certainly I would have more stamina when I was back to my normal stature. My legs still bled so I decided to lick my wounds. Leaving a messy blood trail would not help my evasion.

Just as I cleaned up my first scratch, the tree roots began to shake violently beneath me. *What in the strokes is happening?* I backed away from the tree, ducking behind another stump. *Are the trees possessed? Perhaps the whole forest?*

The worst scenario flashed through my mind when a huge beast manifested in the trunk of the tree, and with it a familiar face.

"Peozleosknowsthingsbecoming," a soft feminine voice trilled from the beast. "Sorceysmustbesprepared."

"Of course, my dear Queen. I will do my best." Sorcey corrected herself, "Cane and I will do our best. What will become of your people?"

"PeozleosQueenshaswillmakesitright. TheRittlesissafesandfriendsSorceysandCanesnowtakesthismagics." The beast handed Sorcey a dagger. "DirksInverness."

"Indeed, we will keep it safe, Queen. Thank you for entrusting us with this task."

"Peozleosdoesnotsentrustitsinthestrokesitbe." With that the beast dissolved back into the tree and Sorcey stood alone staring at the dagger in her hand.

I was not sure what to make of this. *Is Sorcey now doing underhanded dealings? What is this creature she called the Queen?* Before I could decide how to proceed, Sorcey sensed she was not alone and quickly honed in on my presence.

"Gwenora!" She stuck the Dirk of Inverness behind her back and fell to her knees. "What in the strokes are you doing out here alone?" She quickly searched the woods with her eyes. No one was there. "And you are wounded."

She reached down to pick me up. I was too overwhelmed to object. Sorcey still appeared to be the same ally she was before. Whatever she was participating in with that beast must be a different affair—or at least I hoped.

She cradled me in her arms, examining my body, but as she did I felt her embrace get weaker and weaker.

"Gwenora," she almost whispered. "Are you enchanted? I feel incapacitated."

Sorcey fell back onto the ground and I stumbled from her bosom. My blood speckled her arms. I watched on as her eyes rolled back into her head and her body went limp.

Have I done this? I moved around her body, trying to see if she had been injured herself, but there was nothing. No sign of any trauma. Only my blood on her skin. This was terrible. *How can I retrieve help?*

YILLIANA

My wards were intact as I approached. That did not mean that Jolena had not returned—only that she had not disarmed the house. When I got closer I caught her familiar scent, and both anxiety and excitement welled in my chest. *What will she say? How will she explain her odd behavior? What if she bears the mark?* My stomach twisted with that final thought. On one hand it may explain her dishonesty, on the other, I had no idea what these markings were capable of doing to a Conduit.

I swung the door open. Jolena was the other side of the room. I glanced around quickly and saw that Gwenora and the journal were nowhere in sight.

Jolena's mouth spread into a sincere smile, the one I loved, and she ran into my arms. "I have missed you so much, my beloved!" Her familiar embrace brought tears to my eyes. I was overcome with relief and fear all at once. This was my Atoa, my other half. I knew this woman like I knew myself. She was not capable of maleficence.

"I missed you," I said through sobs.

"Yilli, what is it? What is wrong?" She kissed my face gently, starting with my forehead and working her way over my cheeks and finally to my lips. When she started to pull away, I put my hands to the back of her head and held her mouth to mine longer.

Finally Jolena ended the long kiss, cupping my face in her hands and meeting my stare. "It is okay. I am here. I was only coming to change, then intended to meet you in the arena for the Opening Ceremony. Which we may miss if we are not quick on our feet."

I had so many questions. *Why had she lied to me about the Ancients? What errand had she run when she'd arrived home earlier today? How had she known about Kassandra's visions and why had she gone to see her?* But here she was, in front of me, and she appeared normal. There was no cloud about her, nothing to indicate an enchantment. I needed to examine her body for the mark. Changing would be just the way to do it. Once I cleared her, I could tell her everything. I could show her Gwenora and the journal, share the bridge I built.

"You are right; let us change. We will need to be ready for the Champions' Ball."

We stepped into the next room and I took the opportunity to glance toward the enchanted bag. It was not where I left it. Panic surged through me for a moment until I located it hanging beside the door. *Relief.* I could only assume Gwenora was in there.

"You just want to see me naked." She grinned at me from over her shoulder as she untied her pants.

"As a matter of fact." That was true in more ways than she could possibly know. I unbuttoned my cloak and let it fall to the floor as we moved across the room. I met her body from behind and moved her hair out of the way, exposing her neck and kissing it. She moaned gently with anticipation.

"I suppose we have enough time to reacquaint ourselves." She turned around quickly, swooped me up into her arms and cupped my butt cheeks in both her hands with a firm grip. I was immediately wet with yearning.

Jolena shimmied my dress up while she still held me and pushed my back against the wall so that she could slip her fingers inside me. “Oh, how I missed you,” she breathed in my ear. I was swept away with lust and I let my wife take me.

Gwenora

I had licked my own wounds and they healed rapidly, then proceeded to lick the blood off Sorcey's arms—I had laid beside her while she lay unconscious—unable to think of another thing to do. My greatest hope was that whatever was ailing her would pass and she would come to. But she did not need to wander around Atlantis with dragon's blood all over her. That would only create a spectacle. No sooner did I finish cleaning up the last spec than she stirred. *The strokes are finally in our favor.*

Her eyes opened and alarm set in on her face, the same look she had when she initially found me here in the woods. Sorcey sat up. "What are you doing here? Dear original, what overcame me?" She shook her head. "I still feel so groggy, like I am in a thick fog."

She put her hands on her temples and massaged. "Not even my gifts will heal it." Again she shook her head. "But we haven't the time to waste." She got to her feet. "We need to find my husband and your keeper, Yilliana. I will get to the bottom of this episode when we get you somewhere safe."

Once on her feet, Sorcey adjusted the Dirk at her back so that it was covered and picked me up in her arms. "How will I conceal you?" She thought for a long moment. I had no answers and if I did, I had no way of sharing.

"I know. I have an invisibility charm. It is how I will also cloak the Dirk. It will be useless against those who see magic in the strokes but it will shield you from most eyes. We will have to hope I can get you to Yilliana's undetected."

Sorcey placed her hand on the dagger and whispered a phrase in Asagi. The strokes around it blurred and the object itself seemed to melt into its surroundings. I could still see it but I wondered if that was because I was an original.

"Now your turn." She repeated the phrase. The energy around me shifted. "Perfect." Sorcey applauded herself as she nudged me onto her shoulder. "Now stay up here. I cannot look like I am cradling nothing."

I conceded and did my best to balance on her shoulder. She walked out of the grove and back in the direction I had come from. It was not long before the cottage came into view. My stomach lurched. *Will it be safe? Will the trio be lurking about?* I had no way of articulating any of these concerns with Sorcey. I just had to pray to Malarin that all would be well.

Yilliana

Admittedly I was distracted but I scoured Jolena's body for the welt and did not see it. We lay on the floor, both in a heap of satisfaction. Relief and anxiety continued to tug at my heart. If she was not under some spell, *what is her explanation for her peculiar behavior?*

"Jolena…" I paused to make certain I had her full attention.

"Yilliana, what ails you?" She knew me so well.

"Why did you tell me that the Ancients were the reason for your extended absence?"

She got up on her elbow to face me. "Which one of those ridiculous traitors told you?"

"Shiva."

"That yellow-bellied blue beast! I did not wish for you to worry. The weather was fierce and I nearly lost my fleet twice on the voyage there. I had no idea what the strokes had in store for our return and I did not desire to leave my wife in the lurch and fearful. Can you blame me?"

I had wondered if that was why she had not told me. My shoulders relaxed some with her explanation.

"And your errand when you arrived home?"

She threw her free hand up in mocked disbelief. "Is there nothing that those loose-lipped Ancients haven't shared? I took my fleet to the east to collect something I had been wanting to give you for some time." Jolena got to her feet. "I was going to surprise you before the ball because I think it will go beautifully with your gown." She pulled a small sack from the belt loop of her pants that lay on the floor beside us. "I commissioned a water sprite off the coast of Ireland some time back to make it."

Jolena pulled at the strings and a beautiful strand of pearls slid into her hand. I sat up as she returned to sit beside me. "May I?" she asked as she spread the beautiful necklace out between her hands. They were perfect. Each one shimmered with a rainbow glow. "I am sorry it took me away from you for a moment longer." She kissed my neck as she clasped the pearls. "But I thought I would be home sooner. Forgive me?" She kissed my nose.

"All is forgiven." I beamed at my wife. She was magnificent in every way. My anxiety melted away, because now I could tell her what had been happening in her absence and I knew she would have a solution. Jolena was my captain. She would guide me through this. "Let us get ready. We are already late." I got to my feet. "There is something I must share with you."

Jolena began to get dressed as she spoke. "What? Do you have a gift for me too?" she joked.

"I wish I did, my love." That would have been so much nicer to present, instead of the potential for catastrophe. I looked around for the sack, remembering I saw it near the door—I was certain I had left it on the floor, though. *Have I forgotten that I returned it to its place for safekeeping?* I reached for the bag and immediately knew Gwenora was not in it. The journal was the only thing inside. Panic surged through me. *Where has the original gone?*

"Jolena, we have to go now!" I shouted. *How did this happen?*

"What is it that you intended to show me?" she said as she walked out of the room dressed.

"I haven't the time. We must get to the Opening Ceremony."

I put the sack over my shoulder, hoping I could somehow call out to Gwenora if I were to get close to her. I needed to find her. This was all unraveling so quickly. Jolena came closer and put her hands on my shoulders.

"It will all be all right. I am home. How can I help you?"

I wanted to tell her, to spill the whole story out at her feet and have her help me pick up the pieces. But I could not bring myself to do it. A quiet voice tugged at my soul. *Could Jolena have done something with the original?* Gwenora was missing, now that Jolena had arrived home. The sack was not where I remembered leaving it—*coincidence?*

"I know you will help me. Right now I need us to hurry and make our way to the arena. I told Sorcey and Cane we would meet them there." I reached into the bag to make sure I also had the small paralyzing pellets on me. I had never once considered myself in danger among my people, but there was something too sinister to put into words afoot and I had to be prepared.

"Of course. Let us be off."

GWENORA

From what I could tell as we approached, there was no sign of the creature Clive or the other two. He made me the most uneasy. His strokes were different and Apollo and Shatki's account of what had happened to her family was alarming. For all we knew, all the company he kept was somehow entranced. I had been considering such a scenario as we neared the cottage.

"The wards are down," Sorcey noted as we grew closer. "That cannot be good."

I agreed.

Sorcey moved slowly around the grounds until she was at the front door. She knocked several times then let herself in. I jumped from her shoulder as soon as we entered the familiar space. I ran to where I'd last seen the sack with Sorcerer inside. It was gone. No sign of Sorcerer or the enchanted bag anywhere. Despair washed over me. I had abandoned my friend, my child, and now there was no knowing if I would ever see the Stone again.

YILLIANA

Jolena and I pushed through the standing spectators. The Opening Ceremony was well underway and four of the seven teams had already been chosen. Finding Cane or Sorcey in this horde seemed impossible. It would take the luck of the strokes to stumble upon them.

"Jolena! You are finally home," I heard Apollo's voice above the crowd.

Jolena stopped and took Apollo into her embrace. "Apollo! How nice to see a familiar face in this mob."

I reluctantly stopped for them to have their reunion but I continued to scan the faces of those around us.

"The numbers are great," Apollo observed.

"I was gone too long. It is as though they sprung from the ground overnight," Jolena joked. "Where is Shatki?"

Apollo pointed to the platform high above us. It was a long flat plank surrounded by a wall of fire, magically suspended in the air, towering above the spectators. "She has been chosen as Champion for the Mika Sa Katan."

"What an honor."

I interrupted the chatter. "We really must be going."

"Off on another errand, this time with your lover in tow," Apollo teased. "I understand. We will connect at the Champions' Ball."

"That, we will," Jolena cheered back. I took her arm firmly in mine and started pulling her forward. We were nearly to another level of seating when I spotted Cane waving from two levels above.

"Come!" It was a miracle. I said a silent prayer of gratitude to Chitchakor. "I have spotted Cane." But there was no Sorcey, and when I heard Jolena's name reverberate off the arena walls I realized I lost her from my side as well. As soon as her name was announced she was teleported up to the Champion platform to be revered like all the rest.

I took a deep breath and looked up to wave to her in congratulations. She shrugged, as though to say sorry. But I knew it was not her fault. I smiled and continued up to where I had seen Cane.

When I reached him I blurted out the first thing that came to mind, "Where is Sorcey?"

"I do not know and I would be lying if I said I was not concerned." He rubbed his brow.

I gripped his arm, terrified to say the words out loud. "The original is gone."

Cane's eyes got so large I thought they might burst from their sockets. "How can that be?"

I shook my head as tears streamed down my face. "We have to find Gwenora." I looked around frantically, feeling the circle of allies getting smaller and smaller. Apollo's voice came from behind me. He must have followed me up here.

"What upsets the great Alchemist?"

I turned to face him, unable to hide my annoyance. He was

either in the coterie of the one orchestrating this nightmare, or he was extremely nosey. "How can I help you, Apollo?"

"I sensed your angst. I only wish to help."

"Have you seen Sorcey?" Cane spoke over my shoulder.

"No, I am afraid I have not."

"Then I am certain you cannot help us. Good day," I said curtly.

Before he could object, Dagan barged past him and between us. "I need you. Kassandra needs you!"

I turned to Cane, pleaded with my eyes that he find his wife, and left with Dagan.

"Where is she?" I asked as we ran.

"Just outside the arena, but it was too much for her to enter."

"Of course," I agreed as we made our way into the city center quickly enough. Kassandra was sprawled on the ground, her crimson cloak all about her like blood. It was eerie to behold. I knelt beside her as I did the last time but she was more coherent than before.

She gripped my arm when it was within reach. "The mark! You know the mark! Jolena has it. Clive bestowed it. It will all fall."

Her words sent chills down my spine. It was as I had suspected. Jolena was among those cursed. Clive must have them all bewitched—Aurora, Kassandra, Jolena, Cadmael, and who knew how many others. I needed to get Jolena out of here until I could figure out how to remove the curse. And I *would* figure out how to remove it.

My mind put the pieces together rapidly now. Of course the hobgoblins would want to syphon the magic from an original. That would be the ultimate prize. He had only used Aurora as his helpless pawn to get to the Trials and account for his presence on the island while he captured Gwenora. He could have found her in my cottage. I had to get Cane's help and detain this fiend.

"Thank you, Dagan. Take Kassandra far, far away from here. I will get to the bottom of all of this."

Dagan nodded, picked up his wife and headed toward the harbor. I turned to face the formidable Katuanak Arena, where my enemy lurked in plain sight. *I am coming, Gwenora.*

GWENORA

Sorcey squared her shoulders as we approached the Katuan Arch. "This is a risky endeavor—taking you in here under this minimal cloak. But I see no other way. Forgive me if we fail."

We got closer and the Stones began to swarm me with conversation. I tried to make out what was being said. "Gwenora… You are back… Yilliana seeks you… The traitors seek the Alchemist…"

I heard enough to ask some questions. "Who? Who are the traitors?" Although I was certain I knew their names.

"It is the Ramalan and the hobgoblin. They have cursed many."

This was troublesome because Yilliana would likely trust her.

"Where are they?" We were under the arch now, ready to be engulfed in the arena halls.

"They are in the west hall. They approach the Alchemist."

I had no time and no way of explaining where to go. I had to get to Yilliana. I leapt off Sorcey's shoulder. "Show me the way."

"Yes, Gwenora." The Stones began to shake under my feet. I followed the vibration. Behind me, I heard Sorcey searching for me where I had propelled from her person. I did not wish to worry her or leave her behind but I had little choice.

The vibrations continued as I circled the arena. I could hear the spectators cheering and I was grateful that they were busy watching instead of wandering about the corridors.

"You are almost there," the Stones harmoniously said. "Just around this corner."

As I turned the bend I saw Yilliana's back. In front of her were Aurora, Clive and Cadmael. They casually walked toward her but I could feel their intent. They meant to find answers, to find me at any cost.

I spoke to Sorcerer. "I am here. Tell her I am here."

No sooner did the words leave my mouth that Clive looked directly at me. He could see right through Sorcey's invisibility cloak.

"Gwenora?" Yilliana unintentionally turned around, searching for me.

"Yilliana, Feworbusalee!" I shouted.

She did not hesitate. Yilliana repeated the words and the trinket dissolved from my hind leg. My body lit on fire, charged with unmeasurable power—surging through every stroke of my being. My memories flooded back to me and wings shot from my torso, long and expansive. I was growing in size. I needed to get out of these halls before I burst through the walls.

And without a word the Stones knew my need. They folded in upon each other, opening up into a clear blue sky, and I took to the wind with a burst of inertia I would never forget.

YILLIANA

I watched on in utter astonishment. She was magnificent. Gwenora, the original, Commander of the Winds and Sire of the Stones, was glorious as she took to the sky. The crowd in the arena fell silent and I knew they must be watching what I was. Then the Katuan Stones reconstructed themselves and my view was gone. I needed to get into the arena. Distracted as I was, I forgot about Clive. When I turned to see where he was, the three of them were gone. Only then did it occur to me that Gwenora was still in danger.

I ran in to see everyone on their feet, looking up into the sky. In contrast to the bright blue backdrop was the brilliant and cloudlike form of Gwenora. Wispy purple strands followed in the wake of the original's wings. Silver specs sparkled in the sunlight as her tail flickered and her neck stretched like she had been cramped in a box for weeks. And it was, in fact, as though she had.

I turned to my right to see Clive and Aurora standing twenty feet away. There was little I could do. I thought about the paralyzing pebble I had in my bag. It was my best bet for debilitating the monster.

Then I could call on the others and figure out how to break his spell on my friends—on my Jolena.

I took the pebble in my hand and threw it as hard as I could. But it was to no avail. As though to protect her captor, Aurora stepped in front of the hobgoblin. He turned and gave me a sinister grin that made my skin crawl. I watched as he set his gaze on Jolena.

She stood on the platform with the other Champions. The platform itself was high above the arena, circular, and in its center was a huge ball of flame. Each Champion's face glowed with the excitement and now awe of what they were witnessing. All but my beloved's. A crazed look consumed her. She was possessed, and by the look on her face she meant harm to Gwenora.

It could not happen. I would not let it happen. She was not in her right mind. I whispered a spell that propelled me to the platform. I would paralyze her until I could cure her.

"Jolena!" She turned and looked at me but her stare was empty. "My love!"

She cocked her head as though she was listening to someone else. Her eyes set on me and this time it was clear I was the prey.

She moved toward me quickly, quicker than I had expected her to. It caught me off guard and I stumbled, falling backwards.

"Yilliana, get up." It was Gwenora speaking through Sorcerer. I still had the bridge in the bag on my shoulder. "Get out of here."

"Jolena is not in her right mind. She means to hurt you. You must flee," I pleaded, hoping that if Gwenora left we would avert the crisis.

"There is more underfoot here. I cannot leave until you are safe."

But her voice was distracting me and my wife was now on top of me, ready to reach for my neck and snap my head clean off. I rolled to my right. We were very close to the fire wall that surrounded the suspended stage. Jolena did not hesitate; she tackled me. I rolled again, this time losing the bag with Sorcerer in it and my line of communication to Gwenora. I still held the pebble. I gripped it tightly as Jolena came down on me with a barrage of fists and fury.

I let her get in close. I whispered in her ear, "I am so sorry, my beloved. Please forgive me." Then I struck her with the pebble. Her body went stiff atop of me. Over her shoulder I saw Gwenora's fierce form swooping down, commanding the wind as she did so. Champions were leaping off the platform but I was pinned beneath my statue-like wife. A flap of Gwenora's wings and I saw out of the corner of my eye that the bag along with Sorcerer flew off the platform, thankfully away from the center and out of the flames. Gwenora's enormous wings flapped again and this time I felt mine and Jolena's intertwined forms lift from the platform and slide toward the edge. We were going to go into the flames. Gwenora's expression became one of sheer terror but she was already in the bowl of the arena. She either had to catch us with her claws or retreat. Either way, the power of her wings would push us over the edge and into the flames.

Kassandra's prophecy rang in my head. "There will be death and destruction. It is already set in motion."

I was going to die. I looked into Jolena's eyes and saw that the interference of the paralysis had brought her back to me. It was my beloved's eyes I looked into, not the pupils of a possessed minion. She was with me. We would perish together. The wind whipped around us once more and I whispered in her ear, "I love you."

Gwenora

There was nothing I could do. I had caused her demise. I'd killed Yilliana. As I tried to dive down to catch her before the force of my wind threw them into the fire, I simultaneously created a gust that shoved them into the flames.

I screamed with such despair that the entire arena shook. My wings thrashed about in anguish, the physical pain that overcomes you when the devastation is too much for your heart to comprehend.

But there was no time to grieve. Death tainted the arena. The Katuan Stones would have their retribution. The Conduits had fallen from grace once more. The Stones began to crumble upon themselves. Some flung themselves into the sea. Conduits ran in pure terror as the Katuan Stones became missiles of destruction.

I pleaded with my children, "Stop! You must stop! This was my doing. I killed her." I cried through thick sobs, still hovering over the deteriorating platform, fanning the flames that incinerated my savior.

"Gwenora, you were not the one who set the fates in motion. The Conduits have once again fallen from grace," the cacophony proclaimed. "The Stones must hold true to their bargain. It is the way of the strokes."

"But I created you!" I argued. The island shook from the carnage. Tears streamed from my eyes. *What have I done? How did this happen?* I was in shock.

"For that, we will give you our only exception. Speak the word Brilfalti and we will offer one last occasion where the Trials may commence. But today, today we mark the Conduits' fall from grace. There will be no mercy on this day."

"Is there nothing I can do to persuade you?"

The Stones repeated the word, "Brilfalti."

I meant to contest more when I was swiped by flying debris and then heard the gentle voice of Sorcerer. "Goodbye, Gwenora."

No! I could not lose another friend, not on this day. I regained my composure in the air and searched for the journal, for Sorcerer. A flash of movement caught my eye. It was the stone's golden glimmer, about to be swallowed by a chasm in the earth. "I am coming." I swooped down, clutching the journal in my claws just before the darkness would have swallowed it whole.

I screamed again. My grief was consuming me. I could not see straight.

"There are others. You must save the others." Sorcerer's words grounded me. I dodged another missile of debris and swung back around, searching the destruction for familiar faces.

I had to redeem myself somehow. I had to make this right. "Yilliana, forgive me!" I shouted to the heavens. Circling around a second time I saw Sorcey. She was trapped under a large pillar. She clung to the arm of a man who was unconscious beside her. They would be crushed, churned into the earth. I dove once more, quickly clutched the pillar, threw it aside. Sorcey moved ever so slightly. I swept her and her companion into my claws, gently. Sorcey lifter her head and nodded at me. What she must be thinking, I did not know. I was afraid to know.

I placed Sorcey and her friend on one of the ships in the harbor. They would be safest there as the Stones continued their annihilation of the island. Chunks of land were falling into the sea. Fissures weaved their way in and out of the land mass, Conduits were swarming the fleet looking for refuge. I released the ship from its anchor and directed the winds to send the vessel out to sea. I wanted them at a safe distance while I searched for more familiar Conduits.

Franky loved Hephaestus and Celsi. I needed to find them. As I scanned the hysterical faces I saw one I recognized. Clive. He stood strangely still in the center of the chaos. Watching me. I would kill him. I seethed. My blood boiled. I had never desired anything more in my life. This was his doing; he must pay.

I projected my body like an arrow. He just stared on, unmoved. I was nearly to him, my talons outstretched, poised to tear through his flesh, when I heard Hephaestus scream my name.

"Gwenora!" I turned to see him leaning over an abyss, his arms holding tightly to something in the dark. "Help me!"

I did not hesitate. Justice for Yilliana would come. Quickly I veered right, sweeping down and grasping Hephaestus. I expected to see Celsi in his hands but it was a young man. He had Hephaestus' likeness and I realized this must be his son. I identified the ship I'd sent to sea and delivered them to the deck.

Where was Celsi? I must find her. I circled back around. But this time when I did I was met with a huge wall of water. It was coming straight for me. The island had all but collapsed into the ocean. I looked behind me at the ship where I had just placed my friend. This wave would capsize them.

Knowing not what else to do, I changed course once more, commanding the winds, willing them to push the ship out to sea, but it was no use. The sails were not being managed. So I swooped down, picked the ship up and carried it through the sky, rising into the clouds, feeling the moist air on my skin for the first time in what felt like decades. It was the only comfort I would find. My heart was decimated with grief.

When I was certain it was safe to bring the vessel back down to the water, I did. There was nothing for miles in any direction, just a horizon of deep sea everywhere you looked. Sorcey and Cane had come to. Hephaestus cradled the young man's head in his lap. The journal was open and on the deck. I gently picked it up, closing the binding and seeing that Sorcerer was safe. Relief washed through me.

I held the journal out to Sorcey, who took it in her hands.

Hephaestus spoke. "It is the bridge between the dragons and the Alchemist. It holds great power."

His words brought me back to tears. I let the tears fall as I hovered softly in the air.

"Sorcerer, I killed her."

"No, you did not, great Gwenora. It was in her strokes."

I shook my head in disbelief.

Sorcerer continued, "My knowing tells me so."

Hephaestus' son sat up abruptly. "Where is Mother?"

"I do not think she made it off Atlantis, Juccit." Hephaestus reached for his son but the young man pulled away.

"We must go back and look. I cannot lose her too." Tears streamed down Juccit's face and I understood his pain. "We must go back!" he wailed repeatedly.

"We cannot go back, my son."

They might not be able to go back, but I could. "Sorcerer, I will go back. I must look for survivors."

"Very well, Gwenora."

"You must do me a favor. Remember this word. Brilfalti. Put it in your pages and when the time is right, when your knowing incites you, you must share it. It is the last request of the Stones."

"I know this," Sorcerer conceded. "I will follow my knowing."

I nodded. "I have no way to convey to them what I am about to do. I will be back."

"They will understand. We will be here, awaiting your return," Sorcerer assured me.

With that conviction, I sped back to the remnants of the island. I moved as quickly as my wings and the winds would allow me. Debris littered the ocean's surface as I grew closer. The fleet that was once in the harbor was now scattered, sailing in all directions—there were survivors.

I flew down low to the water's edge, scouring the waves. There were no bodies. Either the Conduits had fled the island in time or they were swallowed whole. Celsi was likely lost along with countless others. My feet dipped into the water. I felt a tremendous weight, the weight of shame and blame. The image of Yilliana's body flying into the flames filled my mind. It was too much.

Then I saw a shadow from the corner of my eye. Before I could turn to see what it was I felt a familiar searing pain charge up my right leg and into my spine. My wings stiffened, burned and throbbed—they were pulsating again. *How could this be?* I tried to turn my neck as the shadow grew closer but it had stiffened and I could do nothing with it. My body was useless, suddenly completely limp. I plummeted into the ocean waves.

The End… Or is it?
Start The Queen and see what else may unfold.

www.ingramcontent.com/pod-product-compliance
Lightning Source LLC
Chambersburg PA
CBHW020528310726
48979CB00014B/2250/J

* 9 7 8 1 7 3 3 9 2 5 7 8 5 *